CW00743328

WENDY M. WILSON

Not the Faintest Trace

First published by Wendy M. Wilson in 2018

Copyright © Wendy M. Wilson, 2018

All rights reserved. No part of this publication may be reproduced, stored, or transmitted in any form or by any means, electronic, mechanical, photocopying, recording, scanning, or otherwise without written permission from the publisher. It is illegal to copy this book, post it to a website, or distribute it by any other means without permission.

First Edition

This book was professionally typeset on Reedsy.
Find out more at reedsy.com

Contents

1

1869: Retreat from Otaoto

March 1869: Patea River, New Zealand

Latest from the Front

At the end of four hours the Hauhaus had retired through the dense undergrowth, leaving the bush fairly in our hands. Colonel Whitmore had sent Lieut. Colonel St. John up the opposite bank of the river to Gentle Annie, which prevented the enemy from crossing there. The enemy was consequently forced back with Kemp's volunteers, following him closely up. All behaved equally well: Armed Constabulary, Arawas, and Kemp's men...We captured all the Maori clothing—piles of it, which was burnt— guns, tomahawks, revolvers, money, tents, axes, spades, and shovels; in fact, the whole of the enemy's baggage. Seven dead Hauhau were found, and two women made prisoners. The attack was planned with consummate skill, and carried out without a single mistake...

Wanganui Herald, 15 March 1869

She was lying on her back, wondering if she still had time to sleep, when she saw a large shape come though the reed curtain covering the doorway of the *whare*. She and Matangi

1

had just finished their nightly ritual, he pounding away, out of breath, taking forever, while she lay there wondering if this would mean another child. Surely two boys would satisfy him? Afterwards, Matangi had fallen asleep instantly, still inside her, and she had rolled him off, careful not to wake him, knowing he needed his sleep. They were expecting a battle today if the fog lifted.

"Tuahine, you must get up." The large shape materialized into an equally large man. He picked up her two boys from their sleeping mat and tucked one under each arm. "The soldiers are coming."

She leapt up and grabbed a blanket to wrap around her nakedness, feeling the wetness run down between her thighs. "Matangi, wake up." She leaned down and slapped her husband on the face twice, one forehand, one backhand. He awoke slowly, yawning.

"What is it? I'm tired…"

"The soldiers are coming. We need to go."

He stumbled to his feet, shaking his head to wake himself up.

"Where will we go?" He asked the big man.

"To the Great Ngaere Swamp." The big man pushed through the reed curtain and called back to them. "Follow me. I know the track."

She followed him out of the *whare*, across the clearing and into the dense bush, running softly, the blanket now wrapped around her body and tucked in under her armpits. Matangi followed her, his feathered cloak over his shoulders so he would be recognized as a chief, his gun and his tomahawk in either hand. Outside they could see very little. The encampment had vanished in a dense fog.

2

They ran through the fog towards the river, the boys bouncing under the big man's arms, to where a small fleet of *waka* had been left in anticipation of an attack. She could hear the soldiers behind them, their voices coming from the direction of the narrow track that led into the clearing. Once they reached the clearing they would stop and fight the few warriors who had been left to hold them off while the others escaped. At intervals she heard rifle shots, interspersed with shouted orders. A scream pierced the night, and one of her boys started to whimper.

By the time they reached the river, Matangi had already fallen behind.

"Hurry, husband, hurry," she called urgently.

The big man had tossed the boys into the *waka*, and they huddled together to keep themselves warm, their small naked bodies shivering with cold and fright. They would be hungry before long, and she knew they faced a terrible day. She prayed her sons would live to see the end of it, even if she did not.

Matangi hobbled out of the fog, his thick grey hair standing on end, but wide awake now. He waded into the water, tossed his weapons aboard, and pushed the *waka* out into the river before jumping into it nimbly. He pulled his sons under his cloak and held them to him, sharing his warmth. She watched him affectionately – he was a good father who loved his sons. Her own father had insisted that she marry him, saying the chief needed sons, and it had not been so bad.

On the other side of the river they joined another a group from the camp—a man, a woman and a child from their own *hapu*. She could hear the enemy approaching along this side of the river, probably to cut off their escape, but the fog was thick and concealed both sides. They ran up Gentle Annie and

3

over into a gully, Matangi stronger now that he had his breath, until the sounds behind them were muffled and distant.

"Matangi," said the big man finally. "I must leave you here. Follow along the crest of the hill, then turn towards the mountain. At the Waingongoro follow the river to the swamp." He beckoned to the man with the other woman and child. "We two must return to the fight."

Matangi nodded and took his sons from the big man. "Boys, you must walk. Time to be men now. Do not cry." They looked at him with wide eyes, the smaller one with his thumb in his mouth.

They are not men, she thought, and said to the big man, "Will you catch up to us later?"

He nodded. "After I have killed many soldiers." His eyes narrowed and he stared back towards the camp. "And if God is willing, after I have killed the traitor Kepa and his *Kupapa*."

She watched him run back towards the river. He was fearless, and she loved him. If only he'd been with the rebels from the start.

"Come wife," said Matangi. "We must go. No time to watch your…"

She took a last long look at the big man as he disappeared through the fog back towards the gully, then picked up her smallest son. They would reach the Great Swamp, which had many islands: the soldiers would lose their way, they would drown, they would leave themselves open to attack from warriors who hid in the ditches and trees. And she and her children would be safe.

By the third day they were exhausted. They could hear gunfire in the distance, and knew that it was not their people: their people had guns, but little ammunition. Once, they'd barely managed to hide when the thunder of hooves approached. A group of armed Arawa passed close to their hiding place beneath a clump of Manuka bushes. She had pressed her hand over her youngest son's mouth, fearful he would give them all away; when she took it away, he was gasping for air, his lips blue. But they'd eaten some Manuka berries from the bushes and a few mushrooms, and had drunk from streams. A tiny amount of food, but enough to sustain them until they reached the Great Swamp.

As they staggered away from the hillock where they'd passed the second night, they heard hoof beats again. And this time there was nowhere to hide. As a troop of Arawa, accompanied by three armed constables, came into view, Matangi gave a blood-curdling yell and ran away from his family towards the distant bush. She knew he was trying to distract the soldiers, giving up his own life to allow his family time to escape, but they no longer had the strength. One of the Arawa, a young warrior, raised his musket rifle and felled her husband with a shot in his shoulder. Matangi fell beside a pukatea tree, before struggling back to a squatting position, his empty gun across his knees, blood pouring from his shoulder. Two of the other Arawa placed their horses behind the remainder of the group to keep them in place, while the young warrior forced Matangi down onto his knees and raised his axe. He was going to take his head.

She pulled her sons to her and covered their eyes, afraid to look but unable to turn away.

Suddenly, another man, one of the constables, stepped forward and pushed the warrior aside, briefly raising her hopes that her husband would be saved. But the constable took hold of Matangi by the hair and stretched his neck across the exposed roots of the pukatea tree, pulled a tomahawk from his belt, raised it high, and started to hack away at Matangi's neck. She felt a groan of horror rise from the depths of her soul, and started wailing.

"No, no, my husband, no."

It took long minutes before the man, grinning maniacally, raised her husband's lifeless head in his hand. By then she was doubled over in pain, no longer holding her sons, unable to bear what she had just seen. She heard the other woman scream and looked up. The constable was running towards her, swinging Matangi's head, his eyes wild. He's coming for our heads now, she thought, resigned to her terrible fate.

"Corporal Adams, stop where you are."

She turned her face slowly towards the voice. Two soldiers had ridden up. A captain and a sergeant, both in the blue uniforms of the British – the same uniform worn by Adams. They were looking at the man holding her husband's head with anger in their eyes.

Please God, these men will save my children, she thought.

Adams dropped Matangi's head and stared insolently at the men who had just arrived. "Colonel Whitmore asked us to bring proof of death," he said. "Especially for chiefs...this man is a chief, you can see by his cloak...

"The Colonel specifically said to take ears," said the older man. "And from the bodies of slain enemy. Take his ears if you must, but leave the head and for God's sake don't touch the women and children. What are we, Barbarians?"

Constable Adams shrugged. "Not what I heard. I heard heads..."

The older man shook his head. "You're mistaken. Too late now I suppose. But leave it alone. Put it back with the body."

6

Adams was not to face any kind of punishment, it seemed.

Evading the Arawa, she ran forward and picked up her husband's head, clutching it to her breast. The neck was still bloody, and she could feel his blood seeping into the blanket she had wrapped around herself.

"What should we do with the women and children?" asked one of the Arawa. He was eying her boys. Perhaps they would take them as slaves. Better than decapitation, but not much.

The other *pakeha* soldier, whose face had gone pale, spoke finally. He was a big man, dark-eyed, his skin darker than most *pakeha*.

"Captain Porter, sir, shouldn't we treat them as prisoners of war? Send them to Wanganui or to the redoubt at Patea?"

Captain Porter glanced at him.

"I suppose we should, Sergeant Hardy. But who's going to take them there? We have far too much to do and no horses to spare."

"I could…" began the sergeant, but the captain shook his head firmly.

"Not you Sergeant Hardy. I need you with me. Adams, escort these women and children back to headquarters. I trust you will behave yourself or I'll see you in the stockade."

With that the captain jerked the reins of his horse and left. The sergeant didn't follow him immediately, but held his horse in place, staring down at her. She put her hands together in supplication, the head cradled between her forearms, and looked at him. Please save my sons. Please. She could see he wanted to do something, but understood he was a warrior who must obey orders; he turned and glared at Adams. "I'll be checking on you in Wanganui. I expect these women and children to be in good health. Remember you're a Die Hard.

7

Act like one."

Adams watched him leave, then grabbed Matangi's head from her and shoved it into his saddlebag.

"Not wasting ten quid for that arse," he said. "Look, Parika, you take the children. Do what you want with them." He leered at the two mothers. "I'll take the women back to Wanganui, if that's what he really wants me to do. Or better still, Patea. Much closer – and they'll know what to do with a couple of women like this in Patea."

She was tied by the hands to his saddle, her face pressed against the saddle bag containing her husband's head. As Adams dragged her away from her boys, she struggled around for one last look. Parika and his men had dismounted and were circling her boys cautiously, tomahawks in hand. She felt herself die inside.

2

1877: The Watcher

July 1877, Wanganui River, New Zealand

The annual native scare prior to the meeting of Parliament is apparently being got up, hence we read in a northern contemporary that additions are being made to the Armed Constabulary Force, and that its strength is proposed to be increased in view of certain contingencies which now loom threateningly.
The Colonist, 26 July 1877

He had watched them all afternoon, wondering if it was worth the effort to kill them. He was down in the shallows of the river, humming to himself, looking for eels and saw them come down the path from the logging camp up in the Tararuas. Two young *pakeha* men, one tall with light-coloured hair and a strong build, of the warrior type he respected, the other who reminded him of a *Turehu*, the creature of the forest his mother had used to scare him, small and pale with the strange red hair of the Europeans; both wore the clothing of loggers. He could hear them laughing and talking in singsong voices. *Yaya,* he thought contemptuously. Not part of his mission,

9

but still thieves, cutting down trees with their strange axes, making farms on his people's land.

He put down his net and shrank back into the shadows, saw them drag a small *rimu* log from the riverbank from where it sat drying in the sun. One pointed across the river and said something to the other. A hundred yards down on the opposite bank he could see a broad spit of gravel pushing out into the river. They would aim for that.

The big one removed his boots and clothes, jumping around and shivering in his underwear. The other helped him roll everything into a bundle using his belt, then sat astride the log like a child on a *kite kite*. Laughing and encouraging each other, they maneuvered the log out into the current towards the spit of gravel. The river bore them quickly towards it; they jumped ashore and pulled the log between them, still laughing and pushing at each other. The big, half-naked one dressed quickly, and the watcher could hear him cursing the cold as he did. His passenger, the red-haired *Turehu*, waded back in and pulled the log further up into the shallows, wedging it in the gravel, partially submerged in a secure spot.

He watched them as they walked along the opposite bank, keeping in the shade of the forest, not really caring if they saw him. Even if word had arrived here, he was unrecognizable with his full dark beard and his blue forage cap pulled low over his forehead. He looked almost European. He'd dropped the feathered *kahu huruhuru* that indicated the wearer was a chief, back beside his fire and his eel sack; for now, he wore the clothes of the *pakeha*. It was not yet time for people to learn of his presence. They would learn soon enough.

He watched the boys as they reached a campsite across the river, the tent of another *Yaya*, and called loudly for him.

"Knud, Knud." He saw the *Yaya* come from behind the tent, bottles in hand, and he shrank further back into the shade again. That's what they were after, then, the young men. He should have known. He had seen what *pakeha* cooked up in the bush, and knew what it did to men, even young men like these.

Sitting in the bush across the river from the *Yaya's* tent he kept half an eye on the young men, and half an eye on the river, still looking for eels. He would need to find one soon if he was to eat. As the sun sank lower in the grey winter sky, he saw them come out of the tent. They were laughing still, and pushing at each other as they staggered towards the river. The big one went ahead, and he heard the other call, "Paul, Paul, *vente par mig.*"

The big one took a small bottle from his shirt pocket and waved it at his companion.

"*Komme og fa det*, Jens, or I will drink it all."

"Save me some or I will tell Mette you are a bad man!" said red hair.

They stumbled back to where they had left the log and dragged it into the water. This time the big one did not stop to remove his clothes and bundle them up, and neither of them searched for a landing spot on his side of the river. Red hair fell in the mud as he lifted the log, and stood up sputtering and laughing. The big one took hold of it and pushed it out into the water with the other lying across it awkwardly.

They moved out into the fast-moving part of the river and within seconds of leaving both were in the water, grabbing at each other and the log.

They're going to drown, he thought, the two of them. Good. These intruders were building on the land of his people, cutting down the trees of his people; building roads and railways on the land of his people. They deserved to die. He could kill them himself, perhaps, although that would be a distraction from what he had sworn to do, those many years ago in Otauto.

The river moved them quickly while they tried to stop the log from rolling and turning. He stood and jogged along the track beside the river, keeping up with them. The river curved to one side and the current threw them into the shallows just in front of where he stood trying to catch his breath, near a stand of willow trees. For a moment it seemed that *Atua*, God of the Rivers, had decided to save them, and he rested his hand on his tomahawk. But then the pull of the water caught at them and dragged them back to the centre. They were starting to panic.

The *Turehu* saw him, and called out, his voice hoarse with fear.

"Please help. The water...fast...cannot swim...cold."

He stood looking at the red-headed boy, his eyes half-closed, and said nothing.

"Please *ven*, we need your help or we'll drown."

The log turned in one more, lazy circle as the big one made a desperate attempt to bring it to shore. Both boys were looking at him, spluttering as they tried to stay on the surface. He looked at them with no expression on his face, and he saw doubt forming on theirs.

As they moved along in the water, he walked slowly alongside them on the bank, staring into the eyes of red-hair, who had both arms around the log, making it roll as well as turn. He said nothing. It wasn't up to him. For now, it was up to the river. But he would see what happened, perhaps even do something if *Atua* did not.

Something slithered through the water, not far from the log. An eel, and a good sized one. Later he would have that, when they had drowned. Red hair saw it too, and lunged at it, apparently thinking it was another log. He sank below the water and came up gagging, his disembodied head seeming to float there, mouth gaping. The big one threw himself towards the other to save him from sinking. But red-hair grabbed at his rescuer desperately. The pair went under the water together and came up gagging. They seemed to make progress, but then red hair once again had his arms around the big one's head, holding desperately.

He lost sight of them for a minute as the forest track moved away from the river. When he caught up again, the big one was gone, but he saw a red head pop out of the water. He watched the boy as he found his footing near the far side of the river, where the bush went straight up from the shore. The boy managed to catch a hanging branch and clung to it, yelling for the other boy in a hoarse voice. When the other did not appear, red hair dragged himself to the edge of the water and up onto a rocky outcrop and sat there retching and shaking.

The watcher stood in the shadows, one hand resting on his tomahawk, waiting to see what red hair would do. Eventually, the boy looked across the river and saw him. The watcher contemplated throwing his tomahawk at the boy to kill him, but the river was wide here. He would lose the tomahawk if he missed; even if he hit the boy he would have to swim the river to retrieve his weapon, and he disliked cold water. Instead, he struck a *haka* pose, eyes wide and fierce, tongue extended, hands on knees. The boy looked at him, terror-stricken, and then turned and scrambled up into the steep bush, out of sight.

He laughed and returned to thinking about his mission, the fate of the two young men serving only to remind him of what he must do. He removed his hat, the blue forage cap, and stared at the crest on the front, running his fingers over the numbers there, feeling his rage grow. The old chant came to him: "Kill them, eat them, kill them, eat them, let them not escape. Hold them fast in your hands."

His enemies would not escape from him, none of them. He was *Anahera*, the Angel of Death. He would kill them all, and eat their hearts. And they would not die easy; they would die hard, just as the cap said.

He spotted the eel again, caught it, and put it into his bag. Eel was good, but he wished he could find a pig in this bush. That would last him longer. The fire had burned down and there was no longer enough smoke to dry an eel. He cursed softly. He'd wasted too much time watching the *Yaya*. He walked around in the bush until he found a rotting tree trunk full of large white *huhu* grubs, then returned to his spot and tossed a few handfuls of them against the remaining embers. He would eat the grubs for now, and later he would have some eel.

3

Missing

*These unfortunate men were missing so long ago as last July and not
the faintest trace of their fate was ever discovered until yesterday.*
  Manawatu Evening Post, October 4, 1877

Hans Christian Nissen didn't notice his brother and his
cousin were missing for over a week, and it was five more
days before he sought Sergeant Frank Hardy's help.

He knew he'd seen Paul on July 24th because that was the
day little Claus was born. Paul came to the sawmill in the
morning to fetch him, wild-eyed and scared. Hans Christian
was working on the dock where logs drafted down from the
boom about a mile and a half upstream, pushing totara logs
into the sluice where they were transported to the mechanical
saws and sliced into poles for the telegraph.

Paul had yelled to him over the sound of the saw. "Hans,
Hans. Johanna needs you. I was talking to her and she fell on
the floor. She was screaming. Her dress was all wet. I didn't
know what to do."

Hans Christian had been through this last year when little
Anna was born. Then he, like Paul, was terrified. But when

it was all over Johanna had acted as if she had felt no pain at all so he knew she'd been exaggerating. It would be the same this time. Lots of screaming and then when it was all over the pain forgotten and Johanna all smiles.

Climbing up from the dock, he'd wiped away the sawdust that had accumulated on his boots and trousers, fetched his coat and hat, and followed Paul home at a brisk pace. Johanna was lying on their bed in full screaming hysteria and the women from the clearing were hovering around her unsure what to do other than to tell her she was fine, which did not help. Hans Christian sighed. *Her va ge igen!*

He'd taken the bullock and dray, jointly owned by the families in the clearing, into Palmerston and fetched Mrs. Hansen, who had nine children of her own and had assisted in countless other births. At home an hour later Johanna was still screaming and biting on the twigs and leaves of a willow tree for the small relief it gave her. Paul had stayed until his brother returned, hovering outside the front door, and then, white faced, took off.

"I'm sorry," he'd said. "I can't stand seeing anyone in such pain, even Johanna. I must go. Jens and I, we planned to visit someone anyway, and..."

"Go, go." Hans Christian had said, waving his hands at his brother. "You cannot help. I can see that. Johanna will be well once the baby comes." She is already quite well, he'd thought.

The baby decided to present bottom first, and Mrs. Hansen spent time carefully shifting him into a better position so his head would come first. By the time the baby—they named him Claus, after Hans Christian's father—made his presence known in the small hours of the morning, Johanna was exhausted and barely able to push him out. Hans Christian was also tired after passing the time pacing up and down the clearing smoking his clay pipe and praying that the baby would live and be a big strong boy who would eventually help him at their own sawmill.

By early morning, everyone – mother, baby, Mrs. Hansen, and Hans Christian—had fallen into an exhausted sleep. Awaking well after dawn, Hans Christian had arisen from his own uncomfortable bed of flax rushes to search for some costly Mincasia in town, knowing Johanna would once more not be able to make her own milk. Anticipating Johanna's request, he'd also searched for someone to take care of Anna and the cooking while Johanna recovered from her ordeal.

Finally, Mette Jensen, the sister-in-law of his neighbour Pieter Sorensen, had agreed to stay with Johanna during the day for the next week. Mette and Johanna were not the best of friends, but he knew Mette felt in the way at the Sorensen's house and it would give her something useful to do other than wander in the dangerous bush picking flowers and leaves and gathering strange white slugs with the peculiar idea that the family could eat them. He thought she might be a little touched, truth be told, but she was a capable nursemaid for Anna and a good cook—better than Johanna. The days had flown by, etched in his memory as the time Johanna complained about her lot in life more than ever before, and demanded at least once a day that they return to Schleswig.

The second week was almost over when Mette had asked him casually how his brother Paul was, and he'd realized he could not remember seeing him since that day.

"Johanna," he asked. "Have we seen Paul since little Claus was born?"

She'd shrugged. She was watching Mette stir mutton stew

in the camp oven hanging over the fire in front of the house to make sure it did not catch on the bottom.

"Maybe, I don't know. I have other things to think about."

He'd tramped up to the logging camp, where Paul and Jens occasionally found work, and discovered that neither of them had been there looking for work for several days. No one knew exactly how many days it had been, or when they had last seen the two cousins. From the logging camp, he went down to their *raupo whare*, set on a bluff above the river. He found a long-dead fire and rotting food covered with flies. They'd built the *whare* themselves, and were proud of it, even though it leaned sideways and let in rain. They would not have abandoned it without a good reason.

Then he'd begun to worry. He and his neighbour Pieter Sorensen had gone to talk to Constable Price. The constable had shared their concern, and agreed to make enquiries on their behalf. He'd discovered that the person whom they had gone to see was Knud Jensen, a cousin of Jens on his father's side.

"Knud says the boys came across the river to see him," he'd reported to Hans Christian. "They told Knud they crossed the river on a log and were going back the same way. They were perfectly well when they left, but he didn't watch them cross back and he does not know if they did. Not for certain."

Constable Price had put together a search party who'd searched both sides of the river for a mile or two downstream from Knud's tent down to the *PapaioeaPa*. But they'd found no trace of the boys and the constable told Hans Christian there was nothing more he could do.

Hans Christian had broken down. "They're both dead," he'd

said. "They have been killed and eaten by *Hauhau*. How will I tell my sister that her boy has died? And my mother. Her heart will be broken. I promised to take care of the boys. She trusted me.

"I doubt they've been killed and eaten by Hauhau," Constable Price had said carefully. "Perhaps they took off somewhere. Do they have other friends or family in New Zealand?"

Hans Christian shook his head. "I don't think so. No family, but...." He paused, his face hopeful. "Jens said once he liked a girl on the boat. I think she stayed in Napier. I know he was disappointed her family didn't continue down to Palmerston."

"Talk to Sergeant Hardy, over at the Royal Hotel," Constable Price had suggested. "He's in Napier every week in his Mail coach. And he's looking for investigative work. He'll want to be paid, but not much I shouldn't think. He just wants a change from driving his coach." He'd scratched his head and added, "Used to be in the 57th Foot—the Die Hards—and he's a good man. Tell him what you know and he can ask after her. You wouldn't know her father's name I suppose?"

"Nothing. Just that there was a girl—Hanna, Anna maybe—but I will talk to this Sergeant Hardy about finding the boys, and the girl in Napier." After a moment he'd added, "I have some money in my biscuit tin I can use to pay him."

"I hope Sergeant Hardy will help us," he'd said to Pieter Sorensen later that night. They were sitting outside their cottages on a low tree stump, smoking pipes together. "I know coachmen carry guns and are usually very able men. But perhaps they are not to be trusted."

"He was a Sergeant in Her Majesty's Imperial Army," said Pieter, taking his pipe out of his mouth and poking into the bowl with a stick to make the embers last longer. "However, with our experience with armies that does not mean he will be helpful—just the opposite, in fact. Is not the Queen of England, closely related to Prussian and German royalty?"

"Sergeant Hardy will not be worried about the Queen of England and the Prussian royal family," said Hans Christian. "Let's see what he can do. If he's willing, I will pay for him to search for the boys. I can't believe a coachman could afford to turn down the offer of good money, and we certainly cannot search for them ourselves."

Pieter Sorensen nodded in agreement, squinting through the haze of smoke that was once again rising from their pipes, while both thought of Sergeant Hardy and what they hoped he would do for them.

4

The Die Hard

What induced these men to desert and make their way into Hauhau country is a mystery, for as soon as they fell into the hands of the rebels we are thoroughly convinced they would have been massacred at once. New Zealand Herald, March 25, 1867

Frank Hardy, the one-time Sgt. Frank Hardy of Her majesty's 57th Regiment, sat on the steps of the Royal Hotel and watched two men struggling through the mud of the square towards him. He was smoking a Sweet Three, a habit he'd picked up in the Crimea, and he was almost out, with no chance of finding more. He could buy some up in Napier, when he was up there in his Royal Mail coach, but the turnaround time was brief—barely enough time to change the team and ready the new pair for the return to Palmerston. Maybe he could persuade someone to bring some tobacco and papers over from Foxton and he could start rolling his own. But he preferred the ready-mades; the roll-your-owns left nasty flakes stuck in his beard

It started to drizzle. He pulled off his forage cap, ran his fingers through his dark hair and put his cap back on more firmly. He was bored with his life, longing for action. Once he'd been a soldier, a Die Hard, fighting his way through the Crimea and India. Now he was stuck in a country that was becoming more like his tranquil birthplace every day. And of all places in New Zealand to be, he was stuck in Palmerston, population 800 people, mostly men, mostly Scandinavians, with a few unattractive women, and even those married. What he wouldn't do to see just one good looking woman pass by on the street.

He could see the two men approaching across the Square better now, and he thought they might be Scandies. He dropped the butt of his cigarette and ground it out with the heel of his Hessian boot. As he watched the men struggle closer, staring at him now, he picked a flake of tobacco from his beard. He wondered if they were coming to talk to him.

Life had been exciting, back in '66 when he first arrived in New Zealand, with the Taranaki War in full force and wild-eyed Hauhau fanatics throwing themselves at the British Troops, the colonists and the *Kupapa*—the loyal Maori who fought with them. His regiment had set up camp along the Tangahoe River, near Patea. To the west, the massive white-capped mountain, with its perfect cone shape, soared above the trees. To the south, war chants accompanied smoke rising from *Hauhau* villages. He been longing for battle—it was what he lived for. Too bad that things had gone so wrong.

If he could just find a place to settle, where he would be happy finally, he would stay there. Maybe Napier—some good land up there. He could find himself a shepherd, and a wife perhaps, if he could find the right woman. But he was bored by the idea before it was fully formed. There were no attractive, interesting women to be found in the entire country and he could never be a farmer, with or without the help of a shepherd. He would die of boredom.

He stretched and yawned, still watching the two men approach through the mud. He could see now that they were in fact Scandi—*Yaya* the Maoris called them, for the sing-song way they spoke: *ja ja*. They were both big men with broad shoulders and well-muscled arms. The Scandies had been brought to New Zealand for their prowess with the squaring axe, and their usefulness in clearing away the forests. These two would clear land at a rapid pace, he was sure, and never stop to ask themselves if they were happy.

They stared at him anxiously as if they had come to ask him a favor and expected to be turned down. They were probably right. He took off his blue forage cap, left over from his days in the 57th, and inspected the inside, not looking at them. Whatever it was they were after, he wasn't especially interested. No favors no bribes. He had a good contract with the Royal Mail he was damned if he was going to jeopardize, as much as the job sapped his will to live. He'd been trying to set up a private investigation agency, but that was going nowhere. No one needed anything investigated.

"Excuse me," one said in heavily accented English. "If you are Sergeant Hardy, could you help us please?" The taller of the two, a desperate looking fellow with yellow, tousled hair, had spoken. "I am Hans Christian Nissen and this is my neighbour Pieter Sorensen."

Frank squinted up at him. "Help? What kind?" He couldn't imagine that they would need help with anything. They could break him in half without a thought.

"I must to find my brother Paul and my cousin Jens."

23

Frank stifled a yawn. "Run off, have they?"

"I do not think so," said Nissen carefully. "They would not do that. Maybe they have drowned, or been taken..."

"So just disappeared then?"

"I last saw my brother a fortnight ago," said Nissen, "when my son Claus was born, and he came to fetch me at the mill. But I didn't see him since. I know only that later he went across the river to see someone. I was busy and I didn't think about Paul, or my cousin Jens. Paul should have come to see the baby, and I did not notice for some days that he had not come. I was thinking only of Johanna and the baby, and little Anna, my girl."

"Have you tried talking to the police?"

"We ask for help from the police—Constable Price—and he ask many people. Also many people searched the riverbanks, but they found nothing, no trace of them," said Sorensen. "But we must to know. We think something has happened to them. Someone maybe has..." He stopped and looked sideways at his friend, afraid to voice his thoughts.

"We think maybe that bushwhackers have killed them and left them somewhere in the bush," said Hans Christian. His chin was starting to quiver and he was staring at his feet, his fists clenched at his sides. "Constable Price says you would know about that. We must find the boys, even if they are dead by the bushwhackers."

Frank smiled wryly, thinking, no chance of that. Even I can tell that these people aren't worth robbing. "Maybe, if they were carrying a lot of money, or..."

Nissen raised his eyes and looked at Frank, shaking his head.

"No money, no. They worked sometimes at the logging camp as spotters, but did not make much money. They just

came from Schleswig a year ago and I was helping them until...
they were just boys, seventeen and eighteen and …" his voice
trailed off and he looked away, blinking.

Frank shrugged. "Well then, I wouldn't worry too much
about bushwhackers. They don't kill people for no reason—only if there's money involved, or goods."

Nissen's shoulders relaxed. Frank realized what a young
man he was—probably no more than two or three years older
than his brother and his cousin.

"Maybe they drowned in the river," Nissen said after a
minute. "Constable Price thinks so. But Paul, he was—is
a big man and a good swimmer, I think. And Knud," he paused
for a minute, "Knud is Jens' cousin on his father's side. Knud
is the one the boys visited that day. Knud says they tell him
they have crossed the river on a log with no problems and
would go back the same way."

"So one fell off the log, the other went in to save him," said
Frank.

"Perhaps that is so, but there was no log."

Frank stared at him, irritated. "What do you mean, no log?
I thought you said they crossed the river on a log?"

"Yah, yah," Hans Christian agreed. "But when we went to
look later there was no log, and no marks of a log either. And
the river is wide there."

"Could they have used a log to float across?" said Frank.
He was losing interest, and distracted by a troop of Armed
Constables who'd entered the Square from the Foxton road,
looking dangerous but interesting.

Nissen shook his head. "The logs here don't float well," he
said. "I know about logs in New Zealand. I'm a mill hand at
a sawmill—for now—and I am working with logs every day,

25

the *rimu* and the *totara*. Mostly they sink after a few minutes unless they are very, very dry."

"Hmm," said Frank. The Armed Constables had dismounted and were watering their horses at the trough in front of the general store. "Well, drowning still seems to be the most likely possibility. Sooner or later they'll surface…"

"We don't want to guess," interrupted Sorensen angrily, causing Frank to look back at him. "We want to know. Constable Price said you drive your coach up to Napier. Perhaps you could ask there, or look in the Gorge, just to be sure they are not there—fallen somewhere. You could help us find them. We could pay you. We have so little time you see. We must work always."

Nissen took a small purse out of his pocket and offered it to Hardy. "I have this money I can give you if you find out what happened to my brother and my cousin."

Frank felt for him. He knew that what he was being offered represented savings for the farms these men were working so hard to pay for. But he was looking for work that would challenge him. Searching up and down riverbanks and asking questions up in Napier would lead nowhere. More than likely the boys had drowned and his family would have to accept that, wait until they floated up.

He said, "I'd like to help you, but I can't. I can ask up in Napier for you, but that's about it." Nissen held out his purse to Frank, but Frank waved it away. "Don't worry about money. Asking in Napier is nothing. Help me fill in my time there. But that's all I can do for you." He put his hat back on, low at the front, then pulled it into place from the back with a quick tug, to underline his decision.

They left looking dejected, shoulders down, not speaking

to each other.

Hop Li, the Hotel Royal cook, came out onto the verandah from the kitchen.

"What they want, those *Yaya*?"

"They wanted me to find two lads who've gone missing," said Frank.

"Two *Yaya* men?" asked Hop Li. "I know about that. Read in the paper. Drowned in the river, for sure."

Frank agreed. "Probably. I offered to ask up in Napier. One of the boys was interested in a girl up there. But that's all."

"Your time, boss," said Hop Li. "Do what you want. But you not find them in Napier or anywhere else. They drowned, and…"

He paused. The Armed Constabulary were on the move again, trotting towards the hotel. They were dressed in bush uniform, with shawls strapped around their waists like kilts, heavy laced-up Blucher boots, carbines sitting across their saddles, ready to use at a moment's notice. Still the old short-barreled Calisher and Terry carbine, Frank noticed, like his own weapon. Each of them gave Frank a hard look. He met their eyes steadily, one at a time. Always on the lookout for deserters, the bastards. He wondered what they were doing in the area now. Surely not still looking for a deserter? Did they never give up?

"That remind me," said Hop Li. "The soldiers there with the shawl party. I have card game for you tonight. Two of those soldiers want game. We take 'em good, eh?"

Frank smiled. "Yes, we take 'em good."

He had been in the Armed Constabulary himself for a couple of years, after he left the Imperial Army. He'd been wild back then to kill *Hauhau*, as many of them as he could, to revenge himself for Will. He'd served under the little colonel, Colonel Whitmore, chasing Titokowera around between Patea and Wanganui, then into the great Te Ngaere swamp in central Taranaki. He still had nightmares about it.

The soldiers were a pair of hard-eyed Irishmen who nevertheless lacked the card playing skills of Frank and Hop Li. They telegraphed their good hands with broad smiles and chuckles and Frank soon had a small pile of shillings sitting in front of him. He was assisted by Hop Li, acting as if he had never seen a deck of cards before, who passed information on to Frank with disingenuous comments about his garden or his cooking. They had played this game before, taking money only off men who deserved to lose it, most of the time at least.

Frank could see the men were getting annoyed with their bad luck, and started a conversation to distract them.

"I saw your troop earlier today," he said. "Don't often see a full company in town. Something going on?"

"Not supposed to say," said one, a short chunky man named Wilson, slapping a card on the table.

"A secret operation?" asked Frank.

Wilson looked at his hand, sighed and played a card.

"Looking for someone," he said, waiting to see what Frank was going to play. Can't tell you who. Can't scare people."

"A deserter?" asked Frank, slapping a card down to trump Wilson's card. "Isn't it time you left the poor bastards alone?"

"Whitmore says they'll be deserters until they're dead," said Wilson as Frank scooped up the cards. "He'd give a pretty penny for Kimble Bent." He flipped a shilling at Frank. "Hell's teeth. You're killing me. An unforgiving man, is Whitmore. But it isn't a deserter we're looking for, exactly. Another bastard. Can't say more though."

"I served under Whitmore," said Frank. "Back in the '69 campaign against Titokowera, with your lot. Many from my regiment did. Hard man then. Probably hasn't changed."

"Get to keep any of the heads?" asked the other Irishman, Benson. "I heard he gave bounties for heads. Ten quid if they were chief's heads."

"Never touched a head myself," said Frank, staring at his cards. His hand had started to shake and he slammed a card on the table to make it stop. The images came at him like this, unbidden, unexpected. "Too barbaric for me." He paused for a minute, collecting himself. "But Whitmore asked for ears, not heads. Some men got carried away, I know. Lot of blood lust in that war, on both sides."

He took a deep breath and looked up at the two Irishmen. The heads. It had been a long time ago, the memories buried deep, and he pushed them back to the depths from where they had arisen.

"I did hear of one color ensign who took a head of a corpse, gouged out one of the eyes and took back the head, pretending it was Titokowera," he said, repeating a story many had told back then. "Tito had only one eye," he added, for Hop Li's benefit.

"He get extra money for that?" asked Hop Li, interested.

Frank paused, mostly for effect. "He would have, only he took out the wrong eye."

The two Irishmen roared with laughter and Frank felt the tension ease from his shoulders.

They played on, the Irishmen in a happier mood but still losing.

Eventually they ran out of money and left to return to the Oxford Hotel, where the Armed Constabulary were temporarily billeted. Hop Li had fed them and they'd been drinking his watered-down whisky all night, so they were poorer but happier and possibly a little wiser. Hop Li fussed around, cleaning off the chairs they had sat in with carbolic soap and a hard rubbing.

"What they wear under those shawls," he asked Frank. "Sitting on my chairs with bare bums I bet. Next time I make them wear trousers, or no game."

He counted out the winnings. "Fifteen bob for you," he said, handing them to Frank. A quid for me." He always took extra to cover his expenses.

You have a good eye for a dupe," Frank said, scooping up his winnings. "Almost too easy, those two."

"Could be setting us up for next time," said Hop Li. "Better be careful."

"I'll keep that in mind," said Frank.

"You not deserter, are you, boss?" asked Hop Li.

"No," said Frank. "Not me. My brother was though. Went across the Tangahoe River and vanished. Didn't know what happened to him for a long time."

"Like those *Yaya*," said Hop Li. "Went across the river and no trace. Same story." He stood up and cleared away the cards. "What happened?"

Frank had not told the story to anyone, but he sensed that Hop Li would not condemn his brother for what he'd done. It would feel good to talk about it to someone. It was in his mind now, with the discussion on bounty heads.

"My younger brother, Will, was also a Die Hard," he said. "He wasn't a strong man, couldn't even stand the sight of a horse with a broken leg being put down. Read a lot though. He imagined himself with a bayonet and a sword charging

30

down a valley towards Russian guns. A glorious death. The poets have a lot to answer for."

"He want to die in glory," said Hop Li. "Seems silly to me. Better to live scared and careful, right boss? Watch out for yourself? That the best."

"Just so," said Frank. "My father couldn't talk him out of it. Told him our mother would have hated it. Didn't stop him though. He got into trouble up near Patea. Had a run in with a corporal and would have been sent to the brig for a long stretch. Lashes as well." He paused for a minute, thinking about it, then continued. "He took the coward's way out. Deserted to the enemy. The *Hauhau* rebels."

Hop Li shook his head and sighed. Frank sat there watching Hop Li bustle about, preparing for breakfast the next day, running the shillings through his fingers and thinking about what had happened to his brother, the memory now forced to the surface.

They had been encamped beside the Tangahoe River in South Taranaki waiting for the battle to begin after a long, forced march from New Plymouth. The cold turned exposed skin blue, and the rain left their woolen uniforms permanently damp and smelly. And always it rained, unrelentingly.

Will suffered more than most of the men, who complained loudly but did their best to keep each other's spirits up. He scowled and complained, and refused to have much to do with the other men. One night, with everyone huddled around the fire trying to keep warm, Will's corporal had ordered him to go out into the bush and cut more wood.

"It's your turn," he'd said.

"You can't send a man out to chop wood when it's like this," Will said, his voice rising and getting louder. "I won't do it, and that's all there is to say. I won't be treated like a dog that must always obey its master."

The corporal had looked at him coldly, knowing he was the brother of an officer.

"Refusing an order, hey? You get on out there now or there'll be hell to pay. And don't think your brother will save you."

"I won't do it," said Will. "And you can do what you like about it. It don't matter to me at all, what happens to me. I'm done with it all."

The corporal refrained from doing anything to Will immediately, but reported him the next day to the officer in command. Will was arrested and put in the prison tent. He was sentenced to 25 lashes on the triangle and gaol for a year, which would have meant being sent south to Wanganui Town to spend a year in the Rutland Stockade on half rations, with the worst kind of men to be found in her Majesty's Imperial Forces. Frank went to visit him in the prison tent to plead with him to recant his disobedience.

"Listen, Will," he said. "I can get them to reduce the number of lashes, maybe even get you sent home in disgrace. But you must apologize to the corporal and beg Colonel Hassard's forgiveness. On your knees! On your belly if necessary."

Will had shrugged. "I'd die as soon as apologize to that miserable bastard. I'll take what's coming to me. Glad to be away from this hellish place."

That night under cover of darkness Will had escaped from the camp and crossed the river to join the *Hauhau*. Frank was fortunate that he'd spent the night drinking and playing cards with the captain and two other men, or suspicion would have fallen on him. But he dreaded what might happen to Will with the *Hauhau*.

Nothing was heard of Will for several weeks. A scout came back saying he'd seen a young *pakeha* sitting at a campfire with *Hauhau* warriors, but they could not tell from the description if it was Will or one of several other deserters who'd crossed over in the weeks following Will's desertion. Waiting and wondering had been hell.

"I think I've changed my mind," he said to Hop Li, letting the coins drop to the table one last time. "My brother disappeared without a trace for weeks, and I could hardly bear it. I should help Nissen. Maybe the outcome will be better for him than it was for me."

"That's what I think," said Hop Li. "You like to do good things for people. I know you. You feel better about your brother if you help the *Yaya*."

Hans Christian Nissen was extremely happy that Sergeant Hardy was now willing to help him. Frank rode out to his cottage in the small Scandi community on the edge of Palmerston to tell Nissen he'd changed his mind. The community was set in an area of cleared totara and rimu trees, surrounded on three sides by dense forest, with solid-looking little cottages set along the side of a rutted dirt track, looking almost like a German village, although much wilder. The Scandies had burned down the trees first, then cleared most of the stumps away. The cottages sat behind neat vegetable gardens. Hens and goats, with nowhere to go, roamed freely.

He found Nissen and Sorensen sitting in front of one of the cottages smoking pipes together. They rose to greet him, their faces bright with hope.

"I'll search when I can," he told them. "And I won't take any money for it. I'll report to you from time to time, let you know where I've searched, in case you have time to search yourselves."

As he spoke to Nissen he could see a pair of young women talking in front of the next cottage. They had their backs to him, and one was carrying a small boy on her hip. Every now and then, the other would clutch at her sister's shoulder, laughing. At one point, she half-turned and he saw her face in profile, a strong mobile face with pale golden skin and expressive features. She was tall and slim, with golden hair that caught the sunlight; he could not take his eyes off her. It was if the clouds had parted, the sun had started to shine again—as if spring had arrived.

Nissen saw him staring and said, "They are sisters. Maren and Mette. Pretty girls, yes?' He gave Frank a hard look, which Frank interpreted as meaning keep your hands off them. He dragged his eyes away from the girl regretfully.

"I was noticing how happy they seemed," he said. "You've created a small paradise here I think."

Nissen's habitually gloomy face lit up. "We are very happy to be here," he said. "In Schleswig it was not so good for us, with the Prussians…"

"War is not good," said Frank.

He rode back towards town, his mind on the young woman, wondering whether he would see her again. He distracted himself by thinking about the matter at hand, the disappearance of the boys who had crossed the river. Then, as so often happened, the story of his brother returned.

Will had been gone for weeks, with no news. They had no idea, really, if he'd deserted successfully, been drowned in the Tangahoe River, or even killed himself somewhere. Then, one morning a *Hauhau* warrior had ridden up on the other side of the river. He was a huge man with a full black beard, bare-chested but with a flax cloak over his shoulders, wearing European trousers, but shoeless, with toes tucked around the stirrups in the Maori style. Over his shoulder, he was carrying something that looked like a sack—a dark rope with a round object below it. He dismounted from his horse and plunged a forked stick into the soft sand, hanging the object from it. Looking towards the soldiers across the river from him, he made a sign of with his hand across his throat, pointed at them and rode away grinning.

Silence for a few minutes, then someone said in a choked voice, "By Christ, it's young Hardy."

The head had hung there for days. He was drawn to it with a horrible fascination. What had it felt like for Will? Had they killed him first, or was he still alive when they had started hacking at his head, knowing what was about to happen.

Eventually, he went out early one morning with his Enfield rifle-musket and a box of cartridges and sat on the banks of the river tearing open the packets with his teeth, pouring in the powder, wrapping the paper around the shot and ramming it into the muzzle, shooting towards the terrible disembodied head, without thinking about what he was doing. He'd been trained to hit a four by two-foot target at 600 yards, but that day his hand shook so much that he used a full box of cartridges before the shot blasted away his brother's head in a red cloud. Afterwards he sat there with his head in his hands, his mind in turmoil, his guts roiling.

Colonel Hassard said nothing. Frank's men looked at him sideways, as if he'd murdered his own brother. But he knew that if he had to look at that head for much longer he would have turned the rifle on himself. He almost did anyway, sitting on the bank of the river with his Enfield at the ready, staring across at the smoke from their fires, fingering the trigger, his mind unable to cope with the horror.

Later they heard stories about cannibalism amongst the Taranaki *Hauhau*. How they cut out the hearts of the first enemy killed in battle, and burned and ate them; or how they decapitated enemies and smoked the heads to preserve them. The *Hauhau* leaders began carrying around the severed heads in sacks, as recruitment tools, using them to convince *Kupapa* Maori, those who felt showing loyalty to the Crown was the best way to keep their lands, of the rightness of the *Hauhau* cause. Frank was glad, then, that he had obliterated his brother's head. At least it would not be carried around like an obscenity for the bastards to look at and joke about, or to pull in recruits for their evil cause.

For the next few weeks Frank slept with difficulty, waking every night from nightmares, sweating in his cold tent. The nightmares were always the same; Will screaming as the madmen hacked at his neck with tomahawks. In his dream, he never saw his brother die. But he awoke with the image of his brother's head on the pole seared on his vision. He was ready to kill the man who had killed his brother, or to kill any man who would do what that man had done.

Eventually, the land wars were over. The Imperial Army returned to Britain and he stayed behind, joining the Armed Constabulary to fight in the Taranaki Wars.

5

The Forager

He [George Snelson, Mayor of Palmerston] knew that Palmerston was a wonder to outsiders. They ask, what makes the place progress so? Some have said that it is the public works, but he said not. There is wealth in the place itself. There are large tracts of valuable timber country, and good rich land. The public works had certainly given trade in the place an impetus, but it was to the people themselves, their Scandinavian brethren, with whom they had always been united and the resources of the district that its present prosperity was mainly due.
Manawatu Times, 11 August 1877

At last, after four days of unrelenting rain, the skies had cleared and a thin spring sun had started to dry the mud. Mette Jensen took the opportunity to do some washing in the iron tub in front of the cottage, enjoying the warmth of the sun as she did. Days since Paul Nissen and her cousin, Jens, the boy she had grown up with and loved like a brother, had gone missing, and no one had any idea where they might be.

Mette was frequently overcome by sadness. What could

have become of the boys? She missed them terribly. They were the only two other young people she could talk to in Palmerston, and now she had no one except her younger sister Maren, who was preoccupied with her family. Everyone had thought Mette would marry Paul Nissen, although he was three years younger than she was. He was tall and strong, and nice to look at, but a boy. She preferred to wait for the right man, and she knew Paul was not that man, as much as she liked him.

Maren came out of the cottage and called to her.

"Mette, what are you doing?"

"I'm just finishing the washing," she said. "Then I'll go into the bush to find some greens."

Maren waddled towards her, one hand on her growing belly, an anxious look on her face.

"I wish you wouldn't go into the forest," she said. "I'm scared for you."

Mette smiled. "Really, Maren, there's nothing to worry about. The bush is beautiful and I love to go there."

"I'm afraid a pack of wild *Hauhau* will catch you and kill you and eat you for dinner," said Maren.

"I'm sure I'll be delicious," said Mette. "I'll make sure they save a piece for…" She stopped as Maren's eyes filled with tears. "Please, don't worry about me, Maren *honning*. I'll be quite safe and will stay on the path where I can run home quickly. If I scream loud enough the men will hear me from the mill and come running."

Maren sighed and returned to the cottage. Mette wrung out her apron and hung it to dry over a knot of scrub that had sprung up in the clearing after the trees were removed. The apron was getting rather thin as she had brought it with her from Haderslev two years ago, but she loved the red and gold embroidery that her mother had stitched so carefully on the two aprons, giving one to her and the other to Maren. Clutching it to herself, she felt like she was home again, sitting in her mother's kitchen eating *aebleskiver* with sugar coating her lips. Sugar! If she could have some real sugar just once, that would be wonderful. Powdered sugar would be even better. She might kill someone to have that.

In Schleswig, there were no men. The Prussians had taken many of them for the army, or else they had fled from the Prussians to different parts of the world. A representative of the New Zealand Government had traveled all over Denmark recruiting farm laborers for their skills with the axe. "You will clear the land first, then become farmers," he had promised them. "And the women can work as servants, although they will most likely marry." Eventually the women realized if they wanted to find a husband they would have to follow them to the places they had gone.

When the war had taken the lives of her father and brother, she and Maren had accepted an offer to immigrate. Free passage to young single women. Maren had wasted no time, meeting and marrying Pieter Sorensen on the boat between Hamburg and Napier, already pregnant with Hamlet by the time they disembarked in Napier.

She was still living with her sister Maren and Maren's husband, and a second baby was on the way, a sister or brother for Hamlet. Pieter had built her a little lean-to against the back wall of his and Maren's cottage, beside the lean-to where the milch cow was kept, but she knew with babies coming at great speed they would soon want her to leave, even if they didn't say so. They'd been kind, but it was time for her to find her own life.

Perhaps she could go to Wellington and find work. But she didn't want to work as a maid and she had no useful skills other than finding food in the bush, food that no other newcomers considered food. She didn't imagine that in Wellington they had to eat *huhu* grubs or *wetas* when they ran out of meat.

Not that they ran out of meat these days much. Mutton had become so cheap that even they could afford it—sixpence for a whole leg of mutton that would last them for most of a week, because all the wool was sent to England and something had to be done with the meat. But Pieter was saving every penny to put towards his farm, clearing the land and working at the sawmill at the same time. It was a hard life.

While the apron was drying, she'd planned to go into the bush behind the sawmill and find some food to supplement the cabbage, carrots and potatoes the settlers grew in amongst the tree stumps at the end of the clearing. These had been stored and eaten through the winter, but were almost gone, with planting just starting. Time to find more food, as much as Maren wished she would not.

Before she left, she prepared the camp oven, the heavy three-legged iron pot they used for cooking, for her return, building wood up under the flat pot and partly filling it with water from the water butt. She would light it when she returned from the bush with food. The milch cow she had already milked this morning, and a fresh bucket of milk sat in the two-sided cupboard beside the front door, covered in a piece heavy cotton cloth weighted down with stones sewn into the hem at the corners.

She tightened her bonnet around her head, pulling the strings into a slip knot under her chin, called out to Maren to tell her where she was going, stepped into her clogs and set off along the path through the bush to the sawmill. The path had been trodden down by the men from the clearing who walked to the sawmill every day at first light and back again as the sun was going down. She carried a large woven flax basket that she hoped would be full when she returned. The sun was nice, but she felt hot in her woolen skirt.

She was tall compared to most women she knew, too tall, with white blonde hair tied in two thick plaits, and hazel eyes. She knew she was not pretty, like Maren who had golden hair and enormous blue eyes. Once she and Maren had taken the tram over to Foxton to buy cloth for dresses, back when bullocks pulled the tram and it took forever to get to Foxton. A young man in a dark suit had watched Maren for a long time, and then had come up and said she was the most beautiful girl he had ever seen, and would she marry him?

Maren was unflustered; she looked at the young man kindly and told him she was already married, suggesting he might like her sister who had not yet found a husband. Mette had blushed, as she always did, and looked at the man, smiling. Although she was embarrassed, she was prepared to treat the whole thing as a joke. But she was hurt and humiliated when the man looked back at her, dropped his gaze to the floor, and walked silently back to his seat.

"I'm not pretty enough for him," she whispered to Maren.

Maren had shrugged.

"What good does pretty do in this country? If he knew how you could cook he would come running back."

But a woman couldn't be too choosy. All she wanted to find was a man who would give her healthy babies and make a home for her. Someone who would also enjoy talking to her around the fire in the evening would be nice, someone who would be there when she looked up from her sewing. She imagined a sturdy, fair-haired man with a pipe in his mouth and a twinkle in his eye, a man who would talk to her about books and history and interesting things that were happening in the world. Danish men were not generally talkative types, however, and they certainly did not fit the image she had in her head. Not any that she knew at least.

A group of young boys was playing in the dirt near the entrance to the bush. They stopped what they were playing at and looked at her with wide eyes.

"There's a troldt in there," said one.

"In the bush?"

He nodded, his blond hair falling over his eyes. He brushed it back and said, "We saw him. He was a big troldt and he was holding a sack and a club."

Mette suppressed a smile. She'd seen just such a troldt in a book of fairy tales when she was younger.

"And was he green with orange hair?"

One of the other boys jumped in.

"No, he was brown and he had marks on his face, dark ones, like wings. And he had a big cloak made of feathers."

Well, that was a different kind of troll.

"Why did you think it was a troll then?"

"Because he was very angry," said the first boy. "He looked at us like he was going to put us in his sack and take us away for dinner. We were scared and we ran home."

Mette had nothing to say to that. But she felt a little twinge of nervousness in her scalp as she walked, as if someone were staring at her from behind. Once or twice she spun around to make sure she was alone. The troldt sounded like one of the *Hauhau* Maren was worried about. The trees on the mountain side the clearing were massive, too big to be spanned by the arms of a tall man, and the bush dark and full of things that were unknown to Danish people. She had done her best to explore and understand the plants and animals, but knew she had much to learn. She forced her mind from the troldt, said goodbye to the boys and set off along the path.

She touched the leaves of a fuscia tree as she went by. Later in the autumn it would be covered with konini berries and she would make jam. Pieter loved her jam, and took a jam sandwich to work with him every day. Too soon for the berries yet, but she longed for something sweet. Savory would be nice as well, something with taste, or bite, like the pickled herring they used to eat at home. On that memorable trip to Foxton on the tramway they had visited a small café and she had tasted whitebait fritters, made from the tiny fish that swam upstream in the springtime, cooked in a batter of eggs and white flour. She had never tasted anything so delicious in her life, and she dreamed of a time when she could eat them again.

Perhaps she would find some honey today. *Manuka* scrub was growing at the edge of the forest as well and just beginning to flower with small white buds. Bees loved the pollen from the *Manuka* blossom. She stopped to pull off some leaves for tea, just the very smallest and softest leaves, and tucked them carefully into one side of her basket in a kerchief placed there for just that purpose. The larger leaves made a very bitter tea but the smaller ones were refreshing and you could almost imagine you were drinking real tea. If she could not find any honey she would at least have some leaves for tea.

She could hear the hum of the sawmill in the distance and as she got closer she thought she recognized the voices of Pieter and Hans Christian. Behind the mill a stream surrounded by fern and the occasional kowhai tree, not yet in bloom with its lovely yellow flowers, rose towards the hills and she made her way there. She pulled out some young fronds of *pikopiko* and put them beside the leaves. The roots tasted horrid, but they filled you up when you were hungry. Someone had suggested to her that *pikopiko* tasted like asparagus, but not to her. You might as well say that *huhu* grubs tasted like chicken, which they certainly did not.

She wandered slightly off the path, being careful to keep it in sight. People were always disappearing into the bush and not coming back, especially small children, and she knew she must stay within sight of the path. Maren had put the fear of God into little Hamlet, telling him that the *troldt* would get him if he went too far from the cottage. So far it had worked, although it had also made him nervous about going to bed at night, and he often woke in the night yelling that there was a *troldt* under his little truckle bed. When that happened Maren and Pieter would take him into their bed. Maybe the other mothers in the clearing had told the same story to their boys and that was why they were claiming to have seen a troll.

Still in sight of the clearing she found a large growth of *puha*, which would do for their vegetables. The leaves of *puha*, which was a type of thistle, were quite tasty if they were twice cooked in water—almost like spinach. Beside the *puha* were some red capped toadstools. She had avoided mushrooms and toadstools so far; you never knew which ones would kill you. She knew for certain that the red capped toadstools were not to be eaten. They made you go crazy, and then they killed you.

44

A small sound made her turn and look to one side. A pair of bright eyes regarded her through the undergrowth. She stared into them and drew in her breath.

"*Hej min lille mand,*" she said softly, moving slowly towards the baby pig.

How they would love her if she came home with a little piglet for dinner!

She glanced down, looking for something heavy and spotted a hand-sized rock. Keeping her eyes on the pig, she bent and picked up the rock. The pig kept looking at her, its head on one side enquiringly. She took a minute to look around. If the mother was nearby she would run like a *hone* with its head chopped off to the clearing, but she knew baby wild pigs could become separated from their mothers and she would have heard a large wild pig moving through the bush. She hoped so, at least.

The little pig moved towards her slowly, a conspirator in its own death. It was busy nibbling leaves from the very *puha* she had just harvested when she raised the rock in two hands and brought it down hard on the side of its head. It fell slowly sideways, its eyes glazing over. To make sure, she hit it hard two more times, being sure not to get any blood on her woolen dress and stockings. Then she carefully lifted it and placed it in her basket. It was heavier than it looked and would give them very much meat! She covered it with leaves to keep the smell from the mother if she were nearby, turned, and walked towards home, the pig weighing her down on one side. She had trouble keeping a smile of delight from her face. A pig for dinner. It would last them for days, and the fat under the skin would sizzle and cook into the most delightful taste. She could already imagine it

After only a few steps she heard another noise. She froze to the spot; the mother pig was behind her. Now she was in trouble. Slowly she moved around to see what was there. In the darkness, she could not see well, but the pink skin of a pig would stand out against the green. Instead, she saw something brown. Some legs. Human legs. She raised her eyes and was confronted with another pair of eyes looking down at her from under a blue cap, eyeing her in a way that was not unlike the way she had eyed the pig.

She gasped and almost dropped her basket. The troldt.

A huge, dark-bearded man wrapped in a feathered cloak was staring at her from the bush; or, more correctly, not at her but at her basket. He carried a bag of something that was moving, wriggling, it seemed, to get free, and she thought in horror of little Hamlet, wondering if he was safe at home. This was one of those *Hauhau* who ate little children. He was the troldt the children had seen. The women in the clearing talked about the terrible *Hauhau* all the time and scared the children with stories to make sure they behaved properly, and called them troldt. She had not made the connection.

He raised his arm towards her and pointed at the basket. His face, the part that was not covered by his beard, was painted with blue markings. He looked almost as if he had a butterfly on his face.

"*Poaka*," he said and snapped his fingers at her. She understood what he wanted. He wanted her pig. She backed away slowly.

"This is my pig," she said. "My *poaka*. For my family," waving towards the clearing. "They wait for me, just over there. Many men. Big men." She heard her a quiver in her own voice and bit her lip to suppress it.

He shook his head dismissively. "My pig," he said, taking a step towards her. His voice was deep and gravelly, as if he didn't use it very often.

She was still holding the rock she had used to kill the piglet and without thinking she threw it hard at him. He grunted and took a few steps backward, his hand to his forehead.

Clutching the basket with the pig close to her front, she turned and ran, screaming loudly as she did so. She heard branches snapping behind her, expecting at any minute he would grasp her by the shoulders and seize the pig, but nothing happened. Even in her panic she realized that running back to the clearing would not help—there were no men there—so she ran in the direction of the sawmill, which was a mere hundred yards away. She had the sawmill in sight and could even hear the machines running and men shouting, when a rider on a large black horse appeared in front of her on the track to the sawmill. It was him, she was sure, a big dark man with a blue cap, but for some reason he now wore a long blue-grey greatcoat which came down to his stirrups. She didn't stop to think about why that was so, or how he was suddenly riding a horse, but opened her mouth and screamed as loudly as she could.

"What the dickens…" he said, clutching the reins of his horse as it reared up.

6

The Banshee

HOKITIKA. Mrs. Andrews, mother of the two children who died from the effects of burning at the late fire, died to-day in the hospital, from burning and a shock to her nervous system. Wanganui Chronicle, 15 August 1877

She had appeared out of nowhere, running like a deer and as soon as she saw Frank she started screaming like a banshee and clutching her basket to her front as if it contained the crown jewels of England. He dismounted and stepped towards her, his hands out, unsure what to say or do. But she dodged around him and in doing so, bumped against him and spilled the contents of her basket. A dead piglet fell to the ground, followed by a shower of leaves and petals. She bent to pick it up her bonnet fell to the ground, causing one of her braids to come loose and swing down in front of her face. He leaned down to help her and she reared back, took off her wooden clog and started pounding on the back of his head with it. He stood up and rubbed the spot, staring at her in astonishment.

"That's my pig you *skiderik*. Take your hands off it."

"Hey up," said Frank stepping back to escape the flailing

clog, his forearm in front of his face. She stopped and stood there panting, the clog still in her hand, raised as if to hit him again. Her face was flushed and her hazel eyes were fixed on his, waiting for him to move. He recognized her now. The woman who had lit up the clearing, the day he went to tell Nissen and Sorensen he had changed his mind. He'd wanted to meet her, but not like this.

"I was just trying to assist you," he said mildly. "You dropped your pig."

"Was it, did I…" she stammered, doubting herself. She let the clog drop to her side.

"Did you what?" he asked, retrieving the piglet, brushing away the leaves and wiping off the dirt. He held it towards her and she snatched it and put it back in her basket. "Looks like a pretty fine meal you have there."

"Was it you I just saw in the woods back there?"

He shook his head. "How could it be? I just came from the sawmill, from that direction…"

"He looked just like you."

"You saw someone in the bush who looked like me and who scared you for some reason?"

"He tried to take my pig, and he had something in a sack that wriggled. I thought it might be," she stopped and clutched at her throat, a catch in her voice. "I thought it might be Hamlet."

He was confused. "Hamlet? I thought you had the pig and he—the person who looked like me—tried to take it away from you."

"Hamlet is my sister's little boy, not a pig. I'm afraid because I know that the *Hauhau* take the little children and eat them."

"*Hauhau* don't eat little children. They don't eat anyone any more, if they ever did. What is it with you Scandies that you're afraid of the Hauhau eating you? What about this person in the woods who looked like me?"

She looked at him more closely, then stared back into the woods, as if thinking about what she had seen.

"Well, he wasn't completely like you. He had the the..." she patted her chin, "the hair on the face."

"Beard," he supplied.

"Yah, the beard. And it was big and black, like yours. And he was tall like you, but maybe not quite so tall or hand...." She stopped and looked him up and down. "He was wider than you."

She glanced upwards again.

"And the hat was like yours too."

He took off the forage cap he was wearing. "You mean it was a soldier's hat, like this? What about on his feet? Did he wear boots?" Frank glanced down at his own boots, the Hessians that were an exact copy of those his father had worn when he saw duty with the Duke of Wellington.

"Yah, his hat was just like that. But I didn't see his feet. He was standing in the ferns."

"Could have been a deserter." He looked thoughtful. The deserters he had encountered on his travels often wore vestiges of their former uniforms mixed with Maori clothing; they were fearful of people like him who had been non-commissioned officers. They tended to be hungry as well. A deserter would have certainly taken a pig from this young woman, if she'd let him. Besides, it would explain what the Armed Constabulary were doing in the district. They were looking for men like this, despite what the two Irishmen had said. Memories were long for the army.

"No. He was a *Hauhau*," she said firmly. "He was wearing

a cloak with feathers all over it, and he had drawings on his face. Blue drawings that looked like a butterfly across his nose. And he was dark. Darker than you—a little darker than you, although there was very little light in the bush so I can't be sure."

Frank stroked his beard thoughtfully. "A Maori then? Although deserters often take on *moko*—tattoos. Lots of them around that haven't turned themselves in." He decided against telling her he had *moko* himself, on his upper arm, a wreath of oak leaves with the number 57 in the centre. He'd had it done in Patea, after the attack on Otapawa. Couldn't get rid of it now. Fortunately, he hadn't had the name of some long-forgotten woman etched on his arm, or worse, his mother's name, like many of the soldiers did, so far away from home and lonely.

She shook her head. "No, he was certainly a *Hauhau*. His English was not good. And he said a word that sounded like pig, but wasn't. It sounded like poker."

Frank tried not to smile, wondering how she could tell that the English wasn't good. It wasn't much use arguing about the man. He was long gone.

"A Maori then, possibly, but no reason to believe he was *Hauhau*. Probably someone passing through and hungry. Let's get you home then. Or would you prefer that I escort you back to the sawmill. I presume your husband is working at the mill?"

For some reason she flushed bright red.

"No," she said. "My sister's husband works there. Pieter Sorensen. You know him perhaps?"

"I do," he said, surprised. "I talked to him last week. He and Nissen, about those missing boys…"

She bit her lip and looked away.

"You know them, I suppose," he said, kicking himself. Of course she would know them.

She nodded. "I thought perhaps they'd drowned. But now I think that the *Hauhau* have taken them, now that I've seen a *Hauhau* with my own eyes."

"No, no," he said, shaking his head. "Don't worry about the *Hauhau*. They're not a problem any…"

He saw that her eyes had widened in fear and she was looking past him at something.

"Is someone behind me?" he asked softly.

She nodded, her eyes fixed on a spot behind him.

"Walk towards the sawmill," he said quietly in as normal a voice as possible.

"He has a hatchet," she said softly. "He's looking at your head…"

Frank felt the hairs on the back of his neck tingle.

"Go," he said urgently. "Go, run for the mill." He bent to pick up her bonnet, which had fallen to the ground, and as he started to move he felt something fly by his ear and land with a loud thud in a totara tree. He flung himself up onto his horse, leaned down, pulled her up and threw her across the saddle, still clutching her basket. Both braids had come down now, and she was breathing quickly, starting to panic. He backed the horse up a few steps and yanked the tomahawk from the trunk of the tree. He felt the sharp edge, imagining the job it would have done on his head if he'd been standing straight.

"Go, please go," she whispered.

"He's already thrown his tomahawk," Frank said. "I doubt he has another one. If he makes a move, I'll hit him with his

52

own tomahawk."

"But he may still hurt us," she whimpered. "Maybe he has a gun." She was straining her head backwards to look at him. "Please, let us go now."

He turned his horse. The path was empty, but he thought he could see a shadow moving away deeper into the bush and hear the muffled sounds of ferns being trampled. No point in giving chase, not through the dense bush on his horse, and especially not with the encumbrance of the girl. He held his horse in place, his hand lightly on the girl's back to hold her still, concentrating on looking and listening. But the bush had gone silent. He stared at the spot where he had last seen the shadow. He had the eerie feeling that someone was staring back.

"Who are you?" he called. Then again in Maori, "*Ko wai koe?*" He felt that the bushes shimmered a little, but no one replied. The girl was sobbing now, holding on to his leg with a ferocious grip, and he knew he had to get her away from here and to safety.

He helped her upright on the front of his saddle, and trotted his horse back to the sawmill, the girl clinging on to his arm as if her life depended on him. At the sawmill, he delivered her into the hands of her brother-in-law Pieter Sorensen, Nissen's neighbour who had come with Nissen to talk to him about the missing boys. She explained the story to her brother-in-law in a rush, and, before Frank could stop her, added the possibility that his son Hamlet might have been wriggling in a bag held by the *Hauhau*. Sorensen grabbed his axe and the two ran off towards home, eyes wide with fear, to rescue the boy.

Frank watched them go, bemused, then turned to Nissen and told him what he had found so far, which was nothing.

Nissen nodded sadly.

"I expect they have drowned," he said. "What else could it be? But what about this man in the bush that Mette was in so much trouble about?"

"He tried to steal a piglet that she'd killed," said Frank, realizing in retrospect what an achievement that was for a young woman. No woman he knew would have the grit to hit a piglet over the head with a rock, even if it was standing still in a pig sty fast asleep on its feet.

"She goes into the bush to look for food for her family," said Nissen. "Pieter doesn't like it. Now he has proof that it is not a good idea for a woman to be by herself in the forest. No doubt he will keep her at home after this."

"She seems to be able to take care of herself," said Frank. "But let your women know that there's a suspicious looking character hanging around, a tall dark man who's after food – a Maori or a deserter who resembles a Maori. Tell them to stay close to home."

"They will do that," said Nissen. "They are always telling each other stories about fierce Maori that lurk in the woods just waiting to kill them and eat them. They scare our children with such stories. Most of them wouldn't leave the clearing unless accompanied by men with guns. Mette is different, unfortunately for her."

Not so unfortunate, really. Frank liked to see a young woman with courage. Especially a good-looking woman like – Mette, her name was. "He may be a Maori," he said. "Although that doesn't necessarily make him dangerous. I suspect that he hasn't eaten in a while. Not the most intelligent thing to do, throw a tomahawk at me. But I don't think he's anyone dangerous. Just hungry."

"If he asked us for food we would give it to him," said Nissen. "We would not let someone starve."

"Keep an eye open for him," said Frank. "I have his tomahawk so he isn't armed. I doubt he's dangerous, as I said."

He left Nissen standing at the door to the mill and rode off towards the town to talk to Constable Price, keeping an eye out for the mysterious tomahawk thrower.

7

Monrad's Barn

Every child above seven and not more than thirteen years, must attend school for at least one half of the year. Exemptions: That the child is under efficient instruction; sickness; that the road from the child's home to the school is impassable; that the inspector or master has certified that the child has reached a certain standard of efficiency. Proceedings may be taken before any two Justices of the Peace, to compel attendance, and if the parent or guardian refuses after an order from the Court to send the child to school he may be fined not exceeding £2; and proceedings may be taken week by week. Wanganui Herald, 57 July 1877

After her encounter with the two giants, as Mette thought of them, she was glad to be back at the clearing with the baby pig still in her possession. She had told her story to Hans Christian and Pieter, and then run home with Pieter, both wanting to make sure that little Hamlet was still safe. The thought of Hamlet in peril gave her the courage to pass by the same spot where she had encountered the *Hauhau*. Sergeant

Hardy had assured them both that *Hauhau* did not eat little boys but they found it hard to believe. They had arrived at the clearing out of breath and in a state of high anxiety, only to discover that Maren and Hamlet were nowhere to be found. Pieter sank to his knees and raised his hands skyward.

"Oh Lord, not my little boy. Please, not my little boy."

Mette took a more sensible approach and went to look for her sister and her nephew. She discovered Maren standing amidst a large group of red-faced Danes in front of the Jepsen home, and, much to Mette's relief, holding a querulous Hamlet on her hip. Maren turned to Mette, her face animated, and spoke before Mette could say a word about how she thought she had seen Hamlet wriggling in a sack held by a vicious *Hauhau* man.

"Mr. Jepsen has hurt himself, and serve him right. He pulled down Mrs. Mortensen's clothesline and made the washing muddy."

"Oh," said Mette. "Well, I've had a very scary…"

"Mrs. Jepsen sent her son Pieter to the Mortensen's cottage to ask for the return of a missing axe," interrupted Maren, "but Mrs. Mortensen said they didn't have it. Carl Jepsen came home from the sawmill and went to yell at Mrs. Mortensen and tell her she must give him back the axe, which he knows she has. She's had it for almost a year. When she said again that she did not, he pushed over her new fence, and Mrs. Mortensen's washing fell in the mud. Her shifts and Mr. Mortensen's shirts, all muddy!"

Maren was obviously enjoying the drama, so Mette let her talk.

"Then Mrs. Mortensen picked up a slat of wood from the fence and hit Mr. Jepsen on the head," Maren continued, starting to giggle. "And Mette, it was so funny. He ran off and fell over that tree stump, and he was lying there yelling he would take the Mortensen's to court, he swore he would."

"Why would he ask for money for that?" asked Mette, interested now. "Was he hurt?"

"To pay for the doctor and nurse he must hire, and the time away from work he must suffer. I don't suppose he would win the case, but it would cause trouble for the Mortensen's."

Mette listened to Maren and pretended to be shocked and interested, waiting for an opportunity to tell her own story. Eventually Pieter appeared and behind Maren's back shook his head slightly, so that Mette understood she was not to tell her sister that they had feared for Hamlet's life. She was disappointed; she'd built up a wonderfully exciting adventure in her mind, but realized that a story including the possibility of Hamlet wiggling in a sack belonging to a strange native would probably not interest and amaze Maren, but rather scare her and give her nightmares; she would not be distracted by Mette's rescue by a handsome sergeant.

Mette started to walk towards home but was stopped by Johanna Nissen, wife of Hans Christian, who had witnessed the whole thing and wanted to tell Mette her version of the story. Johanna was a gossip and she would as soon tell stories about Mette and Maren as about the Jepsen's and the Mortensen's. It wasn't a good idea to indulge her if you wanted to keep a few secrets. She got away from Johanna as soon as she could. Two weeks taking care of Johanna and her daughter had been quite enough for her; Johanna was a demanding and unappreciative invalid. But Mette was disappointed not to be allowed to tell anyone about her own adventure, especially the part where she was rescued by a handsome soldier on a large black horse, like something out of a fairytale.

Maren and Hamlet continued to watch the ongoing melee, and clearly little Hamlet had not been eaten by the *Hauhau*, or carried away in a sack, so she left the argument to play out and returned home, first letting Pieter know that she would say nothing to Maren.

Back in her lean-to she settled into her comfortable wooden rocking chair and picked up the only book she had ever owned: a battered copy of Charles Dickens *A Tale of Two Cities*. She was using the book to improve her English, rereading each page until she understood what it said. She had cried when Sydney Carton arrived in the tumbrel holding hands with the seamstress, and both had gone to the Guillotine, Sydney Carton in place of Charles Darnley, the man who looked so much like him; she thought she might be a bit in love with him because of his bravery. "It is a far better thing I do…" she loved it! If she could find such a man…But now, after spending almost a year carefully reading the book and its heart-wrenching conclusion, she was starting it for the second time.

"It was the best of times. It was the worst of times," she read. "It was the age of wisdom. It was the age of foolishness."

She loved the way those lines swung back and forth, like a pendulum! They made her want to dance.

The roast piglet distracted everyone, and there was no talk of the Jepsen-Mortensen fight during *aftensmad*, the evening meal. After it was over she went to her lean-to and dressed for the dance, wearing her freshly washed apron and putting on heavy boots with nails in the soles. It was a long ride to the Monrad property and who knew when she would have to help push the bullock dray out of the mud. She wished she could wear proper dancing shoes, but apart from the fact that she didn't own any, the boots were easier to dance in than clogs, her only other footwear.

It was always exciting to be going to the Monrad's place. Bishop Monrad had been a famous man in Denmark—the Premier in fact—before he came to New Zealand. He had returned to Denmark a few years ago, but his son Viggo now lived at the farm with his wife Olga and their children. Everybody loved Olga Monrad, who was the daughter of a Lutheran minister and a kind-hearted woman. She, like Maren, was now pregnant with her second child and was therefore unable to attend the dance, although Viggo had assured everyone that she had longed to come.

They arrived at the shed, lit up by flames of kerosene lamps, just as the sun was going down. A cluster of men lounged outside the double doors watching the women go in and eying them up and down—like a cattle market, Mette thought. She put her head down and followed Pieter and Maren through the gauntlet of lounging men, feeling a dozen pairs of eyes inspecting her as she passed. Inside, the dance was in full swing, with rosy-faced couples lined up for a Mazurka. A fiddler played Mette's favorite Mazurka, the one from *Coppelia*. It made her feel like a doll on strings, being pulled around against her will, but she loved it and wished they had waited for her before beginning. She stood tapping her boot on the hard dirt floor, humming along with the music. She could see Viggo Monrad circulating around the shed, slapping men on their shoulders and patting children on their heads. He was a tall handsome man with a lean face and an intense expression. Of course, he wasn't as handsome as Sergeant Hardy, who had saved her from the *Hauhau*, but still very handsome.

The music stopped and the dancers were told to find another partner. Mr. Larsen, the manager of the sawmill, but much too old to be a husband, asked Pieter if he could dance with Mette and Pieter gave his permission. She was swept into the dance and joined in energetically, swinging from partner to partner with excited abandon. She could feel her cheeks burning and her heart pounding; she felt alive.

When the mazurka was done, she thanked her companion and went to catch her breath and find a cup of coffee. The Monrads owned a vacuum coffee brewer that was the wonder of the community, and a group of men stood around trying not to stare at it. They were used to the more traditional method in which hot water was poured onto ground coffee and strained into a cup after sitting for a while. Mette poured herself a tiny cup and sat down near to the men. She would have loved to join in the conversation, but knew if she attempted to do so the men would stop talking about anything interesting.

"I don't agree with it at all," she heard Pieter, who was one of the men in the group, say loudly. "It isn't necessary to educate children once they are ready to work. Ten years is more than old enough for them to be lounging around at school. Nothing to be learned after that! I remember when I…"

"Some children should be out to work at that age," said the Pastor, who had soft-palmed sons of fourteen and fifteen away at boarding school in Wanganui. "But others are capable of being educated for more sophisticated work, or even for no work at all, just quiet contemplation."

Pieter grunted his disagreement, and a third man joined in.

"The new law says all children must be in school until they're thirteen. If it's the law, Pieter, we'll have to obey."

"We'll see about that," said Pieter. "My Hamlet will be joining me at the mill as soon as he's old enough, which will be ten to my way of thinking."

Mette had a sudden image of Hamlet, still barely walking, managing a circular saw at the sawmill and she smiled to herself. Imagine poor little Hamlet, who was afraid of the *troldt* under his bed, working at the mill.

The pastor saw her smiling and leaned towards her.

"What do you think, Mette? Should all children be educated until they're thirteen?"

Despite the hard faces of the men staring at her, Mette felt compelled to reply.

"My father was a school master, and so was my mother, a school mistress at least, before she married my father. They taught me to read and write, and to do arithmetic, and I'm very glad they did. All children should at least be able to do that, although I know for some it may take longer than others. I'm pleased if the law now says that children have to stay in school."

"Why do you need to read and write as well as you do," said Pieter, whom Mette knew had a great deal of trouble reading and could barely sign his name. "What good is it doing you?"

Mette knew he was referring to her lack of ability to find a decent husband and to marry and have children. She blushed and looked down, saying no more. The men returned to their discussion, moving on to the merits of the new Land Act and a condemnation of Julius Vogel, the man who'd lured them to New Zealand and had recently been voted in as Premier once more.

A large pair of boots appeared in her vision.

"I would like to dance with you, please."

Without checking to see who was speaking, Mette leapt to

her feet ready to join the dance and get away from Pieter and the group of men who were now ignoring her. Too late she realized it was a Waltz, which she must never dance with an unmarried man, and the man who faced her now was Gottlieb Karlsen, who worked on the road crew breaking rocks, was definitely unmarried and definitely not a man she should dance with. This was going to cause discussion once they returned home. He smiled at her with a large crooked mouth that was missing several teeth, and his breath wafted towards her in a miasma. But she had stood up and was now obliged to dance with him unless she wanted to cause further problems. She winced as he put his arm around her waist and they glided onto the floor together—not exactly glided as Gottlieb, like Mette, was wearing large hobnailed boots. She leaned back as far as she could to avoid the almost visible smell of his breath and committed herself to the dance, which seemed to go on forever. He smiled at her the whole time, obviously very pleased with his own success at finding a partner. When the dance finished, he remained beside her, his arm around her waist, expecting they were together until the end of the evening, if not forever. Mette hastily remembered something important she had to tell Maren, and escaped from the clutches of his arm across the room to her sister.

"You will come back?" he called after her. She gave a vague wave and grabbed Maren's arm in relief. Maren grinned at her.

"I see you have found yourself a wonderful partner," she whispered, looking across at Gottlieb, who was staring at Mette. "But be careful. If he comes courting Pieter will probably be very happy to see him and give him permission to marry you."

63

Mette gave Maren a light punch on the arm.

"Please don't say that," she said. "It was quite accidental that I danced with him. I must now find someone else to dance with right away, before he comes back and expects to have the next dance with me."

Before the next dance began she managed to corral Pieter. He was happy to dance with her, wanting to continue their discussion, or at least his side of the discussion.

"Mette," he said, panting as they twirled around in a Polka. "You don't understand the importance of a man's work. It is physical, and to do it well a man must start working young to make himself strong."

"And what about women," she said. "Should we be educated? If you have a girl next time, will she stay in school until she is thirteen, at least?"

He sighed.

"If she does she will never find a husband," he said. Then, just to make sure she understood he added, "Like you."

"If I do," she replied, "and if I have children, I will teach them to read in Danish, German and English, so that they can read newspapers and contracts, and especially so they can enjoy great literature, like, like *Fru Marie Grubbe*, or a *Tale of Two Cities*."

They danced for a minute more, before he said quietly, "Then I expect you will never marry." She knew he was thinking of his small cottage, and how one day soon he might need more room, so said nothing in reply. Pieter escorted her in silence back to Maren, who was sitting with Hamlet clutched awkwardly against her swollen belly.

Mette sat quietly beside Maren for a while, watching the married couples dancing together, thinking about Pieter and her sister.

"Maren," she said eventually. "Will Hamlet and this new baby of yours go to school and learn how to read?"

"I expect so," answered Maren, jiggling Hamlet up and down to stop him from squirming like an eel. "Pieter says it's the law now, and he always obeys the law. Not that he likes the idea very much."

"He says Hamlet will join him at the sawmill as soon as he is able," said Mette.

They both stared at Hamlet silently. He had hold of the neckline of Maren's dress and was tugging at it, obviously hungry. Maren looked up at Mette, her expression disingenuous. "I hope by the time he starts work at the mill he will no longer need to feed from my breast."

Both sisters started giggling, first silently, and then in full, gasping hysteria, tears running down their cheeks.

When she had finally calmed down, Mette asked, "Does Pieter know that our father taught you to read?"

Maren gazed across the room to where Pieter stood staring at them angrily. They had embarrassed him with their laughter. "I told him that I could read a little bit, but that I didn't really like it. I said I was bored all the time father was teaching us, and that you were his little star. Which was true of course."

Mette was shocked. How could Maren lie so to her husband, about reading of all things? They sat without speaking for a while, the companionship of the previous laughter forgotten.

As people began to tire, the mayor, Mr. Snelson, who was attending the dance in his capacity of mayor, climbed onto a bale of hay and introduced Viggo Monrad, even though everyone there knew who he was. Viggo Monrad was seeking the nomination to the Board of Education and would very much like them all to support him, Mayor Snelson told them, at least those men who had taken citizenship and were able to vote, which was a handful of those present. Mette was very tired at that point and did not pay much attention to what he said, but she noticed that it was very much like her side of the argument she had just had with Pieter. He recommended that all children should stay in school until Standard Six and he hoped they would all agree that the new Education Act was a wonderful idea. Mette tried hard to avoid Pieter's eye during the speech, although she suspected he was glaring at her.

The dance ended at ten o'clock. Viggo Monrad stood to thank them for their attendance on behalf of his wife and himself. Of course, Olga Monrad would not come to a dance like this one. Her pregnancy had nothing to do with it; she was not the type of person who would feel comfortable here. But Mette had seen her at church every Sunday, sitting in the front pew, her husband beside her. And when any of the women from Schleswig had a baby, Olga would send over something nice for the baby to wear, such as tiny knitted booties, as well as food for the parents such as sausage and bread.

They applauded his speech enthusiastically and began to file out towards the carts. Mette had danced with several men she knew from church, but all were older and married. Gottlieb Karlsen's eyes had followed her the whole time from where he sat on a bale of hay at the end of the shed but he had not gathered his courage enough to ask her to dance a second time. She had carefully avoided making eye contact and wondered how she would be able to shake him off in future. But she had enjoyed herself now, which was the main thing.

The trip home in the dark of the night under the stars was

beautiful. Hans Christian and Johanna were crowded onto the bullock cart with them, and Hans Christian pointed out some of the stars, especially the cluster called the Southern Cross, which could not to be seen from Schleswig. They traveled in the company of four families from the clearing, a group of men from the lumber camp, and another from the road crew, so she was not afraid that the *Hauhau* warrior would jump from the bush and steal Hamlet away. Some of the men carried squared axes at their feet and kept an eye on the bush. They could throw them as accurately as any native could throw a tomahawk, and protect the women and children. Hamlet slept in his mother's arms, where he had been for the entire evening, oblivious then to the dancing, or now to the chance of being taken away and eaten by a troldt who was really a *Hauhau*.

She was glad to finally see the clearing again, with its rows of neat wooden cottages and gardens facing the road. Hans Christian's lesson had helped her understand why Pieter had such problems growing vegetables in his front garden, and why she had to use the spot at the end of the clearing. He had chosen to site his cottage facing south, with the garden in front. In the southern hemisphere, it would be necessary for a garden to face north. She longed to point this out to him, but he'd take it as an attempt to win their previous discussion about the importance of education over experience. Silence was the best option.

Pieter pulled the dray up in front of their cottage and they watched as others went on their way. The dray with the men from the road crew was the last to pass, and she saw Gottlieb Karlsen staring at her. She gave him a half smile, to show she understood that he had wanted to dance with her more, then regretted it when he leered back at her.

8

Searching For the Boys

The mail coach passes along the road daily, frequently heavily freighted with passengers and luggage. Strong coaches and horses and skillful driving are necessary to overcome the difficulties and dangers of travelling such roads. It is no less than wonderful that day after day, and regularly about the same time, the coach arrives at the various stopping places on the road. Coachman During is entitled to no small amount of credit for the clock-work like regularity of his appearances, and particularly in wet and rough weather, such as was experienced during the past week.
Patea Mail, August 15, 1877

Frank had not had much time to consider the disappearance of the Scandi boys. He'd asked after them in Napier, with no success, but had managed to track down Anna, the young woman Jens had liked. The Scandi community in Napier was not large, and was clustered in one area. He asked after someone who had come over on the *Inverene* from Copenhagen and tracked down a man working at the stables who sent him to the right family. The young woman's name was Anna Jespersen, and although he did not speak to her, he did speak to her father, Christian Jespersen.

"He was a nice young man," the father said. "Lively, with red hair and a friendly smile always on his face. They were together all the time coming here, and I thought—I hoped—they would marry in New Zealand. But the government sent me here, and Jens was sent to his cousin in Manawatu. She'll be upset to know he's gone missing."

Later he rode up to the lumber camp and checked the boys' *whare*. Hans Christian had cleaned it up, removing all the rotting food, but two bedrolls sat neatly on one side. Clearly, they had not gone anywhere with the intention of not returning. He found a locked metal box underneath one of the bedrolls; shaking it he heard the rattle of coins. He would give those to Nissen and Sorensen. He was sure they would find a use for them.

He rode down the path to the river the boys would have followed, and came out just across from the tent that must belong to Knud Jensen. A rough track ran alongside the river. He dismounted and walked upstream. Fifty yards along he came to the remains of a campfire. Stirring the ashes, he found a few cooked *huhu* grubs, which indicated the presence of someone familiar with the Maori diet, if not a Maori. It could very well be the same man Mette had seen in the bush, but the food did not definitively prove he was a Maori. Deserters were quick to adopt that diet if they wanted to survive. The bush was trampled nearby and he found the imprint of a horseshoe and beside it the print of a bare foot. It was very large. He put his boot against it and estimated a size eleven or even twelve.

Downstream he found evidence of a previous search, a jumble of footprints, shod not barefoot, broken branches, and the butt end of a cigar. He stood for a while staring out across the river.

"Where are you, Paul and Jens?" he said softly. "What happened to you?"

He could imagine them struggling in the water, and then being swept to their death. But it was strange that the bodies had not yet surfaced. And the possible presence of the *Hauhau*, as Mette called him, was interesting. Things weren't as settled as he'd told the settlers; one angry Maori did not mean an attack of any kind was likely, but why was the man hanging around in the bush? There had to be a reason. And had he seen the boys?

He followed the trampled bush further downstream and stopped again to look at the water. It told him nothing. But on his side of the river, under the hanging branches of a willow tree, he saw light glint off something. He removed his coat and boots and lay them on the riverbank. Then, balancing carefully on a lower branch he eased out over the water and leaned down, scooping up a small glass bottle trapped in the branches. It was empty. The stopper, if there had been one, was gone. The bottle had raised letters on one side – HO, which meant nothing to him. He sniffed the opening but could smell nothing. Might not be important, but slid it into his coat pocket.

As he backed along the branch towards the riverbank he heard a horse snickering and froze. His own horse was tethered fifty yards away, his carbine holstered on the saddle. The sound had come from somewhere close by. Very close by. He slid his legs off the branch and into the river, landing thigh deep in water, and ducked down as low as he could. He could see nothing. The sound came again. Someone was on the track alongside the river, not moving. Was someone waiting for him? He thought briefly of calling out, asking who was there, but something felt wrong.

He edged out into the river toward the sound, holding onto the willow branches. A horse stamped softly, confirming someone was there. He moved around the periphery of the willow, feeling his way with his feet, trying not to disturb the water and alert the watcher.

At the far edge of the willow, where the bank curved outwards towards him, he stopped and looked hard, parting branches carefully. He could see a shape through the trees, but nothing more than a dark shadow intermingled with the leaves. He crouched there wondering what to do. He'd stalked fighters in the past, and once, during the attack on Otapawa, he had shot a boy who was hiding behind a tree, not realizing he was armed only with a useless old musket, a memory that still haunted him. He'd not used a gun much since, but carried his old Calisher and Terry carbine when he was in his coach or on horseback. Unfortunately, the watcher was between him and his carbine.

His leg bumped up against something that felt like cold flesh. He glanced down. A dead eye looked back at him. Not now, he thought. Not now. He reached down carefully to touch whatever it was. He felt rough skin, and something moved, maybe with the movement of the water. His mind grappling with the idea that he might have found one of the boys, he pushed against it. Once again it moved away from him, whether by its own effort or with the water he couldn't tell. He edged his foot underneath whatever it was and lifted it upwards.

With a huge thrashing of water a giant eel the size of a small woman reared from the water and lashed at him with huge teeth. He leapt back, cursing.

He heard a shuffle of hooves hitting dirt as the watcher on the bank dismounted. Could he make it to the other side? Possibly. But that would leave him vulnerable. The watcher could be armed, and if he wasn't then Frank's own gun was close at hand for him.

The sound of a troop of horses was suddenly in the air, coming towards him from the direction of the *Pa*. He heard the horseman mutter something, a slap of thighs against saddle, and pounding hooves as his observer galloped away.

He clambered quickly up onto the bank, but was too late to see anything other than a faint disturbance of dust disappearing along the track towards the hills.

Within minutes a troop of Armed Constables crashed along the pathway from town and pulled up in front of him, carbines out and trained on him. He raised him arms slowly, his hands flat and facing outwards, his face impassive.

"S'orlright," said a familiar voice. "I know 'im. That's Frank Hardy. Played cards with 'im just last week. He's a coachman on the Royal Mail. Used to be a Die Hard."

The carbines remained trained on him until the captain moved his hand slightly.

Frank lowered his hands cautiously as the carbines swung away. None of the men let go of the guns, however, but kept them resting across their knees at the ready.

Frank stamped his feet to ease the chill of the water. "Looking for someone?" He was freezing, his wet trousers clinging to him uncomfortably.

The captain stared at him. He had pale blue protruding eyes and a scraggly fair moustache that trailed down each side of his mouth.

"What were you doing here?"

"I saw something in the water and I went in to fetch it."

"By the river," said the captain. "What were you doing by the river."

"Is there some reason I shouldn't be by the river?"

The captain looked at him with narrowed eyes.

"If you refuse to answer my questions we'll take you in and send you upriver."

Frank shrugged. He knew what upriver meant. The Armed Constabulary were rumored to have a secret prison up the Whanganui River from which few returned and none escaped. He knew the threat was empty, but also knew it would do no good argue with the man.

"I was looking for two missing boys who were last seen crossing..."

The captain grunted and signaled for his men to follow him.

"Are you looking for someone?" asked Frank.

The captain reined in his horse and looked back.

"An escaped prisoner," he said shortly. "One of ours, a big man like you. Not in this area that we know of, but..."

"I heard you were looking for someone who had something to do with Titokowera's campaign," said Frank, not looking at Wilson who'd probably told him more than he should have.

The captain stared at him, his eyes popping out even more but did not reply.

"Why now, after all these years?" persisted Frank.

"Had him in prison," said the captain. "But he escaped a few weeks ago and he's gone on a rampage."

An ex-soldier—one of ours the captain had said. Not Mette's *Hauhau* at least. But who was it who'd been watching him? Someone dangerous, or just someone resting there for no reason.

The captain raised his hand and beckoned to the troop to follow him. As Wilson passed him he leaned down.

"Watch yourself," he said to Frank quietly. "This escaped bloke's looking for people like you—old soldiers."

Constable Price was sitting in Hop Li's kitchen enjoying a lunch of slow-roasted mutton flap when Frank returned to the Royal Hotel. Hop Li cut him a slice of meat and handed it to him with a large chunk of damper, bread that he had cooked in the open fire roaring in the fireplace. Frank ate standing beside the fire, drying the dampness from his trouser legs.

"Just ran into our friends from the Armed Constabulary," he said between bites. "Looking for some murderous prison escapee."

Constable Price grunted.

"They don't tell me anything, those buggers," he said. "They come into my territory, they should tell me what they're after."

"All I know is, I fit the profile," said Frank. "They drew their weapons on me thinking I might be him. An ex-soldier I think."

"Big man then," said Price, looking Frank up and down.

"I thought he might be a deserter," said Frank. "But the captain said he's been in prison since the war, Tito's war."

"I don't hold with chasing deserters," said Price, wiping grease from his chin with his sleeve. "Not after all this time. Not a deserter though, you say?"

"There's a man hanging around up behind the mill. I thought he might be the man they're after, but doesn't sound like it," said Frank. "A Maori I think, although someone who saw him thought he was a *Hauhau*." He smiled to himself as he said it. He would tell Price about Mette's scare at some point, although without mentioning the tomahawk, which he'd put into the foot box of his coach for safe-keeping. He'd better buy himself a revolver, something that he could keep in his coat pocket. Legally he was allowed a single gun, but he needed two, to be safe in all situations.

"Don't get *Hauhau* around here anymore," said Price. "Not since '69. I was here in the panic back then, November it was. We were all sure Tito was on his way. Remember the old Bishop? Bishop Monrad, the Scandi? He was so scared he buried his plate in the garden and ran off back to Denmark, his tail between his legs."

"I talk to Captain Monrad sometimes," said Hop Li. "A good man, not scared."

"That's his son," said Price. "He stayed around, kept the farm going."

"You find anything today, boss?' asked Hop Li. "You out looking for the boys I think."

"I searched the river," said Frank. He took out the bottle and showed it to them. "I found this. Mean anything to either of you?"

They both shook their heads.

"I think I'll head out to the Pa as well, after my next trip to Napier."

"You could talk to the men on the road crew, Jackson's men," suggested Price. "They're down by the river picking up rocks quite often. They might have seen something."

"Good idea," said Frank. I know Sergeant Jackson. Used to be a Die Hard."

Sergeant Jackson had left the Die Hards at the same time as Frank and he met him occasionally for a glass of beer or a game of cards. Jackson had found work in road construction when the troops returned to England. Roads were being built all through New Zealand at a breathless pace, and Sergeant "Jack" Jackson worked the roads through the Seventy Mile Bush from Palmerston up towards Napier, so they ran into one another frequently. He would ask him if he had heard anything about the disappeared boys, or if he or his men had any suggestions as to their possible whereabouts. His men were mostly Scandies.

He found Jackson, wearing his old Die Hard blouse as a badge of his past, sitting on a rock on the Foxton road, supervising a gang of men who were breaking rocks to resurface the road in the Macadam style. They'd carried in loads of river rocks and were pounding them to metal. Jackson was watching as a group of tow-headed, red-faced Scandies cracked the rocks into small pieces, measuring the size of each piece by putting it into their mouths.

"Easiest way for them to understand how big to crack the rocks," he told Frank cheerfully. "Luckily they all have big mouths so the metal comes out just the right size."

Frank watched, interested.

"What do you do with the metal when it's finished? How do you decide where to run the road, where to lay the metal?"

Jackson pulled out a clay pipe and a packet of tobacco and started stuffing pinches of tobacco into the bowl, whistling between his teeth as he did so.

After a minute he said, "We just follow the bridle path, mostly, the paths beaten down by people like you on horseback. Then we widen it by chopping down the trees on either side. Big bastards, they are, those trees sometimes. The bullocks drag a grader over the path, an' then we drop on a layer of bigger rocks—bigger'n a Scandie's mouth—then a layer of mullock, and last of all a layer of metal. Other times we have to follow where the surveyor says." He chuckled and sucked on his pipe. "But we don't always do what the surveyor tells us, 'course. What the hell does he know, that's what I ask meself. I spent more time with the army building roads than ever I did fighting, especially during the last couple o' years. Muskets ever at the ready of course, but hardly ever had to use it after '68."

"You were on General Chute's March, weren't you?" asked Frank.

"Near killed me," said Jackson. "All them hills and gullies, the poor bloody pack horses dying. We et a couple o' them. Ever tasted packhorse, Hardy?"

Frank shook his head, smiling inwardly. He'd heard Jackson's story several times before, the March around the east side of the mountain hoping to find a shorter route to New Plymouth, the hardship, the brutal General Chute. It was Jackson's standard drinking story.

Jackson seemed to sense that Frank had heard the story before, and stopped himself, saying, "Well, no doubt you heard me tell it before."

After a minute, Frank said, "I've been asked to look for those boys that disappeared. The Scandi boys—they've been gone a couple of weeks. You haven't heard anything, have you?"

Jackson shook his head. "Can't say as I have. Didn't they just drown? That's what I heard. Happens often enough when you have people who can't swim trying to cross rivers."

"Probably. But we can't find them in the river, or along the banks. The brother of the older boy is afraid some other harm has come to them, that someone has attacked them and left the bodies somewhere."

"More'n likely," replied Jackson, changing his opinion easily "The roads are full of robbers and bandits, not to mention the towns. Did you hear about the robbery at Snelson's store in the Square? Snelson, the new Mayor? He was away for the day and someone bashed in a window and took watches, plate and jewelry, everything they could carry. Five hundred quid's worth I heard. Threw around his furniture as well. And the police raided a house yesterday. A posse of Armed Constabulary from Wanganui Town, looking for booze I heard. Found a hundred-quid's worth hidden in a back room. A lodging house without a license, selling booze to settlers who can't handle it. Be better if the coppers spent their time clearing the bush of bushwhackers, I reckon. Those Armed Constabulary, they don't care about anyone. Do what they want. Seen 'em around here quite a bit lately. Up to summat I reckon."

"But no one attacking strangers that you've heard of," asked Frank. He refrained from mentioning that the Armed Constables were on the lookout for someone specific. Jackson was a talker and would spread rumors in no time.

Jackson rubbed his chin thoughtfully.

"Now that you mention strangers, I did hear that there's someone up in the bush behind the Hokowhitu sawmill. One of these boys says he saw a scoundrel dressed half native half European lurking around." He stopped and looked at the men working for him. "Which of you blokes told me he saw that bastard lurking up behind the Hokowhitu mill?"

The tallest member of the group took a rock out of his mouth where he had been measuring it, and spoke up. "That was me, saw him a few days ago."

"What did he look like?"

"Could of been that bloke there," pointing at Frank. "Looked like him, not quite as tall, beard, dark. Native, I think. Didn't see him close enough to tell."

"I know the gentleman in question," said Frank. "Threw a tomahawk at me, just missed because I had bent down to pick something up."

"So you seen 'im?" asked Jackson.

"I had my back to him at the time," replied Frank. "I'm not sure what he wanted, but he appeared to be after a piglet a young lady had just caught."

"Bit over the top, innit?" said Jackson. "Throwin' a tomahawk at someone to get a pig? Musta been hungry."

Frank shrugged.

"Anything else you can tell me? Have you been down by the river at all?

Jackson looked at his road crew. "These lot are down at the river all the time, collecting rocks. If there was bodies there they would've said. You boys seen any bodies down at the river?"

"Not dead ones," joked the one who claimed to have seen the man in the bush. "Seen a few *puhi*. Can't touch them though, the boys from the *Pa* would come after me."

"And so they should," Frank said. "They should come after you anyway, spying on their young women like that."

The tall man turned away smirking. Frank noticed that he had several teeth missing or hanging loose, detracting from his already disagreeable face.

"Ya know," said Jackson. "You could go up and ask at the *Pa*. They're up and down the river all the time in their *waka*, and if there were a body in the river they'd know about it. Maybe they found a piece of clothin' or summat."

80

"I might do that," said Frank. He'd already decided to visit the Pa.

"Ya know," said Jackson suddenly. "Could be the angel that fella up in the bush Karlsen seen."

"He's seeing angels now?" asked Frank.

"Nah, avenging angel. The one that's killing people up in Poverty Bay."

"I haven't heard of an avenging angel," said Frank. "Who is it he's killing?"

"Not sure," said Jackson. "Soldiers mostly, I think."

"Around here? I haven't heard of anyone like that."

"Not here, just up in Poverty Bay, as I said," said Jackson. "Last I heard of 'im. Killed a couple of men up there, ex-soldiers, and they was on the hunt for Tito, back with you."

"Not likely the same person then," said Frank. It sounded more like the man the Armed Constabulary were after. The escaped soldier. Not the Maori up behind the mill.

He stood up to leave.

"How come you're working for the Scandies?" asked Jackson. "No money there." He stopped and looked at Frank. "Not about the woman, is it? Did I hear you mention a young lady? Got a horn for one of them Scandi girls, 'ave ya? Can't go wrong there, they're all looking for a nice young pommy bloke like you, especially one who has all his teeth."

Frank walked away without speaking. His hand twitched with the desire to punch Jackson's lights out, but he knew it would do no good. Some people's minds could not be changed. Jackson was typical of his kind, and Frank wasn't at all sure that he might have thought the same way, in the past. One day, he hoped, he'd have the chance to change Jackson's mind, although his friend would probably die with his intolerances.

9

The Attack

To arrive in the Isabella Hamilton: Nursery, sponging, hip, and reclining baths; Block tin dish covers, with plated handles; Bidet and washstands with furniture complete; Platow's coffee pots and French cafetieres; Bronzed table kettles and tea urns; Chess tables, patent mangles; 1000 yards galvanized game netting; Stump, French and folding bedsteads.
Lyttelton Times, August 8, 1860

It had been a long and exhausting day and Mette was happy to be back in her lean-to getting ready for bed. She loved her bed. It had belonged to a soldier in the British Imperial Army, was made of good sturdy iron and folded down flat to the floor. On top was a mattress stuffed with straw, so she was very comfortable. Maren and Pieter slept on a solid wooden bed and Maren often complained about the insects that lived in the wood and crawled from the wood and took up residence in the mattress. She would hear Maren through the wall, slapping at them and denouncing them angrily to Pieter. One of the many sounds she heard through the wall.

It was very cold at night, even in spring, and Mette wore a

heavy nightgown, woolen stockings, and a cap that covered her head right down below her ears. She undressed in the dark and put on her nightclothes, not wanting to waste a candle. Next door she heard the soft lowing of the milch cow, which always comforted her and made her feel safe. Pieter and Maren had murmured quietly for a few minutes, and already she could hear Pieter snoring softly. She often read a little before she went to sleep but tonight she was so tired she couldn't keep her eyes open and fell asleep almost as soon as she crawled into her bed.

When she awoke it was still dark. She was surprised as she seldom woke during the night. She lay there smiling to herself, thinking of the dance. She wished there were more events like that to attend. She had enjoyed dancing, especially the Mazurka which had left her breathless and exhilarated.

Something seemed to shift in the shadow, over near the door. She stared towards it, not sure what she had seen.

Someone—a man's voice—said quietly, "Mette?"

She sat up, clutching her quilt to her chest.

"Who is that? What do you want?" Had the *Hauhau* come to kill her? How did he know her name?

"*Du kender,*" someone replied in Danish, and laughed softly.

"No, no, I do not know, I…" She felt relief that it was not the *Hauhau*, but at the same time puzzled that anyone would be in her room. Was it Pieter? No, it could not be. She could hear Pieter snoring on the other side of the wall. The shadow moved towards her. She still could not tell who it was, but she was beginning to be afraid. Should I wake Pieter and Maren, she thought? Pieter needed his sleep so he could leave early in the morning for the sawmill. And Maren, Maren was having a baby and was always tired.

She was still deciding whether to scream when a hand was clapped over her mouth and a face pushed near to hers. A smell of rotting teeth washed over her, and now she knew who it was. If I call him by his name, she thought, will he think I am happy to see him? Her body was starting to shake and she felt cold and numb all over.

She managed to put both her hands on one of his and tried to push it away. It came loose briefly from her mouth, and she gasped, "Don't, please don't."

But he was already pulling the quilt away from her body and clutching at her gown.

"You want me to, I know you do," he whispered. "After, we will get married because no one else will want you. That will be good for both of us."

He's right, she thought fatalistically. And it was my own fault. I did not look first, but stood up without thinking. Nevertheless, she kept pushing at his hand and struggling against the other hand as it pulled at her nightgown. His hand was still tight over her mouth; she grunted as loudly as she could, a sound from deep within her, praying silently that Pieter or Maren would hear and come to help.

He leaned on her heavily, his elbow on the bed and his hand over her mouth, pressing her down. She felt him fumbling with his own trousers, and something hard pressed against her stomach. Her heart pounded and she thought she might die of horror and shame. She tried to shake her head loose from his grip, but it was held fast in place. She wrenched her whole body from side to side in a fruitless effort to dislodge him. He laughed, seeming to enjoy her struggle. He pulled her nightdress slowly up, pushing himself at her at the same time. She braced herself for what was to come, her eyes closed tight so she could not see his face.

Then the bed did what it was supposed to do, and folded down flat. They landed in a heap, him on top of her still, his hands now out on the sides of the bed.

"Pokkers!" he blurted out, unable to stop himself. Then he whispered harshly, "You must be quiet, or your family will hear." His hand slapped onto her mouth firmly once more. She tugged at his hand, noticing as she did that blood ran from the side of her own hand where the bed rail had hit it. The collapse of the bed had happened too quickly, and she had not had time to scream for help.

But through the wall she heard Pieter or Maren stir and stay something. Her attacker's hand tightened over her mouth so she could barely breath, but she made one more noise deep in her chest. She knew this was her single chance for rescue.

"Mette?" called Pieter tentatively. "Is everything well?"

The hand tightened even more and through the pain she managed another sound.

She heard Pieter say to Maren, "I'm going to see if Mette is all right. I'm hearing some strange noises through the wall."

Maren said something quiet and she heard Pieter get out of bed and walk across the room. Her attacker swung his legs around and sat up and the hand on her mouth loosened briefly.

"Pieter, Pieter, help me," she said. Her voice came out as a hoarse whisper, but Pieter had heard and started to run. Her attacker leaped to his feet, pulling his trousers back on.

"*Taeve*," he snarled at Mette. "I will see you later, when you are walking in the bush. And you will like it and we will be married." He began tucking himself back into his trousers, his face a mask of hatred and lust.

85

Mette was too distraught to reply. I will never, never marry him, she thought. I will die first.

As her attacker opened the door to her lean-to Pieter came into view. The intruder pushed at Pieter's chest and Pieter fell backwards with a grunt of pain. They heard the intruder plunging into the bush, breaking branches and swearing.

Pieter struggled upright and Mette waited for him to chase after her attacker. He was a big man and strong, and would easily overtake and punish the man who had attacked her. Instead, he turned to her.

"Who was that?"

"I don't know," she said, and burst into tears. "I could not...tell." If I tell Pieter who it is he will either kill him or make me marry him, she thought. I wouldn't be happy about either of those things.

"Someone from the dance?" he asked. When she did not reply, he said, "What did you do, Mette? Did you encourage someone at the dance?"

"I don't know. Perhaps I did," she said through gasps. "But is it permitted that he could come to my home and attack me like that, because I looked at him at the dance?" She stopped herself from saying because I danced with him at the dance, because that would allow Pieter to work out who it was.

Pieter shook his head, standing there looking at her his face full of reprimand. It was almost more than she could bear.

"You mustn't be childish, Mette," he said. "A man cannot sometimes help himself. There are many men here who do not have women, and you are a very nice woman. Not pretty, but a good cook and some men would be happy to have you."

Mette had regained some of her composure.

"I would never marry a man who came into my room in the

night and attacked me," she said. She plucked at the middle of her nightdress and held it against her hand to stop the bleeding. Pieter didn't seem to notice. Instead he asked shrewdly, "How would you know, if you didn't see who it was?"

She had no reply to that and thought for a minute of telling him who it was. But before she could speak, Pieter added, "We can't report this to the police. It would cause too much trouble in our community. I'll ask Sergeant Hardy what we should do. He's like a policeman, and very helpful. For now, I will make a bar for the door. When you come in you must place the bar across and you will be kept safe."

"Is it necessary to tell Sergeant Hardy?" asked Mette. "He'll think because I have been attacked twice that it's my fault when someone attacks me."

Pieter looked at her, frowning.

"It is a lot your fault Mette," he said sternly. "You must be more careful."

He left to report back to Maren, and Mette wondered what he would tell her. Maren would understand, at least she hoped she would. She pulled her rocking chair in front of the door and wedged it under the handle. The smallest sound and she would scream her head off. Then she sank onto the bed and gave way to a flood of tears. She would try to sleep, but knew it would be very, very difficult.

Morning came eventually, and she awoke to the sounds of roosters crowing, amazed to realize she had slept. Her body ached and the hand where she had cut herself had crusted over. She lay there for a long time before she gathered her strength to dress and go outside to gather feed for the cow.

10

On the Riverbank

On Sunday afternoon, a little girl was run over by a horse up the river bank. When picked up, it was thought that life was extinct, but after a little time animation returned, and it is hoped that the little sufferer is not seriously injured. We learn that the horses were being driven down the road by a man behind them on horseback, and were going at a fast pace when the accident occurred.
  Wanganui Chronicle, 7 August 1877

Frank listened to the story Pieter told him with growing disbelief.

"This is not the fault of your sister-in-law," he said finally. He had ridden out to the clearing to talk to Nissen, but finding him not home had stopped to talk to Pieter Sorensen, half hoping he would see the young woman again.

"She encouraged him," Pieter said dismissively. "A woman should not dance with a single man unless she is willing to consider marrying him."

"You know who it is then?"

"She wouldn't say, but she danced with an unmarried man at the Monrad's shed, one of the men on the road building crew. I expect she gave him the impression she would like to marry him and he came to her room to visit her."

"In the middle of the night? And he attacked her? That's not a visit, that's an invasion."

Pieter nodded reluctantly. "Perhaps he went too far. But still, he's a man. That's what she should expect if she flirts with someone."

Frank could feel himself growing angry, but he could see there was no point in arguing with Pieter, any more than there had been with Sergeant Jackson.

"Would she talk with me?" he asked. He didn't think it was the best idea, but at least something would be done about it.

"I do not see why she shouldn't," said Pieter, to Frank's surprise.

He went to talk to Mette, who was washing linen in a large tub. She was looking tired and stressed and his heart ached for her. He brought up the subject cautiously.

"Your brother-in-law tells me you had a problem the other night."

She nodded without looking at him, scrubbing at the washing as if her life depended on it.

"I told him that the person who attacked you was despicable," said Frank. "Personally, I'd like to see him go to gaol for a good long time. And horsewhipped first."

She glanced at him sideways, but said nothing, continuing to scrub the same spot on her wet clothing.

"Pieter seems to think you did something to encourage him, but…"

"No, I did not," she spoke up, still scrubbing at the same spot on her garment. Frank glanced at it and saw that it was a nightdress, and that it was stained with blood in the front.

He felt a jolt of cold horror, soon replaced by intense anger. Momentarily he was too angry to speak, but said, finally, "I don't think for a minute that you did anything to encourage him," he said. "But Pieter doesn't think like us."

She looked up at him finally, letting the nightdress fall back into the water.

"He does not have the education," she said.

He smiled.

"So I noticed."

He stood there for a while in silence, wondering what he could do. Finally he said, "If you wish, I could have a talk to the man who…"

"No," she said quickly. "I don't know who it was."

"Pieter seemed to think it was someone one the Foxton road crew, a person you danced with at the dance."

Her face reddened.

"How would he know that if I don't know?"

"What do you know then? Was there anything about him that seemed familiar, or that you could describe?"

"He had bad teeth and very, very bad breath," she said.

Frank nodded, remembering his discussion with Jackson and his crew. Now he was sure he knew who the bastard was, and was not surprised.

"Lots of men around here with bad teeth," he said, not letting her know that he had guessed whom it might be. "Probably difficult to narrow it down to one."

"I don't want you to try," she said. "Pieter has made my door secure and I'll be more careful about where I walk. I won't have a problem again."

"Best to avoid the bush paths now anyway," he said. "Our friend from the other day, the piglet thief, is apparently hanging around up behind the mill. One of the...someone I spoke to the other day said he'd seen him there."

She sighed. "I must stay in the clearing at all times, I suppose. That will make for a very dull life." Her hand pushed absently at the washing as if she wished it would just go away. He watched the pink spreading in the water, mesmerized. If he ever had the opportunity he would kill the bastard who'd violated her.

"Tell me about the boys," he said after a while. "Paul and Jens. I'm trying to find what could have happened to them, for Hans Christian and Pieter."

She stopped pushing at the washing.

"They were happy boys, full of life. Jens – he's my cousin, or at least the cousin of my cousin, and I've known him all my life. He's like a brother to me. Paul was his friend. They did everything together, but Paul was the leader. They came from Schleswig in the last year, Paul first so he's learned more English. They built themselves a *raupo whare* up near the logging camp and they lived...to tell the truth they lived like two pigs. But happy pigs." She smiled slightly at her own joke.

"What do you think has happened to them?" Frank asked, not mentioning he had been to the *whare* where the boys had lived.

"Sometimes I think they must have drowned, but then I know they could swim a little, or at least Jens could, and it seems strange that they would both drown. I've started to think that someone killed them and hid them somewhere. Like perhaps the *Hauhau* who tried to take my piglet."

"If he <u>was</u> a *Hauhau*, which may not be the case," said Frank. "More likely a deserter who's been living in the bush for years. He would still face a disciplinary hearing if he was caught, probably be sent back to England to be hanged."

91

She put her hand on her neck.

"That seems to be a terrible punishment for someone who doesn't want to fight. Is it right, do you think, to hang someone who runs away from the fighting?"

He was torn for a moment, and then found himself telling her the story he'd told Hop Li.

"My own brother deserted," he said. "He was in the 57th, the Die Hards, with me, but the discipline was too much for him and he went across the river to the enemy camp."

She put her hand over her mouth, her eyes wide.

"And they—your soldiers—brought him back and hanged him?'

He shook his head.

"It was worse than that. He deserted to the enemy—the *Hauhau* you are so afraid of—and they killed him."

"Then I'm right to be afraid," she said triumphantly. "Did they shoot him?'

Frank looked away from her questioning eyes.

"They cut off his head and displayed it to us, from across the river. On a pole."

She reached her hand out towards him, as if to comfort him.

"I'm very sorry. If they've done that to Paul and Jens, then I'll kill them with my own hands."

He shook his head, unable to speak for a minute.

"The beheadings and the cannibalism lasted a couple of years, mostly during Tito's war in '68 and '69. It's been years since they've done anything like that. You shouldn't worry about *Hauhau*." He thought about the man the Armed Constabulary were chasing. Could he be a Hauhau? Why would he be killing soldiers now, so many years after the Tito pursuit. Despite the brown legs he'd seen on the rider at the river, it still seemed more likely to him that the man was a deserter.

Mette interrupted his thoughts.

"But you think they're dead, don't you, the boys?"

He nodded. "I'm sorry, but I do."

"And will you find them? Find the bodies? We would all be happier if you could. It's not knowing that's so difficult."

"I'm trying," he said. "But there's not much to go on. I found a bottle...maybe you recognize it..."

He handed her the bottle with the initial H.O. and watched her as she Mette examined it.

"It's one of Knud's, I think," she said finally. "See these letters? H.O? That's for the House of Oldenburg, the royal family of our country...our real country," she added.

"Why would Knud need bottles like these?" he asked.

Mette blushed. "If I tell you, you can't say anything to Pieter or Hans Christian."

"Not if you don't want me to."

"At our church, we aren't allowed to drink alcohol. But Knud, he makes beer from the *matai* tree in his tent across the river. That's why he stays there sometimes...why he was there when they went across."

A sly grogger. He should have thought of that. And the foolish boys had gone across to buy the grog from him, and probably been drunk when they came back...

"You know about this, but Sorensen and Nissen don't?" he asked.

"Knud is my cousin," she explained. "Not on the same side as Jens, who was also his cousin. Jens and I are...were not cousins. As I said before, Jens is the cousin of my cousin, and that cousin is Knud."

93

He smiled. "I think I'm following this…"

She smiled back self-consciously. "Well, one of the older woman told me Knud was making alcohol from *matai* and asked me to say something to him, and I did once, at church. He didn't deny he was making it, but told me not to tell Pieter or Hans Christian. I said I wouldn't if he didn't sell it to any to the younger men as they aren't used to alcohol at all. A neighbor of mine back at home made himself very sick by drinking…what do you call it when it's made like that?"

"Sly grog," said Frank.

She nodded. "Yes, sly grog. I didn't want the younger men to start drinking sly grog. Perhaps he didn't think Jens and Paul were—are—younger men."

"Do you think Knud would talk to me honestly about it?"

"Probably not…but I could talk to him. We could go to him together…"

"Now?"

She looked up at him, her face more animated than it had been since he arrived.

"I'd like that," she said.

Her sister Maren had come from the cottage, little Hamlet on her hip, walking awkwardly with a belly swollen from a second child she carried.

"What would you like," she said sharply. She had a round golden-pink face surrounded by a halo of white blond curls and, unlike her sister, bright blue eyes. A pretty woman, undoubtedly, thought Frank, but not as interesting and intelligent-looking as her sister. Rather bland in fact, now he saw her up close.

"Sergeant Hardy has asked me to…go down to the river to see what I think about how Paul and Jens went across," improvised Mette.

Maren glared at Frank and then at Mette. "Pieter would not like you going off with this man," she said.

He saw a long look pass between the sisters, a look he found impossible to read. Finally, Maren said reluctantly, "If he asks I'll say you went into town to fetch some seeds from Snelson's. He won't like that either…but better than saying you went off with Sergeant Hardy." She gave Frank a hard look. "You will take care of my sister please."

He nodded. "Of course I will. I will protect her from the *Hau…*"

He saw Mette shake her head slightly and stopped. "From bushwhackers and murderers and wild pigs, and any dangerous creatures lurking in the bush. I swear." He put his hand on his heart and grinned at Maren to show her he was just joking. Maren's frown faded slowly. She shook her head and turned to go back inside the house, shooting one last look at Frank.

Mette wrung out her washing and hung it over the scrub.

"You'd think she was my big sister instead of my little sister," she said. His horse had wandered over to where they were standing, and pushed her head against Frank. She was ready to leave.

"Would you like to ride?" he asked Mette.

"I've never been on a horse before," she said nervously. "Except for…she won't jump up and down, will she?"

"I'll walk beside you and make sure she doesn't try to buck you off," he said, and was surprised to see a quick look of disappointment flash in her eyes. "Now I'll make a step for you with my hands, and you can hold onto the saddle and pull yourself up. She managed to get herself into the saddle, after initially falling across his back, and laughing heartily at her own clumsiness, which he rather enjoyed.

The river was over a mile away and he strode along in silence, leading his horse and thinking about what she had gone through, wondering what he could do about it that didn't end with him in the lockup. They arrived at the spot where the track ran down from the logging camp, the place that Hans Christian had told him was where the boys crossed the river. Across the river, they could see Knud Jensen's tent. Jensen was busy working on something out behind the tent.

"This is where they probably crossed," he said as he helped her from his horse, which involved more laughing and physical contact. They walked down to the water, which was now low to the point of being walkable most of the way.

"There's no place where a fallen log could span the river," he said. "It's wide here and when the water was up, as it was that day, the only way to get across would be to float holding on to a log."

Mette looked up and down the river. She seemed to have forgotten that they were on the way to see Knud.

"If I was going to use a log to float across," she said, "I would push it in right here and try to land on that gravel down there."

"Good suggestion. The curve in the river would throw you over to that side and you'd be swept right onto the gravel. What about coming back though?"

They both stood looking.

"We can't see from here," said Mette finally. "Perhaps there's another gravel patch they could aim for further down, if they started at that one."

"No, I checked down that way. "Once the river goes around this bend it's straight all the way down to the *Pa*."

She looked at him sharply.

"There are *Hauhau* in this *Pa*?"

Frank sighed. No, there were no *Hauhau* in the Pa. They were traders, bringing fresh fish and vegetables up the river from Foxton in their *waka*, their dugout canoes. The town would probably starve without them.

"I don't think so. It's just a *Pa*, with people going about their business like you and me. I'm going to go and talk with them soon. You can come along if you like."

"Perhaps," she said nervously. "If Pieter…"

He patted his horse. "I'll talk to Pieter," he said. "But we need to get across to see Knud. Hop back up on Copenhagen, and we'll…"

"Copenhagen? Your horse is named Copenhagen, from my country? That's a peculiar name for a horse," said Mette. "Why have you given him that name?"

"After the Old Duke's horse," said Frank. "Nothing to do with your country. I should have realized that when I told you his name. The Duke of Wellington was riding a War Horse named Copenhagen at the battle of Waterloo, and seeing he won, I thought the name would be a positive influence on this horse. She's a good horse, but probably not one you'd want to ride into battle. She can take us both across the river, however."

Mette looked at the horse nervously.

"Are you sure she's strong enough to carry us both? Won't we fall off and get swept away?"

"Don't worry, the water's barely up to the horse's stirrups. It would take more water than this to move her."

She grabbed hold of the saddle and hopped up onto the horse as if she had been riding all her life. "Come on up then," she said. "Don't fall in and get swept away...I can't swim."

He eased the horse into the water, and she leaned sideways to watch the water as it rose slowly up towards the stirrups. After a few minutes, it began to recede.

"The water didn't even reach my feet," she said. He was holding her firmly around the waist, but she didn't seem to notice. On the other side, the horse stopped and shook its mane, showering them both with droplets of water.

"See," said Frank to Mette, who was laughing softly, her hand over her mouth. "She wouldn't make a good war horse—she isn't smart enough. I'll tie her up here to reconsider her actions while we visit your cousin Knud.

"Yes, that is my bottle," said Knud. "Where did you find it?" He was sitting by a large kettle of boiling water with leaves and branches floating on the surface. He was older than Mette, in his thirties Frank thought, his hair darker than his cousin, and with heavy eyebrows that joined in the centre and hung over light blue eyes. Deep lines gouged his cheeks giving him a hangdog look.

"It was caught in the branches of the willow tree hanging over into the river, down that way" said Frank. "I was wondering if the boys could have dropped it. Did they have a bottle from you when they left here?"

Knud's eyes shifted away from Frank's gaze, then returned.

"No," he said without conviction. "They were just boys. I would not sell them my, my tea."

"*Warten Sie ein minute, Knud*," said Mette. "*Wir beide*, I mean to say both of us know that you do not sell tea. Did you sell alcohol to the boys, when I specifically said not to do it? How could you do that?" She paused for a minute and glanced at Frank. "Well, they're gone now and it will make no difference, except that knowing if they were drinking would help us find them as well as give us a possible reason for them to have drowned."

Knud looked downcast. He squared his shoulders and admitted, "I gave them a bottle, yes, I did give them a bottle—maybe that one there, which is certainly mine. What was I to do? They were cold when they arrived at my tent. They came across the river holding on to a log and the water was freezing. I could hear Paul's teeth chattering."

"You gave them a drink before they crossed back?" Asked Mette looking stern. "Surely that was not a good idea because ..."

Frank interrupted her. "You say they were in the river when they crossed it? They didn't walk across on a log?"

Knud shrugged. "As I said, they were wet."

"But you didn't tell Hans Christian this," asked Frank, "that they were in the water and not walking across a log?"

"He didn't ask. I assumed he knew what I meant."

Mette was frowning at her cousin.

"You gave the boys a drink and then you let them cross the river holding on to a log, knowing only Jens could swim?"

Knud looked uncomfortable.

"How was I to know they both couldn't swim good," he said, his voice rising. "Anyway, I cross the river all the time and it's easy here. I have never drowned, not even almost. The river is calm and shallow."

"Not that day," said Frank. "So you gave them a drink while they were here, and a bottle to take with them."

Knud nodded, looking more miserable by the minute.

"And the stopper was missing, so if this is the bottle you gave them, they had opened it and drunk more—possibly all—of it."

Knud was practically shrinking into his own body, staring at the brew in the kettle, no longer stirring it.

"I, I suppose that is true," he said.

Frank looked at Mette.

"So," he said. "We have two young boys who were probably not at all used to drinking alcohol with a couple of drinks in their bellies jumping into the river to float across it on a log. They'd already come across and landed on the gravel spit down there, as you guessed, and when they tried to go back, half tanked at that point, they had nowhere to land and were swept downstream."

Mette returned his look, her eyes filling with tears as she imagined the scene.

"That Maori chap was watching them when they came across," said Knud suddenly, evidently thinking that he could redeem himself with the information. "Thought I couldn't see him skulking on the other bank, but I could."

Frank and Mette both stared at him.

"He had a tomahawk too," added Knud. "Not that I was worried about him, but he could've helped them if they got into trouble. Don't know why he wouldn't." He took a closer look at Frank. "Kind of looks like you, come to think of it. Big like you, but with blue moko on his face so I could tell he were a Maori."

"The *Hauhau*," exclaimed Mette. "Perhaps he saw them in the river and went in and killed them."

Frank frowned. He wasn't ready to give up on the idea that the man was a deserter, and *moko* did not necessarily make him a Maori.

"It seems rather too much to think that they were drinking

and possibly in trouble, and then someone tried to kill them," he said.

"I suppose so," said Mette. "But Sergeant Hardy, how do you explain that the search party couldn't find their bodies. Something must have happened—something more than just drowning. Someone found the bodies and hid them, at least that much must have happened."

"Mette, you may call me Frank," he said, as if Knud was not there. "Sergeant Hardy sounds very formal and makes me feel as if I am still in the army."

Knud watched them, his eyes narrowing suspiciously. That will set the cat amongst the pigeons, thought Frank. Now they will have me courting the girl before you know it. Once the idea was in his head, though, it didn't seem like such a bad idea.

"Of course," he said, trying to undo the situation, "you could always call me Mr. Hardy."

Mette laughed loudly and it made him feel better than he had for a long time.

"I'll call you Sergeant Frank," she said, her eyes sparkling. "A, what do you call it, a compromise."

He thought that was probably the moment that he realized that he could very well be in love, but he looked at Knud and said, "If the boys were swept downstream, where do you think they would be?"

Knud spat into the dirt and stood up.

"Likely down by the *PapaioeaPa*," he said, gesturing down-stream. "Course, if they found them they would've told Constable Price. Or at least, one of the Native Constables woulda told him. Nothing in it for them to hide a couple of bodies. Not like they were carrying money or anything."

"Perhaps they blamed them for the Government action on the Manchester Block, the one where many of the Scandi are building farms," said Frank.

Knud shook his head, dismissing the possibility.

"Don't see why. They've been causing a bit o' trouble over there, in Feilding, like. But I can't see them coming up here and looking for two boys and killing them, just because they looked like Scandi and happened to be in the river."

"Sergeant Frank, you said we should go down to the *Pa* and talk to them," said Mette eagerly. "Why don't we do that? Perhaps you will be able to tell if they seem bloodthirsty and likely to kill two of my people. Could we go there right this minute?"

"It's getting late now," said Frank. "What about tomorrow?" Would you be able to come? Would Pieter stop you? I could come and fetch you around midday."

They started to walk back down to the river while Mette thought about it.

"I think I am able to come," she said after a few minutes. "But not tomorrow. Tomorrow is Sunday and I must go to church. I could come with you to the *Pa* on Monday."

He shook his head.

"I'm off to Napier on Monday," he said. "I'll be back late Tuesday. We'll go to the *Pa* on Wednesday. I'll come and collect you early, as soon as the sun is up."

"I'd like that." She smiled at him. He felt his heart lurch and smiled back.

"If you promise they won't hurt me, and if you are there Sergeant Frank, I'd enjoy seeing the *Pa*."

"I promise," he said, seriously this time. "Mette, I noticed you spoke German to Knud back there. Why did you not speak Danish?"

"It's very sad," she said. "My land, Schleswig, now belongs to Germany. That is why Hans Christian, and Pieter, and many people from Schleswig, came to New Zealand. We don't want to be Germans or to fight with the Prussians against France, and the young men, they don't wish to be forced to join the Prussian army. In Schleswig, we—the Danish people—speak Danish at home and German everywhere else. Except for at church of course, but even there...there are German people living in Schleswig as well and they go to church with us."

"How terrible that Paul and Jens left home to avoid conscription into the army, and then died doing a simple thing like crossing a river," he said.

"That's true," she said. "But their mothers would rather have them die here than die in the Prussian army. We do not love General Bismarck and his troops in Schleswig."

"Has Hans Christian written to his mother about his brother and his cousin?" he asked. "The mothers must be very worried."

"That's why we must find them," she said. "He can't write when he doesn't know for certain what's happened to them, and every day he feels more and more guilty because he hasn't told them."

Frank looked serious. "I intend to try very hard to find them, Mette," he said. "Dead or alive."

She gave him a questioning, somewhat calculating look, and said, to his bewilderment, "Do you smoke a pipe, Sergeant Frank?"

He shook his head. "Just cigarettes when I can get them. But I'm out right now."

They came to the river where Copenhagen stood waiting

patiently. Mette pulled the back hem of her skirt forward and up, and climbed astride the horse. Frank mounted behind her and put one hand around her waist to hold her steady, holding the reins with the other. He felt her lean back against him. It felt right, and he wished they could ride further like this.

Half way across, Copenhagen stopped and tossed her head, whinnying softly.

"What is it girl," said Frank. "Something there?" He leaned out and looked down beside them. The water was muddy, but he could make out something on the bottom. He backed the horse up and took a different route. On the other side he helped Mette down, sat on a log and took off his boots.

"What are you doing?" she asked.

"I'm going out to see what was stopping her," he said. "Seems to be something there. Might be nothing."

"Oh," said Mette, understanding. "I hope…"

She paused.

"If I get swept away, make sure my boots go to a deserving person," he said, making her laugh. He stepped out cautiously, feeling around with his feet.

"Is it cold?" she asked.

"Bloo…very cold," he said. "Ah, here's something. He pulled up his shirtsleeve and bent down, pulling something up. He dragged it ashore and threw it up onto the track.

"It's an old boot," he said. "I thought it might be something important, but…"

She was standing very still, staring at the boot.

"It's Paul's boot."

He put his arm around her shoulder and looked down at the boot.

"How do you know?"

She knelt and picked it up.

"See here? The laces are not threaded through all the way to the top. Paul always wore his boots like that. And this mark? He burnt his boot in a fire, just a few weeks ago. A spark came out of the cooking fire and set light to the brush, and he stamped it out. I remember him joking about the shape of the burn. He said it looked like the Kaiser with his moustache and…"

She clutched it to herself and started to cry.

"He must be in the river," he said. "I'm sorry…"

"Someone could have thrown his boot into the river to make us think that," she said, wiping her eyes with the back of her hand.

"Possibly," he said. "But at least we know he was in or near the river at some point, and however he left he wasn't wearing his boot."

He helped her back onto Copenhagen and walked her back to the clearing. He had enjoyed holding onto her on Copenhagen as they forded the river, and thought perhaps he shouldn't have. She was a young, innocent woman, destined probably to marry someone much like the missing Paul, and to have many blond children. She was not for the likes of him, with his warrior past and his nightmares. She should do better.

He left her at her front door, still holding the boot to her chest. She planned to show it to Pieter and let him break the news to Hans Christian.

11

The Papaioea Pa

A somewhat serious accident occurred on Wednesday afternoon during the election. Mr. Owen was driving his buggy rapidly through the Square, and in rounding the corner opposite the Post-office it unfortunately capsized, precipitating him and four other occupants to the ground. Mr. Owen, we regret to say, sustained a fracture of his collar-bone, and remains very unwell.
Manawatu Times 11 August 1877

"You are not going to the *Pa*," said Pieter later that day. They were sitting over the last of the piglet nibbling on the bones. Pieter had not believed that the boot belonged to Paul, and had refused to mention it to Hans Christian.

Mette's eyes widened.

"Excuse me Pieter, but you are not my father. I believe I can do what I want."

"I am not your father, but if he was still with us he would say the same as I do. You should not go riding off with a strange man to a village of natives who may do who knows what to you."

"Sergeant Frank says they are quite safe. They trade with

the people in town, and bring fish and vegetables up the river in their canoes. He says..."

"Sergeant Frank!" exploded Pieter. "Mette what are you thinking. If you spend time with this man people will start to talk. It is worse than dancing with Gottlieb Karlsen at the dance. And look what became of that."

Mette felt as if Pieter had struck her, and it must have shown on her face. He went red, then said quietly, "I am sorry I said that Mette, but it's true that you should not be seen too much with this man. I know he's looking for Paul and Jens, and that you can assist him with this, but please think about what you are doing."

Mette looked down at her plate, at the piglet that had reminded her of Sergeant Frank each time she had another meal from it. She had been thinking what she was doing, very much so. She was thinking of little else, especially since they had forded the river, with Sergeant Frank's arm around her holding her tightly. She was feeling something she was not sure of, but it was a good feeling. It made her think of the sounds she heard through the wall in the night, soon after Maren and Pieter stopped talking.

"I'll think about it Pieter," she said, not looking at him. "Perhaps you're right. I'll go to the *Pa* on Wednesday with him and then that will be enough."

Pieter grunted his approval and returned to the piglet bone.

Frank arrived at the cottage in the clearing early Wednesday morning, shortly after Pieter and Hans Christian had left for work. The sun was just rising over the trees at the end of the clearing, making the dew sparkle like the diamond necklace that Mette had once seen at Rosenborg Castle in Copenhagen, where the Danish royal family kept their jewels. Frank was not mounted on his horse, but riding in a two-seater, black-painted pony trap, pulled by a pretty little light grey pony. Mette was disappointed that she was not to ride in front of him on his horse, but at least she would be beside him, and the pony trap would be fast and exciting, much better than riding in a bullock cart.

"I borrowed this from the mayor, George Snelson," he told Mette as he helped her aboard.

"That's very kind of the mayor," said Mette. "To let you use his pony trap."

Frank grinned. "He's in Wanganui," he said. "He has no need for it himself. The pony was sitting in the paddock behind the Royal Hotel and the trap was behind his shop. He'll never know."

They rattled off in the pony trap, Mette feeling as if she was royalty, towards the Palmerston Square, which was about two miles from the clearing. Mette hadn't been into town for some time and was amazed at the number of buildings that now surrounded the Square, even a very nice Bank of New Zealand, which was an imposing building made of brick with a high front door and large windows. In no time at all the square would be surrounded by buildings and the mud in the centre would disappear under grass or a pleasant park. By the end of the century they would be living in a real town and perhaps she would be near the Square, in a house of her own with children. There would be a blond girl she would name Katerina, after her mother, and a dark-haired boy…she glanced sideways at Sergeant Frank and blushed, hoping he couldn't read her thoughts.

From the Square, they trotted down towards the river and along the path towards the *Pa*. Frank sat upright smiling and using his whip to move the horse along quickly. The *Pa* came into sight, raised above the surrounding landscape on a low hill, surrounded by a wooden palisade and a high grassy bank. Mette could see a darker space, which appeared to be a gateway, but without the drawbridge that she had been expecting, like the one at the Rosenborg Castle. As they neared the entrance, a group of women came out and walked towards them. They carried flax baskets under their arms and chatted happily. Frank slowed to speak to them, taking off his forage cap and putting it under his arm as his did so.

"*Ra pai,*" he said. "*Kei hea te rangatira o tenei iwi?*"

The younger women giggled and looked up at him under their eyelashes, but a woman dressed in a long flax cloak, her hair parted in the middle and held back low on her neck, stepped forward and looked at him enquiringly.

"Why must you see our chief?" she said in clear English.

"Greetings," Frank answered. "You speak my language very well. Much better than I myself speak the language of the Maori."

She bowed her head slightly in agreement. Mette could see she looked amused.

"I am Sergeant Hardy, late of Her Majesty's Imperial Forces, and this young lady is Miss Mette Jensen. I wish to speak with your chief to know if he can tell me anything about two young men, relations of Miss Jensen, who have gone missing. Two young Scandinavian men—*Yaya.*"

"Ah," she said. "*Yaya.* We have not seen any *Yaya* here. They seem to be afraid of us. They do not trade with us or buy the food that we bring up the river from Foxton."

Frank looked sideways at Mette, and then said, "These young men will probably not be alive. We believe they drowned in the river but we cannot find their bodies."

"And for some reason you think my husband, the Chief, will know something about what happened to these men?"

Frank drew in his breath sharply. "If anyone else knows about the young men I am certain your husband will be able to find out. He will know all that his people know."

"That is true," she said. "Very little happens at this *Pa* that Hakopa doesn't know. If you will follow me I'll take you to him and we will talk to him together." She smiled at Frank. "As with you and the Maori language, he speaks very little English and I must translate for him."

She gestured to the other women to continue towards the river, and spoke to them sharply. They avoided her eyes and looked at each, heads lowered, as if trying not to laugh.

"What is she saying to them," asked Mette in a whisper.

"She's telling them to behave themselves at the river," said Frank. "They're on their way to wash clothing there, and she would usually accompany them to supervise."

The Chief's wife strode briskly back towards the gateway to the *Pa*, and Frank and Mette followed slowly in the pony trap. The gate did not lead immediately into the *Pa*, but moved in a three-step pattern of fences, which was somewhat awkward to negotiate in the trap. Mette watched as Frank maneuvered carefully through, impressed by his skill.

Inside the gate, a large open area was surrounded by buildings with elaborate carvings. Young boys tossed sticks back and forth, chanting as they did so, and didn't missing a single stick thrown to them.

"They're very good at that," exclaimed Mette. "Each one must throw and catch at the same time."

"Like juggling," said Frank. "I could never manage that,

although I've seen people who do it very well."

"We have a game called Koob in Denmark that uses sticks," said Mette. "Each person throws a stick at the king, or a line of Koobs. It's an easy game, and not as skilled as that one. What is this area?"

"This is the *Marae*," said Frank, indicating the entire area with his whip. "The place where the *hapu* gather. The *hapu* is the family or group of families, and families belong to a larger group called an *iwi*, which is a tribe of connected families. Maoris don't believe in individual ownership. The family or the tribe owns the land. Over there is the meetinghouse, with the carvings on the front."

"The *Marae* is like our clearing," said Mette. "Many of us are related, and we all live in an open space together. Of course, we don't have a palisade around us, just trees. What are the women doing over there? They look as if they are digging something up."

"Cooking, I believe," said Frank.

"But they're pulling something out of a hole in the ground," said Mette. "How is that cooking?"

"They're taking out stones and ash. They'll put them back later when they've built up layers of wood. That's how they cook, that or on a spit."

The chief's wife, who was listening to them as she walked in front of them, turned her head and smiled at Mette, "They are making a *Hangi*," she said. "The food is buried in the ground, wrapped in leaves inside *tete*, or baskets, and covered with hot stones. Afterwards, the women will bring it to us in the meetinghouse. The food takes a very long time to cook which is why they are starting in the morning."

"I would very much like to learn how to cook food in such

a way," said Mette earnestly, as Frank helped her down from the trap. "What food do you cook today?"

"We have a pig," explained their hostess, causing Frank to smile. "And potatoes and kumara, and *puha* leaves."

"I cook *puha*leaves as well," said Mette. "But they're very bitter unless I boil them twice. Does this way improve the taste?"

The woman nodded and stopped paying attention to Mette. A tall, handsome older man with gleaming white wavy hair and an erect stance had come out of the meetinghouse. A group of young men stood behind him, glaring suspiciously at Frank and Mette.

"Hakopa," said Frank. He strode forward to meet the man, and to Mette's surprise they appeared to kiss. Her escort put her hand lightly on Mette's arm and said quietly, "They're greeting in the Maori way, which is to rub noses together. We call it a Hongi, which means to share your souls."

"Sergeant Hardy has worked with your people before," said Mette. "He seems to know very much about everything."

"Worked with us?" asked the woman. "When was that?"

"During the wars...up in Taranaki I think he said."

The woman gave her a sharp look. She looked angry.

"I have not introduced myself to you," she said after several awkward minutes. "I am Moana o Te Maunga of Te *AtiAwaiwi*. Hakopa's *iwi* was not my *iwi*, but I came here when we married." She looked at Mette, her eyes calculating, and then added, "I am a princess of my people."

Mette gazed at her with wide eyes. She wondered if she should curtsey. As if reading her mind, Princess Moana said, "However, it is not necessary to bow to me. Our royalty is not like the English royalty."

Mette found her voice finally. "Your Majesty…"

"You may call me Princess Moana," said the Princess.

"Princess Moana how is it that you speak such perfect English? I have been trying very hard to learn English and find that it is a difficult language."

"I was educated in England," said Princess Moana. "I was sent to Cheltenham Ladies' College where I learned excellent English, as well as many other things that have not been at all useful, Latin for example, and playing the pianoforte."

Mette had been on the verge of telling the princess that she had assumed everyone in the *Pa* would be a savage, but she stopped herself just in time. The Princess would not be amused, she was sure.

Frank was chatting with Hakopa and his men, obviously having some difficulty. Princess Moana signaled to the men to wait for her and said to Mette, "Would you like to see how we cook?"

"I would like that very much," said Mette.

The Princess called out sharply in Maori and a woman dressed in a traditional reed skirt and embroidered top came over and smiled at Mette, who stood there wondering if she should rub noses with her. The Princess said something to the woman, who took Mette's arm and pulled her towards to *Hangi*.

"She will show you the *Hangi*," said Princess Moana. "You will not need to understand what she says, as it will be evident. I must go and translate for my husband."

The women were still clearing ash and cold stones from the hole. One came up to Mette and touched her hair, stroking her plaits and pulling them gently forward.

"*Hine-raumati*," she said. The first woman nodded, turned

113

to Mette and repeated the other's words. *"Hine-raumati."*

Mette touched her own hair. They were intrigued by the colour, it seemed. The two women returned to the *Hangi*. Mette watched as they continued piling stones beside the oven, removing any ash that had accumulated from a previous meal. Once all the stones and ash were removed they began to rebuild the *Hangi*. A pile of Manuka logs lay nearby, and the women piled them in the pit, first one way, then another in a crisscross pattern until the pile reached almost to the top. Twigs and dry grasses were pushed down the side and lit with a flint struck sharply against a rock. Once the fire took they tossed the stones onto it and stood back, satisfied.

A movement between the whare caught her eye and she glanced over. Someone was standing in the shadows watching her; she looked away, embarrassed to be caught staring back. Before should could sneak another look the Princess returned, looking annoyed. The men seemed to be talking to each other without her assistance. She nodded her approval at the way the *Hangi* had fired up, and said to Mette, "When the logs burn away and the stones sink, we will place the food in flax *tete* on the hot stones."

She spoke briskly, and although Mette had a thousand questions she did not think that the Princess was interested in answering them. One of the women, the same one who had touched her hair, said something to the Princess and pointed at Mette.

"They've given you a Maori name," said the Princess. "You are *Hine-raumati*, the Summer Maid, because of your hair, which reminds us of the summer and the golden corn. *Hine-raumati* is the wife of *Tama nui te ra*, the sun god. Sergeant Hardy is not a sun god, however. He is more like the god of war, so we must choose a different name for him."

"*Hine-raumati*," said Mette, relieved that Sergeant Frank was not to be given the name of the husband of the Summer Maid, "What a wonderful name. I'm proud that your women have given it to me." As she turned to smile at the women, she saw the man between the whare again. He had come out of the shadows and was staring across at Frank and Hakopa. The smile froze on her face. Surely that was the *Hauhau* who had tried to take her pig. What was he doing, standing there as if he belonged? It could not be him. But she had seen the blue butterfly on his face. It must be him. She had not seen another Maori man with a butterfly *moko*. She held her smile and looked at the women and past them, her head fixed in place, her eyes darting back and forth. As she stared, he slipped out of sight. But as he did so, she realized was not bearded. It was not the *Hauhau* then. But the *moko* was the same.

"I would show you our gardens now," said the Princess. Mette jumped and turned to her. "But I see my husband and Sergeant Hardy are returning from the river."

Mette's heart was pounding. Why would the *Hauhau* be at the *Pa*? Had she just imagined him and his butterfly moko? Was it him without his beard, or perhaps another man with the same *moko*? She saw Frank separate from the group of men and come towards her telling her it was time to go. I won't tell him I saw the *Hauhau*, she thought. He'll think I imagined it. Perhaps I did imagine it.

She said goodbye to the Princess as best she could, nodded towards the women and climbed aboard the trap.

"Did you learn anything about Paul and Jens?"

"Hakopa suggested I look down in the estuary, near Foxton," said Frank. "He said if they got caught in the current and drowned they could have been carried all that way down past Foxton. He says he's seen it happen before when the river is running high. Seems unlikely to me, but I'll ride down there if I don't find them soon."

"Was he a friendly man?" asked Mette, thinking of her possible sighting of the Hauhau.

"Friendly?" asked Frank. "He seemed friendly enough. Why do you ask?"

"I mean to say, do you think he would be friendly to settlers? Would he have any reason to lie to you if he had found the boys' bodies, or even if he had found them alive?" She was struggling with the idea of telling Frank that she had seen the *Hauhau*, at the same time as she was starting to doubt that she had seen him at all.

"He seemed to be less aware of the world than his wife," said Frank. "We were his guests, and he treated me as a guest, but after meeting his wife I was expecting him to be sharper."

"He was blunt?" asked Mette, looking puzzled.

"By sharper, I mean that he seemed less aware of the world, considering the obvious intelligence of his wife. He's been a very good friend to the government though and is influential with many of the *iwi*."

"Ah," said Mette. "Then he's a good man who wouldn't hurt us?"

"I am sure he would not," said Frank, looking at Mette. She could see he was wondering why she had asked.

"I asked him, through his wife, if he knew of anyone living up behind the sawmill," added Frank. "He said one of the younger men had mentioned a man called *Anahera* who visited the *Pa* at night sometimes, who could be the man I was referring to. But the Princess broke in and said *Anahera* just meant

116

angel, and they were probably talking about visions they had when they prayed. I didn't believe that either. Did you ask the Princess anything about your *Hauhau*?"

"When she came back from translating for you she seemed angry about something," she said. Should she tell Frank about the man she had seen? She would eventually. "She spoke in a sharp manner to the women, and answered my few questions in a very—what did you call it—in a very blunt manner. I didn't feel able to ask any more questions then."

"I have more questions than answers at this point," he said. "Not about the boys and where they might be, but about this *Anahera* who visits the *Pa* at night. He could be your *Hauhau*, but there's also someone from Poverty Bay the Armed Constabulary are looking for. It's a long way from here, but if it's the same man there could be trouble. Not for you or your people, but for ex-soldiers like me."

Mette decided to say nothing. It was not possible that she had seen the *Hauhau*; she remembered his beard very clearly. She had described it to Sergeant Frank that first day, when she ran in front of his horse. She must have imagined the resemblance.

12

The Ka Mate Haka

The Maori element is a striking feature in town just now, many of the natives now lining the foreshore with their tents, not having been in town for some years, while others for the first time gaze upon a pakeha kainga. A suggestion has been made to us, that with the assistance of Mr. Booth and Mr. Woon, the natives could be persuaded to perform a war dance. Many of the inhabitants of the town have never seen a Maori dance, the last one of any importance having taken place at Putiki on the occasion of the opening of the Bridge, and was arranged in honor of Sir George and Lady Bowen. There are a fair number of natives down now who are proficient in combined movements, and who might be persuaded to give their pakeha friends a sample of their skill.
Wanganui Herald, 10 July 1877

"The Maori people were not as frightening as I thought they would be," admitted Mette as they left the *Pa*. By now she had pushed the possibility that she had seen the *Hauhau* to the back of her mind. "I liked the cooking in the ground with the heated rocks--the *Hangi*—although I saw only the preparation of the rocks and not the cooking. Princess Moana did tell me something of how it's done though. I'd like to try cooking with heated rocks when I'm back at my...at Pieter's house." She paused for a minute, and added, "Of course I couldn't tell Pieter about the *hangi*, or show him one. He already believes that the Maori intend to roast us on a spit over the fire, like the piglet, if they have the opportunity."

They traveled in a companionable silence for a few minutes, and then Mette asked, "How did you come to learn to speak Maori, Sergeant Frank?"

"I don't speak Maori, not really," he said. "But I understand it somewhat, and I can speak a few words. I worked with the loyal Maoris, *Kupapa* they were called, back when we were chasing Titokowaru back into the great swamp."

"These *Kupapa* were fighting with you against the *Hauhau?*" asked Mette. "I thought you were fighting natives? The natives were also fighting natives?"

"They were afraid they'd lose their land," he said. "So they swore allegiance to keep it safe. At least that's what I've always believed. Of course, some of them lost it anyway. The Government was brutal, back in the 1860's."

She looked back at him. "You think the government was wrong then. That they should not force people off their land." It was not a question.

"You're right. I don't," he said. "I've come to realize that the people who live on the land have rights to that land, like the estate where my father lives, which has many small tenants who farm the land and pay the landlord rent. The landlord would never clear them off the land."

"But he—the land owner—could die," she said. "And what then? His sons could clear away the tenants."

"No, there are laws protecting tenants now. There weren't

in the past. In Scotland, the landlords evicted the tenants during the Highland Clearances in the eighteenth century and the early part of this century. Small tenant farmers were pushed off land they had farmed for centuries but didn't own so that the landlords could farm sheep. Sheep are easy, they can roam free without being tended like cows or crops." He remembered his idea that he would farm sheep one day, up near Napier, and how he would find a wife and a shepherd. Perhaps he had found one of them already.

"In Schleswig, as well," said Mette. "The land was owned by a *gutsherr* and the small farmers—the *grundholden*—leased the land from him, but there were reforms many years ago, and…" She stopped. Before them was a horse, standing idly in their way, without a rider. As she looked at it a figure rose from the bank above. He was in full war gear and carrying a Maori spear, raised in their direction.

"Get down, Mette," said Frank urgently. "Down by my feet."

She slid down behind the footboard and Frank put one foot onto her shoulder.

The *Hauhau* Anahera stood there, naked except for a plaited flax belt around his waist. His eyes bulged and his face was a mask of surprised rage, his arms raised with elbows bent and fingers splayed.

"The *Hauhau*," Mette's voice quavered. She was looking through a gap in the footboard just above the footboard. "He has come to kill us. Again. He looks very angry. I should have told you…"

"He has a *taiaha*," said Frank softly. He must have got it from the *Pa*. I still have the tomahawk he threw at us in my possession…"

"Does that matter now?" Mette whispered. "He can kill us

with his spear."

"One of us," said Frank grimly, "if he's lucky. He only gets one shot."

Anahera squatted down lower, his legs spread wide, and Mette waited for him to leap towards them, but instead he began to chant, slapping one hand against his thigh rhythmically and stamping one foot. The spear was held in his other hand, above his shoulder, pointing towards them. After several slaps, he raised his other hand towards them at waist height, with fingers shaking. "Ka mate Ka mate, Ka ora, Ka ora…"

"Why is he dancing like that," whispered Mette, clutching Frank's boot. "It's a very angry dance. Is he going to kill us?"

"It's a war dance, done before battle," said Frank, his eyes fixed on the *Hauhau*. "A *peruperu*—a *ha-ka*. Mette, he's looking at me, only me, and there's a revolver in my coat pocket. Pull it out and drop it on the seat. I'll keep my hands on the reins where he can see them. Do it very slowly and don't let him see you."

Her hand shaking, Mette eased her hand upward into his pocket. She could feel his heart beating slowly against her hand. He was not afraid. She lifted the gun slowly from his pocket and slid it down onto her chest. Her own heart was beating very fast. *Anahera's* stamping and chanting grew louder and he slapped his thigh with increasing forcefulness.

"Hurry," said Frank. "He's almost done." His eyes were fixed ahead, his hands on the reins, unmoving.

Mette threw the gun up onto the seat and closed her eyes.

"When I pick up the gun and shoot, get yourself down as low as you can," said Frank. "He's going to throw the *taiaha*, and once he does he won't have a weapon. Then we'll have the advantage. I have six shots in my weapon. He won't get near us alive."

The *Haka* came to an end: *"Kotahe, e rua, e toru e fa! He!"* Anahera thrust his tongue out at them and stood there, holding his crouching position, eyes still bulging.

Frank picked up the gun from her in one smooth move, and she heard a click, She looked up and saw his arm pointing forward. He was staring down his arm, his eyes narrowed, focused on the *Hauhau*.

"Shoot him!" she said urgently, looking up at him. "Sergeant Frank, shoot him before he kills us."

He shook his head. "I can't shoot first."

Anahera drew back the hand with the *taiaha* and threw it towards them. Mette heard a bang, then Frank fell on top of her and gave a grunt. He is dead, she thought. He is dead. But she felt his elbows dig into her as he rammed home another shot, followed by a loud bang that almost deafened her. There was a yell from *Anahera*. Mette saw him leap down onto his horse, holding one arm.

Frank was upright again, his gun aimed towards his adversary as he rammed another bullet into the chamber.

"He isn't going," said Mette. Her heart was almost leaping out of her chest, partly from fear, partly from relief that Sergeant Frank was still alive.

"I have three more shots left," said Frank. "If he comes at us, I'll shoot him again. One of the shots will hit him." His hand was steady now, raised so he could sight down his arm towards the Hauhau.

Anahera stared at them for a few seconds, then pulled the reins back on his horse, turned. And rode away.

Frank let the gun fall to his side and looked at Mette.

"Are you all right, Mette?"

"Aren't you going to chase him and shoot him Sergeant Frank?" she asked.

He helped her up from the footboard.

"Not in a pony cart," he said. "And I don't intend to kill anyone again if I can help it."

"I saw him at the Pa," said Mette. "I should have told you. I thought it was him but I wasn't sure; his beard..."

"Hmm," said Frank. "I wonder what he was doing there?"

"Why would he want to kill you?" asked Mette, trying to remember if the man who had attacked them had a beard. It had all happened too fast. She didn't want Frank to think she was a confused woman, and surely he would have noticed if the Hauhau had shaved his beard.

He shook his head. "I have an idea, but I need to talk to a few people first. It's nothing for you to worry about. I think it's me he's after, or someone like me."

He set gun the between them on the seat, and flicked his whip at the horse. "I'll take you home and then go back to town to talk with Constable Price. See what he wants to do. Hang on tight, I'm going to travel fast."

Mette clung to the seat and they set off at high speed. She did not think that a human could travel so fast and not die, but she'd had so much terror and excitement today that nothing more could scare her. She knew now that as long as she was with Sergeant Frank she would be safe. He could manage anything the world threw at him, and at her. One thing she was sure of, though, was that she would not be telling this story to Maren and Pieter. Especially not Pieter.

13

The Posse

Capture of Horopapera: Constable Hughes... selected a trustworthy young fellow named John Stagpoole, and they started off on Saturday morning last in pursuit, previously arming themselves with a loaded revolver each. After travelling three miles on the Mountain Road they struck into a narrow track, and, crossing numerous gullies and creeks, also two rivers, got to the expected retreat a small native village in a clearing a distance from the road of about six. miles. They took the precaution of concealing themselves by lying down, as well to elude the dogs, which began barking, as if to scan the country round in search of their man. After creeping on hands and knees for some distance, they spied the object of their search near a whare. Then came the anxiety for it was known that Horopapera was well armed. With a little manoeuvring, however, Stagpoole and the policeman pounced on him quite unawares, and after a short struggle the Maori's hands were placed behind his back and the handcuffs put on.

Taranaki Herald, 6 August 1877

Constable Price had no reservations about what was going on.

"A *Haka?*" he asked. "I doubt he was trying to kill you. All this about an avenging angel is tommyrot. He's probably just someone from the Pa with a grudge against *Pakeha* and he wants to make it look like it's some kind of ceremonial revenge."

"You haven't heard about him before, *Anahera*, the avenging Angel?" Frank asked. "Have the Armed Constabulary still not spoken to you?"

"Don't tell me anything, those chumps," said Price. "Not unless I have something they need. But we can talk to Constable Karira from the Pa. He may know something. You've met him, have you?"

Frank shook his head.

"He's distantly related to that Karira fellow who was the first Native Constable, up in New Plymouth. He's a fine chap, almost European. He was educated in England was Wiremu. Knows a thing or two."

Constable Karira was, as described, a fine chap. He came out of the station when summoned, wearing a grey suit, his boots polished to a high gleam, his thick wavy black hair brushed straight back from his clean-shaven face, and cut shorter than most Europeans cut their hair. He shook Frank's hand firmly.

"I've heard about an angel," he said. "*Anahera.* Seemed like a wild story to me, someone wanting to kill people for some misdeed from the past. Wishful thinking, I expect. But the man coming to the Pa is not *Anahera*, the angel, if there is such a person."

"That's what I told him," said Constable Price. "A local using those stories to create fear, thinking it might help drive the settlers away. Some of those Scandies, it wouldn't take much."

"He comes to the *Pa* now and then to pick up potatoes from

one of the women there, or at least that's what I've heard. She feels sorry for him I think."

"You're sure the man in the bush isn't the *Anahera?*" asked Frank.

"Not likely," said Karira. "Doesn't sound too angelic to me. I can't imagine anyone calling the man I've heard about *Anahera*. He's just a crazy local Maori with a bee in his bonnet. Wants to live in the bush and scare people."

"Not the Avenging Angel, then" said Frank.

"The Angel of Death, more like," said Constable Price. "We should go root him out, see what he thinks he's up to."

"You'd best be careful," said Karira. "He's a big strong man, I hear, over sixteen stone, all muscle and bone, and a man who has seen fighting in war time. If you go looking for him take some backup. I'll come with you if you need me."

"And so will I," said Frank. "Especially considering I'm the one he seems to be after. No idea why. I did run into him with Miss Jensen, however. Perhaps that bothered him. I wasn't scared enough, or I protected her."

Constable Price locked the door of his Police Station and sent his Assistant Constable, who had just finished conveying two deadbeats to the lockup, to fetch other members for a posse. A few of the local shopkeepers who belonged to the Reserve Force were rounded up, as well as the recently elected Mayor, Mr. George Snelson, and Sergeant Jackson with his road crew. Frank noticed the Scandi with the missing teeth was not with them. Just as well. He would deal with that cretin in due course. He went out to the paddock behind the Royal Hotel and managed to find a horse for everyone, although the mayor decided he would rather take his pony cart. They mounted and headed up the bridle path towards the sawmill.

Hans Christian Nissen and Pieter Sorensen were standing outside talking when they arrived. The saw mill seemed to be in full operation, with men yelling and logs coming at them through the chute from the back of the mill, but Hans Christian, his face a mask of worry, soon disillusioned them.

"We've had an accident," he said. "On the mechanical saw. We're waiting for Dr. Rockstrow to arrive."

"What happened?" asked Frank.

"One of the new men, from Schleswig, he just arrived last week with his young wife who he wed on the boat coming here. He cut off his hands—both of them—with the mechanical saw. When he realized what he'd done he threw himself on the saw and let it take him in the throat."

Frank was appalled. "Why the dickens would he wish to do that?"

"I don't know. He would have bled to death quickly anyway," said Hans Christian. "But he'd want to make sure he died. Without him his wife will be able to find another husband. But without his hands he will not be able to work, and they would have no means of living his family would have great difficulty in surviving."

"But the heartache, man, how will she recover from his loss?"

Hans Christian shrugged. "She will forget him, I'm sure, eventually. She will need to forget him if she is to have a life. They have no children, you see, and she will be used to marriage but still free to begin a new family. Someone will marry her."

They left the mayor at the mill to await Dr. Rockstrow. He looked relieved—his pony trap would be used to transport the body into town. Frank arranged the group into single file, with Constable Karira in front, and Constable Price at the rear, and went ahead to see what he could find, avoiding the bridle path as much as he could in case a trap had been left for them.

In a few hundred yards, just out of earshot of the sawmill, he found a deserted camp, with signs that someone had recently been there. A large eel was smoking over embers of a fire. He stooped to check it, to estimate how long it had been since the fire was fully ablaze, but as he did he heard a loud thump followed by a high-pitched scream. He spurred his horse back towards the sound. The men had all dismounted and surrounded one of the shopkeepers who lay on the ground, his face bleeding profusely, curled up in agony.

"He's not dead," said Constable Karira, who was kneeling beside him. "It's a *tawhiti*, a trap. He sprang it just off the path there. I was concentrating on the track itself so I didn't spot it, unfortunately."

Frank climbed down to look. A small black *matipo* tree had been stripped of its lower branches and bent backwards. Frank could see, about ten feet away, the place where it had been fastened to the ground with flax.

"See here," said Karira, patting the trunk gently. "Anyone touching the stripped trunk at any point would release the flax, causing the tree to spring upwards and hit him. He's lucky it didn't kill him." The shopkeeper lay on the ground beside them moaning. Karira knelt beside him and patted his shoulder. "You're going to be fine," he said. "You're just experiencing some shock. You'll live."

"There could be more," said Frank.

"He would have set more than one," said Karira. "Constable Price should keep the group here while we continue up the track to check for more. Any sign of him up ahead?"

"I found the camp," said Frank, as the two men moved cautiously along either side of the track. Looks like he's gone, and not very long ago. Ah, there's another one."

He squatted down at the head of a smaller *matipo* tree, tied down almost parallel to the ground, and took out his knife. It would have been difficult to spot for anyone not looking carefully. When he cut the flax, the tree sprang forward then whiplashed back towards him. If it had hit him on his horse, the horse would have been terrified, probably rearing up and hurting, if not killing, both of them.

By the time they reached the camp with its smoldering fire they had found and released three more. He called back to Constable Price to bring the rest of the men, who trotted nervously to the camp. Frank could see that they weren't going to be much use to him if it came to a fight, other than Sergeant Jackson, who was carrying a carbine across his saddle, and the sturdy Constable Price, who was now leading the wounded shopkeeper behind him on his horse, lying over it like a blanket roll, still moaning.

"One of these men needs to take Mr. Barnard back to the sawmill," Price said. "Dr. Rockstrow will be there soon to attend to the body of the Scandi who threw himself onto the saw. They can take him back to town on the mayor's pony trap."

"I'll take him," said Sergeant Jackson. "Needs to be someone who can fight off the *Hauhau*, if we run into him."

The rest of the shopkeepers, who had obviously thought returning to the saw mill would be an escape, looked at each other nervously, happy to leave the job to Sergeant Jackson. The Sergeant wheeled his horse around and they watched in silence as he led the wounded man, trussed to the saddle of his own horse, back towards the sawmill.

The fire was almost out, and they could see that little remained at the camp. Constable Karira leapt from his horse. "Might as well have that eel," he said. He scooped it up and thrust it into his saddlebag. It was a tight fit and he had to cut it in half with his knife. The group watched him, varying signs of distaste showing on their faces. Very few of them had tried eel and they had no idea how delicious it could be, smoked over a fire, Frank thought, remembering the eel they had eaten while they camped at the river, after his brother had been murdered.

He followed Karira from his horse and they explored the area together. It took a while to find the place where Anahera had been sleeping, but they eventually located a branch about ten feet up a massive Totara tree with a flax bedroll still stuffed against the trunk, but visible from the ground. He had been taking no chances. Beneath the tree were signs that a horse had been tethered there, and hoof prints led away into the bush.

The rest of the group sat on their horses looking around nervously.

"Why don't the rest of you return to town," suggested Frank. "Looks like he heard us coming and took off. We'll never catch him now. Constable Price, you escort them, and Karira and I will explore the area more, see what we can discover."

They posse rode off, a palpable air of relief emanating from them; Frank said quietly to Karira, "Fewer potential targets for him. Let's hope they make it back to town without incident."

Karira grinned at him. "Some of them, a hatchet would bounce off their heads and fall to the ground."

Frank laughed, and looked at the bedroll up in the tree. "Any idea how we can get that down?"

Karira said nothing, but nudged his horse against the tree, tossed the reins to Frank, and stood up on the saddle. As Frank kept the horse calm he reached up and took hold of the branch and swung himself up and onto it. Frank was impressed.

"Finding anything," he called after a minute.

Karira said nothing for a minute, then leaned down and held a feather out to Frank.

"A feather?" asked Frank. What does that tell you?"

"Comes from a cloak," said Karira in an overly loud voice. Then, more softly, "I heard a horse snicker."

"Is a cloak important?" said Frank loudly. Then quietly, "Which direction."

"Looks like something that belonged to a chief or a Tohunga. Behind me and to my left. Hand me my carbine. I'll keep you covered."

Frank admired the feather with one hand, and with the other slipped Karira's carbine from its holster on the saddle and handed it to him, keeping his arm between the gun and the noise of the horse.

"It's a kiwi feather," said Karira loudly as he took the carbine from Frank. "From the bird. The feather comes from a *kahu huruhuru*, a cloak."

"What does a cloak like that mean then?" asked Frank, edging forward. "Many Maori wear cloaks. What does it tell us? That this man is somebody important?"

He pulled his revolver out from inside his coat and cocked the trigger. He had ordered it from Wellington after he had felt the presence of someone watching him at the river, an Adams New Patent Double Action breech loader, not as good as the Colt single action, but more practical in the bush. He'd kept it inside his coat and used it when Anahera had attacked him and Mette. He knew that legally he could carry only one gun, but he wasn't taking any chances. And two certain shots were always better than six uncertain ones. He moved around behind the tree and towards the sound of the horse, holding the revolver straight out in front of him, moving it from right to left as he scanned the bush. As he got further away from the track the bush darkened.

"The *kahuhuruhuru* is worn only by chiefs and *Tohunga*," he heard Karira, his voice further off now. He sounded quite insincere and Frank hoped he was fooling anyone hiding in the bush nearby. "The kiwi feather is prized because the birds are difficult to catch. They come out only at night. The feathers are somewhat rare. Kiwi can't fly, so a feather could not have got up into the tree without help. I think it comes from a cloak, and the cloak is a *kahu huruhuru* and thus belonged to a chief or a *Tohunga*. Now I must ask myself, why would an important man like that be hiding up behind a sawmill in a small town in the Manawatu? If he were a local chief, I'd know him."

Frank paused and listened for a minute. He too now heard the faint snicker of a horse. He moved slowly towards it, keeping both hands on his gun. The shape came out of the gloom, the white blaze between the eyes, and the whites of the eyes themselves, standing out against the darkness. He backed against a tree and scanned the area carefully. Nothing. He had two bullets chambered and was ready to shoot at the smallest sound as he crept towards the horse, scanning the area. The horse greeted him with a loud whinny and stamped its hoof lightly on the ground.

"Where's your master then, eh?" Frank said softly. He took

hold of the reins and looked around again. Nothing stirred.

"I think he's gone," he called softly to Karira.

Something that felt like a load of bricks hit him in the back and knocked him to his face. His gun flew from his hand, exploding loudly, and he felt a foot press heavily on his back.

"*Mate i teie nei*," a voice snarled. "*Matepakeke.*"

A huge hand grabbed his shoulder and flipped him over. *Anahera* stood above Frank, holding a greenstone *mere* in his other hand, raised high. The man was staring at him with absolute rage in his eyes. Frank flinched, waiting for the blow. Instead, he heard a shot. The *mere* flew from Anahera's hand and he clutched at his arm. Frank crawled back and stood up. He felt like he was escaping a building that had just fallen on him. He heard a clang as Karira chambered another bullet.

"Leave," yelled Karira. "Or I'll shoot to kill next time.*Ka kopere i ki te patu.*"

Anahera lunged for his mere, losing his forage cap in the effort. Karira fired again. His shot went wide and Frank heard it ping against a tree.

"*Muri*," said Anahera. "*Muri.*"

He picked up his mere, leaped onto his horse and disappeared between the trees. The sound of the hooves faded quickly. Karira appeared within minutes, astride his horse.

"Which way did he go?"

"Too late," said Frank. "A couple of minutes' head start in this bush, and he knows his way around. We won't catch him now. At least we know he's still in the area."

Karira dismounted.

"He was in the tree," he said. "Dropped right onto you."

"Felt like a giant *kauri* tree fell on me," said Frank. "Thanks for stopping him. I thought I was dead this time."

"He said 'You die now,'" said Karira. "Then he said, 'die hard.' He wanted to hurt you as well as kill you, apparently."

"Die hard?" said Frank. "I don't think so. That sounds like a reference to my regiment. The Die Hards. He could be the man the Armed Constables are looking for, although I thought that man was a *pakeha*. One of ours, they said."

Karira was looking around at the flattened fern around them.

"What's that?" he asked. "Behind you on the ground."

Frank turned. "His cap," he said, picking it up. "He wears a forage cap for some reason." He turned it over. "It's a Die Hard cap, like mine. See the insignia?"

Karira said, "Do you think he's after Die Hards for some reason?"

Frank squinted at the inside band. "There's something written here. I can't read it…"

Karira took the cap. "Adams, I think. Do you recognize that name?"

"It sounds familiar," said Frank. "Adams? I knew most of the men in my regiment, but I can't remember an Adams. But something's there in my memory. It'll come to me."

The rode back towards Palmerston, side by side in a companionable silence, but the name Adams kept surfacing and disappearing. Who was it? Why was the faint memory accompanied by a feeling of dread, or revulsion?

The body of the young sawmill worker and the wounded shopkeeper had both been returned to Palmerston, and the sawmill was running smoothly again. Nissen and Sorensen were nowhere in sight. They parted ways, Frank to the Royal Hotel and Karira to the Pa.

14

Frank Finds Gottlieb

There is a well-authenticated record of a Kupapa, under Whitmore, being shot quite through the head with a rifle ball; stopping the hole at both ends with clay, — and recovering. It is well known, too, that Maoris hardly ever die of wounds, but generally get well again if they are not killed on the spot. Thus, an Arawa, who climbed the palisades of a pa on the West Coast, was shot through the stomach with slugs; a wound that would have killed any European. Yet he recovered, and got the New Zealand Cross for his bravery, if we remember rightly.
Timaru Herald, 26 March 1877

Constable Price called in the Armed Constabulary and talked to them in Frank's presence.

Captain Andrews, the man to whom Frank had spoken during his search of the riverbank, confirmed that they had been on the lookout for the so-called Avenging Angel who had already killed up in Poverty Bay, suspecting he might have come down through the Gorge to this area.

"But the man I saw was Maori," Frank said.

"We were looking for a Maori," said the captain. "I told you that."

Frank shook his head.

"You said he was one of ours."

"In a manner of speaking," said the captain. "A *Kupapa*, a Maori loyal to the crown. But like many of them did, he changed sides in the Titokowaru uprising. The land confiscations got to them in the end."

"One man then," said Frank. "The same man who killed up in Poverty Bay is down here hiding in our bush." He shuddered, thinking how close Mette had been to a murderous killer on two occasions.

"But we'll keep looking for him…"

"Not you," said the captain. "I have reinforcements coming. We'll blanket the area and keep a close watch on the Gorge. He won't get through there without us knowing. You stay out of it." He glanced at Constable Price. "And you as well, sir, if you don't mind. This is a job for professionals."

Constable Price bristled, but said nothing.

The Armed Constables scoured the bush and found no sign of him, but several of them settled down in Palmerston North, determined they would take him if he showed his face anywhere, while others, including the reinforcements, were stationed in pairs along the route to the Gorge. The people of Palmerston were stoic, accepting that there might be a killer in the district, but relieved that he was apparently out to kill soldiers and not settlers.

Banned from searching for *Anahera*, Frank's thoughts returned to Mette's nighttime attacker. He was positive that the man who had attacked her was the same man he had seen on the road crew. Pieter had let slip that he suspected someone from the road crew, and Mette had mentioned his bad breath and missing teeth. Those facts, together with the comments about watching the young Maori women at the river added up for Frank. It was just a matter of tracking the man down and making him understand that he should never go near Mette again. How he was going to achieve that, Frank was not sure. An old-fashioned man would use a horsewhip to teach the lesson, but Frank had seen enough violence and would not use it easily. Even so, he replaced his dual action revolver with his Colt single action, putting it in the inside pocket of his greatcoat. Best to be ready if he met the man. And Anahera was still out there somewhere as well.

As luck would have it, he encountered Sergeant Jackson picking up supplies for his team at the Snelson's General Store, and asked him where his team was at that moment. Sergeant Jackson mentioned a site near the *Pa*, on the Foxton Road about half a mile from where Frank had seen them previously. He took his horse out along the track towards Foxton and soon found the crew. They were dragging rocks from the river and doing the first break, making sure they were small enough to load onto the dray; the next step was to cart them nearer to the road, where they would smash them again into metal. Three men were busily at work, their muscles bulging and faces red as they pounded on the rocks with iron mallets. The fourth man, the one with missing teeth, was nowhere to be seen.

Frank hailed the men. "When I was here the other day, one of you said you'd seen a man camping up behind the sawmill. Where's the man who said that?"

The three straightened up, stretched, and looked at each

other. After a minute one said, not looking at Frank, "Karlesn? Reckon he's down yonder by the river. We haven't seen him for awhiles."

"He goes down there sometimes," added a second man. "Dunno what he does, but he goes there. When the boss isn't here."

Frank thanked them, tied his horse to a tree, and moved in the direction the men had indicated. About two hundred yards further along the river curved in an arc, leaving a pool with a rocky outcrop just below a higher spot on the bank. He could see a group of Maori women washing clothes, squatting down in the shallow water, probably the same group he had met with Princess Moana. Taking care not to intrude on their privacy, he stepped cautiously around the curve below the bank. He spotted his prey above him about fifty yards further down.

Karlsen was crouched on the edge of the rise, looking down towards the women in the river. Frank could see his forearm moving up and down, his face and neck red with the exertion. Karlsen did not appear to hear Frank as he leapt the last few steps up the bank roaring in anger, but grunted in surprise as Frank grabbed the back of his shirt with both hands and pulled him backwards down the bank with one swift tug. Frank's heart was pounding and his whole body was filled with rage.

"You scum. You're an offence to your manhood and your people. What the devil do you think you're doing."

Karlsen was lying on his back, his moleskin pants gaping open at the front. His penis had shrunk back inside his pants and he clutched at the opening, trying to do up the buttons with one hand.

"What do they care," he said. "They're down there in the

water paying no attention to anybody. I'm up here, and they don't know it. I need some fun. It's not as if I'm touching them."

"How do I know that? From your word of honour? These women are going about their daily duties and they don't deserve to be used for the fantasies of a sick mind."

Karlsen smirked at him. "Don't tell me you don't think about women. Done more'n that, I wouldn't be surprised. I've heard about you soldiers, and the way you rape women when you've won a fight. You're just a bunch of rapists pretending to be the defenders of the British Empire."

"That's another thing you've been accused of—raping a woman," said Frank. As soon as he said it he wished he hadn't but there was no taking it back. A flicker of comprehension showed in Karlsen's eyes.

"If you mean that whore from the dance, she wanted it. She came to this country looking for a man, her and her sister. What did she expect? She would meet a gentleman who would come courting her with a bunch of roses?"

A red haze dropped in front of Frank's eyes. He leaned down and picked up Karlsen by his shirt, stood him on his feet, drew back his fist and punched him squarely on the nose. Karlsen reeled back but did not fall, blood spurting from his nose. He tottered there looking at Frank for a minute, leaned forward with his hands on his knees to catch his breath, and then righted himself again, sneering. *"Skiderik. Du er endes fancy mand.* What, do you fuck her yourself?"

He took a breath and launched himself at Frank. His flailing fist found its target and connected with Frank's face just below his right eye, a glancing blow that was still capable of leaving a mark. Frank stumbled back as his head whipped sideways, catching himself just before he fell. Panting, he recovered and stared at Karlsen, then threw his arm across his own body and whipped it back towards the face of his foe. The back of his hand caught Karlsen square on his right cheek, leaving a bright red mark.

Karlsen retreated again, rubbing and holding his face, but did not give up. He stood there swaying, his legs wide apart to help him stay upright.

"I'm right, aren't I?" he said. "You want to fuck her but she won't have it. She had a taste of a real man and now nothing else will do for her."

He had made himself a perfect target, and that, along with the surging rage, helped Frank with the final blow. He took a step back, and then came forward standing on one leg; with the other, he kicked Gottlieb squarely between the legs, his leather Hessian boot with its pointed toe connecting fully with all that was exposed there by Karlsen's stance.

Karlsen stayed upright for a full minute, his face blank, and then crumpled to the ground, moaning in agony and clutching his injured manhood.

"*Ah, min gud!*"

Frank stood there panting for a bit. When he had his breath back, he said in a growl he did not recognize as his own voice, "You touch her again you bastard and you die. Understand? And you'll die hard, to boot."

When Karlsen did not answer him, Frank pushed his booted foot against his head and said again, "Understand?"

Karlsen nodded, his face still contorted with pain, rocking backward and forward on the ground. As Frank walked away, Karlsen yelled, "I'll get you, you bastard."

"Just try," answered Frank. "I'll look forward to it."

The men from the road crew were still working on the rocks where Frank had last seen them.

"He'll be a while," he said curtly to them. "Leave him be."

They nodded, not making eye contact. He wondered if they had heard anything of what Karlsen had said. He would not be able to tell Mette what he had done to Karlsen, but he was sure the man would not attack Mette again. Men like him were usually cowards. Frank and Mette had seen the last of him.

15

Mr. Robinson's Book Shop

E. METARD Begs to announce to the inhabitants of Palmerston, that he has just received a large stock of Books, Stationery, Fancy goods, Tobaccos, And cigars. He would draw especial attention to his well-selected stock of Stationery as supplying a want long felt in this township and district. The stock of Books has been carefully selected, and will furnish reading, both grave and gay, for the millions. The Tobaccos are of the best brands, as a trial of them will prove and the lovers of a good weed will find no difficulty in suiting their tastes at his establishment.
Manawatu Times, July 7, 1877

"I have received a letter from my sister Agnete, who lives in Woodville," Pieter told Mette, holding a folded page of paper towards Mette.

"What does it say?" asked Mette.

"See for yourself," said Pieter, avoiding looking at her.

She wiped her hands on her apron and took the letter.

"Do you want me to read it aloud?"

He shrugged. "Please yourself. I know what it says."

Mette covered her mouth with her hand so that Pieter could

not see her smile.

"I'll read it aloud," she said. "Then we can discuss it together as I read. I'm sure she must have something very important to tell you." She cleared her throat.

"My Dear Brother," she began. "I know you cannot…" she stopped and glanced at him.

"Cannot what?" he asked impatiently, blind to what was coming.

"I can't make out what the first part says," she said. "I'll jump to the next paragraph."

Pieter rolled his eyes. "I thought you could read," he said. "Go on, tell me what she says."

She started again, carefully avoiding the words "you cannot read" and "you will find someone to read this to you."

"My dear brother. I hope you are well. I am well and my two little ones are also well—Dotte and little Pieter. Yesterday, my dear husband Mads was in the bush and a tree fell upon his head. He was unable to jump out of the way. The doctor came and told me that Mads was dead, and…"

"Mads is dead? My sister's husband is dead?" interrupted Pieter, abandoning all pretense that he had read the letter. He snatched the page from her hands and stared at it, then thrust it back towards Mette. "Please, tell me what it says. I cannot read her writing. She was never good at hand writing, I…"

Mette saw that tears had formed in his eyes, and she took the letter from him gently.

"I'll read it," she said. "You are too upset."

Pieter nodded wordlessly, biting his lip.

"…that Mads was dead," she repeated. "And now I must leave my house by the end of the month as it is owned by the logging company. Dearest brother, I need your help."

143

Mette and Pieter stared at each other wordlessly.

"What can you do?" asked Mette. "How can you help her?"

Pieter looked at his feet for a minute, then looked back at Mette.

"I have some money," he said finally. "I could send it to her."

"But what will she do when the money runs out," asked Mette. "Will you send some more? What about Maren and Hamlet, and the little one coming soon?"

Pieter clasped his hands together under his chin, fingers locked, almost as if he were praying, but did not reply.

"She could come here," said Mette. "She could stay with you."

"How? Where would she sleep? How would we provide enough food for her and her children with the money I make at the sawmill?"

"She will stay in my room with her children," Mette said hesitantly. "I'll move somewhere else. I'll find a job and move to wherever that job is—maybe I could be a housemaid." She could feel her heart sinking even as she said the words.

Pieter's eyes lit up. He reached forward and held her hands tightly.

"Thank-you Mette, thank-you. I can see this is the only thing we can do. It will be difficult when the baby arrives but we will manage. And gradually I will make this house larger for the two families."

I'm doomed, thought Mette. I will become someone's maid and I will have no more freedom. It will be worse than getting married to someone who does not love me or cannot read and talk about what we have read. Aloud, she said, "Would you like me write her a letter telling her about this idea?"

Pieter started to nod, and then his eyes brightened. He'd

had a better idea.

"You could go to her. The Royal Mail coach goes tomorrow, and if you take it to Woodville you could stay until she is ready and then bring her back with you when the coach returns. I would go myself," he added, "but I must work at the sawmill, as you know. I am not able to stay away or I will lose my job and then everything will be lost." He looked sad as he said it.

Sergeant Frank, thought Mette. I will ride the Royal Mail Coach with Sergeant Frank. I would like to do that very much. She smiled at Pieter to show she thought it was a good idea.

"I'll give you some money," said Pieter, proud of his own generosity. "You can stay at a hotel in Woodville and wait for the coach to return. Then when you come back with her you can stay in a hotel until you find work. Perhaps you could go to Foxton. I know there will be work there. Many families require servants, or perhaps you could work in a shop—sell fish even. I'm sorry you did not learn to sew well. That would have been excellent work for you. However, if you are very lucky you will find a nice man to marry you in Foxton."

Mette was ready at first light the next morning. Pieter was to take her into town before he went to the sawmill, and she would wait there until the Mail Coach was ready to leave—an hour or so. Although she would not have a home to return to she was excited at the thought of the adventure that awaited her through the Manawatu Gorge to Woodville. She'd been to Woodville once before, on the way up from Wellington when they first arrived in New Zealand and she remembered that it was a larger town than Palmerston, with a main street with shops and several hotels. A real town, in other words, just like the one where she and Maren used to live before they came to New Zealand.

She purchased her ticket and left her bag at the Royal Hotel. Frank was out the back in the paddock getting the horses ready and did not see her, even though she stood around on the verandah for as long as she could without looking foolish. The Square was somewhat dry today, so she decided to walk around and look at the shops: a butcher, a greengrocer, a saddler, a photography studio, then, much to her surprise and pleasure, a bookshop. *Robinson's Fine Paper, Books, and Tobacco,* it said on the sign above the door. She went in, overwhelmed at the sight of so many books in one place. Her hand clutched the purse that Pieter had given her, with the precious coins inside; ten shillings of English money, five Danish Crowns, and some more in tradesmen's tokens, which she would be able to use at the hotel in Woodville. She'd never in her life had so much in her possession, but even so she would not be able to use any of it to purchase another book for herself. Pieter would demand an accounting of every penny spent, and with good reason. He'd worked hard for this money.

She stood in the bookstore and touched the books carefully. So many beautiful books with leather bindings and gold-edged pages. She ran her hand along the spines of the books in wonder. So many books! She was afraid to pull one from the shelf, in case the owner of the store expected her to buy it. However, one lone book sat on a table, a piece of paper marking a spot in the middle as if someone had been reading it. She picked it up. It was a volume of poetry by a man called Robert Browning, someone she had not heard of. Opening it, she read a verse:

I smile o'er the wrinkled blue-
Lo! the sea is fair,
Smooth as the flow of a maiden's hair;

And the welkin's light shines through
Into mid-sea caverns of beryl hue,
And the little waves laugh and the mermaids sing,
And the sea is a beautiful, sinuous thing!

So beautiful! It made her think of her and Maren's sea voyage from Copenhagen to Wellington, although they had not seen any mermaids. Did they exist, she wondered, or had Hans Christian Anderson simply made them up? She hadn't seen much of the sea on their way to New Zealand as they had been cramped up in the hold of the ship with all the other Danes who were emigrating to New Zealand in a fetid crush in which it was difficult to breathe. Maren and Pieter tried to spend time up on the foredeck, their only chance to be alone together for a few minutes, but Mette never went there. Everyone agreed that the foredeck was a place for young couples to spend a few minutes of privacy.

Many people had died on the voyage, including several young children, some just barely born. Typhus had swept through their ranks and it had been very unpleasant. But still, the idea of travelling across the sea swept her away, especially as even now she herself was going somewhere. Woodville by Mail Coach was not as exciting the mid-sea caverns of beryl hue, but it was an adventure all the same.

"May I assist you, madam?" said a voice behind her.

Mette closed the book and placed it gently on the table, and then turned to look at the speaker. An elderly man with round eyeglasses and a shock of bright white hair was looking at her questioningly.

"I, I'm very sorry," said Mette. "I was looking at the books. I have no money, and I can't buy one. But the poetry in this book is very fine. And I am especially fond of Mr. Charles

147

Dickens."

He smiled.

"As indeed one should be," he said. "And what have you read by Mr. Dickens?"

"Only one book, but I've read it twice, almost. *A Tale of Two Cities*. It is a most wonderful book."

"One of my favorites," he said, smiling. "You enjoy reading, I take it?"

"I love to read, but I don't have much opportunity, especially in English."

He reached towards the shelf of Dickens' book and pulled one out. It was smaller than the others and not nearly so fine looking, with a green cloth cover with the name in gold lettering but no gold on the page edges. She took it hesitatingly, opened it and started to read, then looked up at him, her eyes glowing.

"*A Christmas Carol*," she said. "I've heard of this book. I would like so much to read it."

"Then please do," he said. "Please take it."

"But I have no money, even for such a book that is less fine than the others, and smaller as well."

"I would not ask a penny from you," he said. "There are so few people who love to read in a town like this, and books deserve to be read. That one does not look as fine as the others because it's a Colonial Edition."

"What's a Colonial Edition?" asked Mette, interested.

"Publishers print special editions to be sold only in the Colonies, especially Australia, New Zealand and India. Sometimes they're even printed before the first edition in Britain. The New Zealand people are great readers, especially those who have come from Home and don't expect to return.

Mette did not like to ask him what he meant by Home. Did not everyone in New Zealand come from a home somewhere? This man sounded as if he was referring just to England. She said, "These books are not as expensive as these other ones with the lovely gold edges?"

"Indeed no," he said, smiling again.

"In that case I will take it," said Mette. "But when I have finished reading it I'll return it."

She held the book tightly and explored the shop further. Against one wall was a stand of paper. Beside it stood a glass case filled with pens. They did not look like the pens Mette had grown up using, and she looked enquiringly at Mr. Robinson, who was watching her with an amused expression on his face.

"Those are fountain pens," he said. "I expect you have used a dip pen—a pen that you dip into an inkwell before you write. Would you like to see one of these?"

"I would like that very much."

He unlocked the case and took out a pen, handing it to Mette. She rolled it over in her hand and asked, "Where does the ink come from?"

He picked up a bottle of ink, the kind she knew well, plunged the pen into it, and slowly pulled a small lever on the side of the pen. When he had finished, he wiped the pen on a handkerchief, took a piece of paper from the shelf, and slowly wrote his name.

"Now you try."

Mette put down her book and took the pen. She wrote her name slowly and carefully. He handed her a piece of blotting paper and she pressed it against the words so they would not smudge.

"That is a wonderful pen," she said. "No need to keep

stopping and dipping the nib in the ink. I could write so much faster if I had one of these."

"Now that I cannot give you," he said, smiling.

"Oh no," she said, shocked. "Of course, I didn't expect you to. But I'm making recipes from the things I find in the bush, and would like to write them down."

He looked at her thoughtfully. "Are you staying in town? I don't think I've seen you in here before."

Mette explained her situation, wondering why he had changed the subject so suddenly. He was trying to get rid of her, she was sure of that.

He took the pen from her, and said, "When you return to town, after your trip to Woodville, please come and see me."

She nodded, wondering what an old man like that would possibly want to see her for. At least he had given her a book, so that made it a wonderful day for her, and she hadn't even gone through the gorge with Sergeant Frank yet. She was a little worried about the dangerous *Hauhau* who had tried to take her piglet and done the angry dance—the *haka*. But she knew the soldiers had made sure he was gone. Fortunately, Pieter was not given to gossip and had not heard the stories, or he would never have let her go to Woodville.

As she left the store she noticed that there was also a case filled with cigars and tins of tobacco. Perhaps Sergeant Frank came here as well, and she would meet him accidentally, possibly when she returned the book.

16

Through the Gorge to Woodville

Notes by a Man About Town
  I was present during a discussion as to where the best scenery was to be had, and after hearing the whole North, Middle, and South Islands talked over and anecdoted, and (as I before observed), being located in Masterton, I thought that I and my bag might as well see the romantic scenery of the Manawatu Gorge.
  Manawatu Times, 14 April 1877

She walked from the bookshop, smiling to herself, and found Frank outside walking up and down as if she had conjured him up with her thoughts. He was looking unhappy, rubbing his bunched up right hand with his left. She noticed he had a bruise under one eye, but thought it best not to mention it. If he'd been fighting with someone, well, she did not need to know about it. Maybe he'd been drinking at the hotel and got into a fight. She had heard that the hotel was a place where people got drunk and fought with each other. Not that she could imagine Frank getting drunk and starting a fight with anyone—not unless he had a very good reason.

"Look what Mr. Robinson gave me," she said, ignoring the

bruise and the rubbing. Perhaps I can read it on the coach on the way to Woodville, if the coach doesn't bump around too much. Did you know I am coming on the coach with you today? I'm going to fetch Pieter's sister from Woodville as her husband has died."

"They told me at the Royal," he said, his eyes not meeting hers. "I hope Pieter knows what he's doing, sending you off on a venture like this by yourself."

"You'll take care of me, I'm sure, and save me from the *Hauhau* and the bushwhackers, and the wild pigs," she said with a smile.

She had expected him to smile at that, but instead he looked downcast.

"I will, of course, I'll always take care of you when I'm able. But when I'm in my coach I must also take care of the horses. The road's rough and the coach not at all comfortable. You'll find it hard going and I doubt that you'll manage to read on a moving coach."

"Then may I ride up the front with you?" she asked. "That would be an interesting trip I think, if I can't read. I'll look at the wonderful scenery instead."

They were in front of the Royal Hotel and he answered her with a brief nod. One man, a traveling bible salesman wearing a green coat and sporting large mutton chop whiskers, stood beside a box of his wares, ready to board the coach. His arms were wrapped around his middle to fend off the chill of the morning, and he was stamped his feet to warm himself. The coach stood nearby, with two enormous light grey Percheron horses yoked and ready to pull it. The coach was black, with large wooden wheels, and a coat of arms on the side Mette did not recognize. Probably something to do with the English

Royal Family. The English liked to have royal in everything.

Frank left her to fetch her bag from the hotel and walked round to check the horses. When she returned, he was seated up on top of the coach, holding the reins and a whip. He wore his usual grey-blue greatcoat but had added a tall hat, and looked very large as well as very handsome. A Chinaman stood beside the door of the coach and indicated that she should give him her bag. He was quite short, with long hair tied back in a pigtail, very much like her own plaits, and she handed him the bag reluctantly. She was sure she was just as strong as he was, and could put the bag wherever it needed to be put without any help, especially from a Chinaman.

"I'm going to ride up in front with Sergeant Hardy," she said to him slowly and loudly, as she handed him the bag.

Frank glanced down at them.

"Shove it up here, under the seat, Hop Li," he said.

Hop Li pushed her bag under the seat and helped her climb up beside Frank.

You should put some raw steak on that eye, boss," he said, to Mette's surprise. Frank gave her a quick smile. "Hold tight," he said. "It's bumpy up here."

She clutched the side of the seat with one hand, and her bonnet with the other, and they took off with a little flick of his whip above the backs of the horses.

"That was Hop Li," he said after a minute. "He's the cook at the Royal Hotel. He's a friend of mine. He's also one of the best cooks in New Zealand. I've known him for quite some time."

"He seems to understand English very well," said Mette.

Frank grinned, his face crinkling in the way she enjoyed seeing.

"I should think he does," he said. "He's been in New Zealand since the West Coast gold rush, over ten years ago. Before that he was in Victoria, Australia, until the gold ran out there."

"He dug for gold?" asked Mette. "Does that mean he's very rich? Why does he need to be a cook as well?"

"Rich, but not from gold," replied Frank. "Probably one of the richest men you'll ever meet. He fed the prospectors, seduced them with his cooking and ended up with more gold than many of the diggers."

Mette understood the appeal of food very well, and she nodded her understanding.

"His food was the best they'd ever had, and he always had a garden full of vegetables and fruit trees," Frank continued. He was looking forward as he spoke, his eyes on the road ahead and the horses. "As a matter of fact, he has a garden right behind the hotel, across the other side of the paddock. He's been buying land around the Square, for a market garden. The hotel job gives him a chance to keep his eyes open for possibilities."

Mette craned around in her seat, even though they had come too far to see back to the hotel.

"Oh, I'd so much like to see that. I'm finding new plants here all the time, and finding ways to use them instead of using the plants we were using at home."

"He has a new fruit he brought with him from China," said Frank. "Oval shaped, and brown with a fuzzy skin, about the size of a large egg. It grows on a vine. You should taste it if he offers it to you. He calls it a Chinese gooseberry—it's sweet and delicious. He says it'll do very well in New Zealand."

"I wish I could return and talk to him right now," said Mette. "I would so much like to see his garden."

She craned around to look back again and saw someone come out of the bush and stare after them. Was that Gottfried? She hadn't seen him since that terrible night, but had mistaken someone for him several times. Thankfully, she was with Sergeant Frank, and if that was really him this time she would be safe. She looked back one more time, but the figure had gone.

They continued in silence, Frank concentrating on his horses on the rough, rutted road. The scenery soon calmed her, and she began to enjoy herself. The metalled road ran mainly through bush, but also through desolate landscape covered in totara and rimu stumps stretching off in the distance. They forded several streams, the horses straining to pull the coach up and out of the water each time, coaxed carefully by Frank. A few times she and the bible salesman had to climb down from the coach to lighten the load and walk in the muddy track behind it. Walking made a nice change from the bumping and swaying of the coach.

At one point a group of armed men rode by, wearing blankets around their waists as kilts, blue jackets and broad-brimmed hats, rifles but with shorter stocks resting across their saddles.

"Those are the Armed Constabulary," said Frank, seeing that Mette looked nervous. "They're keeping an eye on things. They'll be guarding the entry and exit to the Gorge as well. We'll be safe from Anahera as we pass through."

Within an hour and a half, they arrived at Ashhurst, where the tributary Pahangina River met the Manawatu River. Here they would cross the Manawatu on a ferry punt. The stagecoaches between Wellington and New Plymouth met here to exchange passengers, but Frank's Mail Coach would cross the river and continue through the gorge carrying the same passengers the whole way.

The Bible salesman and Mette climbed down once more from the coach and watched as Frank maneuvered the horses aboard the ferry punt, dismounting to keep them calm as the ferry was drawn across the river on a rope. Once the coach was safely on the other side, the ferry punt came back for them, pulled by a team of bullocks roped to a turnstile. Looking down at the water, Mette was reminded of Paul and Jens. They could be right here, below her feet, stuck under the dock, and she would not know. She peered down through the wooden planks, just in case they were there, but could see nothing but a kind of green slime that gathered around the pylons.

Once across the river the Mail Coach entered the road adjacent to the gorge. The Manawatu River, which she knew well from Palmerston, ran here between two mountain ranges, the Tararuas and the Ruahines, the ranges ending one each side of the river. Initially it was not much more than a pleasant ride alongside a very fast and narrow river, but gradually they climbed higher until the road was the height of a tall building — a cathedral, for example, like the Church of Our Lady in Copenhagen, which she had visited once, or the Haderslev Cathedral, which she knew very well — and ran beside a steep drop.

She could see Frank concentrating, his whip constantly ready to snap above the horses' heads, careful that they did not put a step wrong as they strained to pull the coach along the rutted road running up the slope. She was glad she was sitting on the bank side of the coach and not the cliff side, so she did not have to see what lay below. Being in a high place made her body feel very strange, almost as if it could float up into the air. She felt she held her breath for the whole two hours it took to pass through the Gorge.

They hit the highest point of the Gorge, and Frank stopped the coach for them to step down and look over the edge at the water. Mette did not want to let him know she was terrified, and so stood as near as she could to the drop, half-closed her eyes to blur the view, and hoped Frank didn't notice that her hands were clenched tightly by her side. Had she looked down she would certainly have fallen to her doom, unable to stop herself.

The road leveled out and dropped slightly towards Woodville, and she could see before her the plains and forests of the Wairarapa. They stretched in front of her, green and wonderful, as far as the eye could see under a beautiful blue sky with just the tiniest of fluffy white clouds. This was the Seventy Mile Bush that ran into Palmerston, that the Scandinavians were in the process of chopping down to make farmland. As they came nearer the forests seemed less thick and impenetrable, with large areas where trees had been cut down or burned, with only the blackened stumps remaining. Eventually, Woodville came into view, first as some columns of grey smoke, then gradually the town itself with its metalled streets and wooden sidewalks. The trip had been scary, but they had made it through alive, which was all that mattered.

The coach pulled up beside Murphy's Hotel, and Mr. Murphy himself came out to greet them. He was a short, round bald man with tufts of hair above his ears and a twinkly smile; he wore a leather apron and his sleeves were rolled above his elbows, as if he had just that minute been cleaning off the counter or scrubbing the front step. Mette asked him if he had a room for the night and was pleased to hear that he had several. Sixpence a night for room and board, which meant that she had a place to stay until Frank returned the next day. She asked Mr. Murphy if he knew of Agnete Madsen, a young Danish woman with two small children whose husband Mads had just been killed in an accident in the bush.

"Indeed I do," he replied. "In fact, her husband is currently resting at the church across the street. I believe the funeral is this very afternoon. You may find her there later in the day—four o'clock I believe."

"Do you know what happened?" asked Mette. "She sent a letter to her brother in Palmerston, and said only that a tree had fallen on her husband and he was dead. Was her husband not used to the working in the bush?"

"That's not the case at all," answered Mr. Murphy. "He was a very good bush man. In fact, he was a crew leader and known for being a careful and hard worker. Nobody knows how he came to be under the tree when it fell. Usually there's a warning, with time enough for everyone to get out of the way."

"So how did it come to fall on him, do you think?" asked Mette, curious.

"They said he tripped," answered Mr. Murphy. "They yelled that the tree was coming, as always, and he was standing on the side where it was to fall. He started to move away, and then tripped over something. Before he could get up again the tree was on top of him and he was crushed. They wouldn't let his wife see him, he looked so terrible. They say his head was almost completely flattened."

"How terrible for her," said Mette. "To lose her husband, and not be able to see him one last time."

A strange expression came over the innkeeper's face.

"You would expect her to be sad," he said. "But she seems to be coping with it very well. Best for her, I suppose."

Mette put her small bag in her room at the hotel, marveling at the sight of the bed, which had a feather tick mattress and was covered with a large quilt. It would be like sleeping on a bank of moss, she thought. Such luxury! How could she go back to the little bed in Palmerston after this? Once her bag was stowed safely, she ventured out to walk about the streets of Woodville until the funeral was to start. The smell of bread baking permeated the street and she followed it to a small bakery, tucked behind the hotel on the main street.

A plump woman with rosy cheeks, her hands covered in flour, greeted her.

"Good morning my dear. What can I find for you today?"

Mette pointed to a large round loaf with a crispy golden crust.

"How much is one of those?"

"Sixpence for one loaf, and ninepence for two," said the woman, wiping her hands on a cloth in anticipation of the sale. "Or one of these larger loaves, the four pound loaves, for ninepence."

"I'll take two of the smaller ones," said Mette. Pieter wouldn't mind if she spent his ninepence on food, she thought. She would have some of the bread tonight, and would share the rest with Frank on the coach ride back to Palmerston tomorrow.

"Are you a visitor to town?" asked the woman.

Mette nodded. "Just for the day. I expect to be returning to Palmerston tomorrow if my task is completed."

"I hope you're staying at Mr. Murphy's establishment. Mr. Murphy is a fine man and one of the original settlers in the area," said the woman. "I hear he does very well by his guests."

"It is a very nice place," said Mette, wishing she could speak English as well as the baker woman. "And at a good price."

"We did used to have a less expensive place down the street a way, but the owner, Mr. George Ollandt, was cruelly murdered just last week by Henry Thompson, his partner," said the woman, clearly happy to have someone new to listen to the tale.

"Mette put her hand over her mouth. "Murdered, how..."

"An axe, I expect," she said. "They say the face of poor George was quite mangled, and found covered in flies. The inquest is to be held here tomorrow afternoon, and of course Henry Thompson will be remanded to trial. And now the police are searching for another man who is missing, a Mr. Peter Kane. He left Sandon in June to find work, carrying all his fortune on his person, ninety pounds, imagine that, and his wife has written to him and advertised in the newspapers to no avail. We're all fearful that he's been killed for his money and his body thrown into the woods, probably by the same Henry Thompson. The Armed Constabulary arrived here the day before yesterday, but they took off early this morning. Thieves and robbers, and murderers, what is the world coming to? I have no idea."

Mette felt her little hoard of glowing coins in the pocket of her dress, enough that anyone who passed her must be able to see it clearly. She thanked the woman, took the two loaves of bread, and returned to her hotel room, afraid to venture further into town. She would stay in her room until it was time to go to the church across the road where the funeral was to be held. She had no desire to risk her life on the dangerous streets of Woodville, as harmless as they had looked at first.

She was carrying the two books by Charles Dickens in her

bag, and she withdrew *A Tale of Two Cities* to read while she ate a piece of the bread with jam she had brought with her. She had forgotten that the opening passages of the book spoke of a ride in a Mail Coach, and reread that section with pleasure. It was wonderful to read something you had recently experienced yourself.

With drooping heads and tremulous tails, they mashed their way through the thick mud, floundering and stumbling between whiles, as if they were falling to pieces at the larger joints. As often as the driver rested them and brought them to a stand, with a wary "Wo-ho! so-ho-then!" the near leader violently shook his head and everything upon it—like an unusually emphatic horse, denying that the coach could be got up the hill. Whenever the leader made this rattle, the passenger started, as a nervous passenger might, and was disturbed in mind.

The passage reminded her of the ride over the Gorge and the way the horses had dragged the coach up the incline towards the highest part of the Gorge, mashing their way through the thick mud, just as the horses did in Mr. Dickens' novel. Once she had talked to Pieter's sister she could start thinking about the trip back tomorrow with Sergeant Frank. She very much looked forward to the return journey, even though they would no longer be alone. She would have to sit inside the coach with Pieter's sister and her children, and the children would probably whine and protest.

17

The Funeral

A party of five, settlers, had the contract for clearing in the bush there [on the bank of the Manawatu] *on the line of extension of the railway. Two of them were engaged in felling a tree; in coming down it struck another tree, breaking it short off. The latter in its fall struck one of the men on the head, and killed him instantly. The deceased was a Scandinavian, Laurenz Christiansen by name, about 50 years of age. He leaves, we regret to learn, a wife and six children totally unprovided for. The settlers are doing all they can for the bereaved. The inquest was to have been held to-day, and the funeral is to take place on Sunday.*
The Manawatu Times, August 29, 1877

The time came for the funeral to begin, and Mette put her book back into her bag, and hurried across to the church. She was pleased she'd been able to find Pieter's sister so easily. Woodville was a small town, although larger than Palmerston, but Scandinavians often only knew other Scandinavians. She'd expected to have to find a Scandinavian before she could hear about the accident; finding Mr. Murphy was an unexpected gain. She could hear singing from inside the church and entered quietly.

A group of people stood clustered at the front. Before them lay a plain wooden coffin, painted black, with the lid closed. The church was decorated with pine branches and a wreath of pine lay across the coffin. It was quite grand, almost as if one of the Monrad's had died. Mette stayed at the back of the church, as it was clear that the funeral was in progress right this minute. She had arrived at just the right time. She was somewhat surprised to see the funeral conducted in the church, as her people would usually hold the funeral at the graveside unless the person who had died was important. She wondered if Agnete had been so upset that she had spent too much of her remaining money on the funeral. That was not the way a widow should behave, as she had to think of herself and her children and how they were going to live.

Someone began to sob, and Mette saw that the sobbing came from a young woman with two young children. She was dressed in normal Sunday clothes, but had a black shawl around her shoulders, which she clutched tightly to herself. Beside her stood a tall fair man with a reddish beard and a moustache that curled up on either side of full red lips. He was holding his hat in his hands and looking very solemn. When the woman started to sob, he put his arm around her and whispered something in her ear, stroking her shoulder. She looked up at him and said something that made him smile, as she wiped away her tears with a kerchief. The two young children, a boy and a girl, stared at their mother with wide eyes. The boy, a little older than Hamlet, had his thumb stuck firmly in his mouth and a terrified look on his face. Something big was going on, and he had no idea what.

Finally, the ceremony finished and the group turned and

walked slowly towards Mette. She could see that this was Pieter's sister Agnete, as she looked very much like him. However, she was short and plump with rosy cheeks, whereas Pieter tended to be tall and pale. She looked at Mette sharply as she drew near.

"Are you looking for someone?"

Mette hesitated, and then said, "I believe you are the sister of Pieter Sorensen, my sister's husband. He received a letter yesterday, which I…"

"You read to him," she interrupted. "Can he still not read? Our mother tried so hard to teach him to read, and to write, but he was determined to work with our father and would not sit still to learn. I suppose he's had no success in Palmerston because of that."

"His reading is not perfect," said Mette cautiously. "But he can certainly read a little. And he's doing very well for himself in Palmerston."

She had taken an instant dislike to this woman and felt she had to defend poor Pieter. He'd sent money to help her, and she was criticizing him to Mette, a stranger.

"He is, is he? Why are you here then?"

"I am Maren's sister, the sister of Pieter's wife," said Mette. "Pieter wanted me to come here and offer you somewhere to live—at his place. He would like me to escort you and your children back to Palmerston. I've come to take you back to Pieter and Maren. They have a place for you and your children."

"Take me back?" she said. "Take me back indeed. I don't want to live with Pieter and his foolish wife." She had apparently forgotten that the foolish wife they were discussing was Mette's sister. "Did he send money?"

Mette fingered the purse full of coins in her pocket.

"A little," she said. "But just enough to pay for your fare on the mail coach back to Palmerston."

Agnete made a sound with her tongue against her teeth and looked upwards. "For the Lord's sake. Did he not understand? I need money, not charity. I thought you said he was doing well? You can give me the fare, but I have no intention of returning with you to Palmerston." She eyed Mette up and down, sizing up her wealth and finding it wanting. "I don't suppose you have two pennies to rub together, and neither does Pieter if he sent you to find me."

Mette removed the ten-shilling note carefully from the purse, without taking it from her pocket. "What will you do if you don't come with me to Palmerston?" she asked. "How will you live?"

Agnete glanced at the man beside her who had been standing quietly, listening to the conversation, and smiled confidently. He smiled back, rather like the way a wolf that was about to eat someone would smile, Mette thought.

"Mr. Williams has kindly offered to take me—and the little ones, of course—to Wellington to stay with his, his *sister* Daphne. She has a lovely home overlooking the harbor with several rooms. A parlor, a room for a maid." She leaned forward. "Her house even has an indoor watercloset." Clearly the indoor water closet had helped persuade her to go to Wellington. Although why she would not be happy with a chamber pot and an outdoor privy was a mystery. Those were good enough for most people.

Mr. Williams clasped both Agnete's hands in his, and said, "Of course, if Mrs. Madsen's brother wishes to take the *children*, that would be very acceptable. My sister is somewhat poor in health and finds it difficult to handle noisy young children."

Noisy! Mette looked at the two children cowering beside their mother. "Mrs. Madsen's brother has one tiny extra room with a small bed and barely room for his own family," she said. "And the water closet is outside in the bush, where there are dangerous animals and Maoris lurking at all times. I myself was attacked by a *Hauhau* just a few weeks ago." She stopped herself saying that the room was hers and she had offered to leave it for this woman standing there with her fancy man. She removed her hand from her pocket with the note folded in her palm. The purse would not be coming out. The ten shillings she held was quite enough for this unpleasant woman.

"Well then," said Mr. Williams, looking disappointed. "I'm sure we can find good care for the children in Wellington."

For a minute, Mette almost relented. These poor children were going to be torn from their mother to live who knew where: the workhouse, and orphanage. They would be far better off with Maren and Pieter. But then she remembered the tiny space, little Hamlet, and the baby that was coming in a few weeks, and she kept quiet. She would tell Pieter what she suspected, and if he wished to go to Wellington and bring the children back to Palmerston, he could do so. She would even go herself. But she could not arrive home with the children in tow and expect Pieter and Maren to make a home for his sister's children. That was asking too much of them.

She handed the ten-shilling note to Agnete, who turned it over and looked at in disgust.

"Pieter isn't a very generous person," she said. "I see he wants me to live like a church mouse in Wellington, and does not care if my children starve. Goodness, I will have to resort to living like a ladybird just to feed myself and my children."

Williams stroked her wrist and said softly, "Not as long as you have me my dear."

Mette choked back her revulsion. She had almost reached into her pocket and pulled out more money to give this woman for her children, but the sight of Mr. Williams soft white hand stroking Agnete's, a hand she noted that was the exact opposite of Frank's strong brown hand, strengthened her resolve. Pieter and Maren and their children would not go wanting so that this woman could live in a house with an inside toilet and a view of the harbor.

18

Ringiringi

BENT, THE DESERTER.

Patea, Nov. 27. Kimbell Bent, a deserter from the 57th Regiment 13 years ago, and who has ever since lived with the Maoris about 50 miles up the Patea River, and up till Monday had not been seen by any Europeans since he deserted, was interviewed by a Patea resident, and said he intended to lay his case before the Government, as he is anxious now to go back to his native country (America.) Bent deserted after being flogged, and in 1866 was believed to have shot Lieut. Colonel Hassard in an engagement near Hawera [Otapawa] and a large reward was offered for his capture. The Maoris treat him as a slave, and say he was never allowed to carry arms. He has kept a diary the whole time of his absence from civilization.

Grey River Argus, November 28, 1878

Frank left Napier early on Wednesday morning and headed for Woodville to collect Mette, stopping in small towns and settlements to drop off and pick up the mail. He passed quickly through Waipawa, Waipukurau, and Dannevirke, and then stopped in Norsewood, where the Manawatu River started its journey towards the ranges and Palmerston, to water his horses. He walked around the town to stretch his legs, and noticed for the first time how many Scandinavians lived there. Stood to reason, of course. Norsewood. They were sturdy people, he thought, well suited to the task of clearing the bush and building the roads. But they had done it for land, and they deserved to be given land. Shame on the government in Wellington, and especially on Sir Julius Vogel for bringing them to New Zealand with vague promises of land.

Of course, the Maori deserved to keep their own land as well, but he had been at Mawhitiwhiti in '68 when the *Pai Marire*, Mette's *Hauhau*, had slaughtered four sawyers over cutting rights, and then killed a loyal native who came to negotiate, cutting him to pieces with their tomahawks. Sometimes it was hard to find it in his heart to forgive the extremists even though they also just wanted land. He'd been recruited into the Constabulary a few months after the incident, and helped confiscate the land of rebels. And then had come the pursuit of Titokowaru and the terrible things that had led to. This country was a difficult place to live. He thought about his talk with Karira and was momentarily overwhelmed with the emotions of the memories that returned to him. Some day he would have to tell Mette about what he'd seen that day. But for now, he couldn't bear the thought of her looking at him in the way that Karira had looked at him. He wanted to say, it wasn't my fault. But it was, he knew. He was part of it.

With his horses fed and watered, and ready to go again, he took off towards the next stop at Matamau. There, two roads formed a T-junction, with small farms being carved out of the bush along the road running up to Ormondville. He could see that in this place, as in so many others, England and Scotland and Wales would be rebuilt here in the colony, and the natives would be displaced, moved out to who knows where. A lone building stood at the place where the roads met, containing a post office, a police station, and a general store. The mail flag was not up, but he stopped to see if they had any cigarettes. Sometimes he got lucky, and he needed a cigarette right now.

A group of Maori men were squatting in front of the door to the post office, sitting in a companionable silence, each enjoying a smoke from a clay pipe. They were clad in European clothing, but were barefoot. He nodded in greeting, "*Kia ora.*"

They nodded back to him, muttering greetings. As he was about to enter the post office a familiar voice said, "Sergeant Hardy?"

He turned. "Yes?"

One of the "Maoris" rose to his feet. He was looking at Frank with a lopsided grin, half friendly, half nervous, his pipe clenched in his hand a few inches from his chin, which was covered by a full beard, reddish brown and streaked with grey. His forehead was tanned dark by the sun, but pale blue eyes looked out at Frank. It was clear that he was not a Maori. A deserter by the look of him.

"Private Bent, that's who I am," the man said, confirming Frank's suspicions. "Or was. Kimbell Bent late of the Die Hards. Ringiringi they call me now."

"Good Lord, so it is," said Frank, smiling. "How have you found yourself in these parts? I thought a deserter like you would have been killed years ago. Didn't Her majesties' Imperial Forces come looking for you? Or the *Pai Marire*?"

Bent shrugged.

"I'm one of them now. I have a Maori wife and an *iwi*—a tribe—I belong to. I work a little, but I rest as well, on many days. No waiting for Sunday, the day when my body can recover from the aches and pains of work. It's a pleasant, carefree life, although I miss talking to Englishmen."

"I'd talk to you if I had the time," said Frank. "But I'm on my way to Woodville with the mail, then on to Foxton and Palmerston. Can I take a message from you to someone? Your family must wonder if you're still alive, surely."

"My family is gone, those that care. But I'd appreciate a ride down the road to Tahoari," said Bent. "I don't need to go there for any reason, but I'd surely like the opportunity to talk with an Englishman again."

Frank nodded. "You're welcome to ride for those few miles. I'd appreciate the company as well."

Ringiringi climbed up onto the front seat of the coach, smiling happily. *"Hei kona ra,"* he said to the group he had been sitting with. "Tomorrow."

Frank settled the horses to a steady trot before he said anything. After a while, he asked, "They treat you well, the *Pai Marire?"*

Ringiringi shrugged. "Well enough. I was a bit of a plaything for them at first. Owning a *pakeha* was quite the thing for them, and they paraded me around to tribes to show me off. But once they were accustomed to me they started to trust me. They gave me a wife, but she didn't stay around long. An ugly woman, but nice enough. Daughter of a chief. I have another wife now. Titokowaru's daughter. Friends, we were, Titoko and me."

"You were with Titokowaru," asked Frank. "Until the end?"

Ringiringi shook his head. "Just until Otauku. He sent me

171

off, said it were getting dangerous. Then they chased him into the Great Swamp. I weren't part of that. Just as well. The Kupapa and the colonists, they were nasty. Lot of people died on that chase. Old people, women, children, even babies. They didn't give no quarter to the woman or the children."

Frank felt sick.

"I was with Whitmore for the chase," he said. "But believe me Bent, I did nothing to the women and children. I was not a part of it."

Ringiringi looked at him, his expression unreadable.

"I expect not," he said. "You were always a decent chap."

"What about other deserters," asked Frank. "Were they with Titoko as well?"

"Some," he said. "One or two tried to desert back, but that didn't go too well for them. Don't like traitors, the Hauhau."

Frank hesitated for a minute, and then asked, "I don't suppose you heard about what happened to my brother—Private Hardy, Will Hardy. He deserted before you."

"I heard about him yes. But he were already dead by the time I went over," said Ringiringi. "I heard about the beheading. That was a bad thing. Even the *Hauhau*—my *Hauhau*—thought so. Not something they would've done, they said."

Frank said nothing, and after a few minutes Ringiringi continued, "He wasn't one of ours, you know, the feller that did it. Came down from the north, up near Waitara, where the wars started. Your brother would have been fine with my lot, so long as he swore he would stay with them, like I did, but that big feller, he came to our camp the same day your brother came over the river. He wanted the *pakeha* to die, and the chief couldn't say no, especially after the ceremony. The chief, he left your brother in a hut, so he told me, and the big feller went in there and cut off his head. He were screaming something terrible, so they said."

Frank felt his gorge rise. His worst fears confirmed. Will had been beheaded alive. The image of that warrior riding up on his horse, Will's head hanging from his hand by a hank of hair, sprang into his mind and choked him up so that he was unable to speak. Poor, poor misguided Will. Frank would never be able to tell their father about this, and he knew the secret would weigh heavily upon him.

"Sorry to be the one to tell you," apologized Ringiringi. "Best to know the truth, don't you think?"

"Did you ever see the man who killed my brother, the big fellow, after he killed Will?" asked Frank. Was it possible that Anahera was the same man? The description seemed similar.

"From time to time. He came by every few months to make sure my lot wuz being warlike enough. We weren't you know. We didn't really like to fight. We ran like headless chooks from Otapawa. Lot of us died first as well. Were you there as well?"

Frank nodded. "Was that you who called out to us? Someone yelled from the palisade at us that day, in English."

Ringiringi looked sheepish. "That were me," he said. "I were thinking you had no chance against us, and would just run off. But it were us that ran off. The five pounders scared us. But it weren't me that killed Colonel Hassard. I know they said I did, but I didn't."

"Must have been 300 died in the *Pa* that day. It was a slaughter."

"Not 300 hundred," said Ringiringi. "Not near 300, but it were a slaughter, that it were." He added, "Someone killed his brother."

"Whose brother?" asked Frank, confused.

"The big feller," said Ringiringi. "I just remembered he were living with us. His brother I mean to say. That's partly why the big feller came to visit so often. He wanted his brother out of the way of the fighting, but of course it worked out just the opposite, and his brother were killed."

"What made him think his brother needed to be protected? Wasn't he a fighter?" Frank asked.

"Too young," said Ringiringi. "He were just a boy, about thirteen or fourteen. He were supposed to be with the woman and children, back in the bush at the hiding place, but he came back to the *pa* to bring us a musket—a very old one, not much use to it really—and on the way he ran into one of you blokes and was killed."

Frank said nothing. He knew who had killed the man's brother. He had done it himself, and it had haunted him for years. A young boy he had encountered in a clearing who had pointed a musket rifle at him. He had given the boy a chance to drop the gun, and when he raised it and pointed it at Frank, Frank had shot him. He beheaded my brother, he thought, and I killed his brother. There was no point to it all, the fighting. People got killed who were not supposed to be killed, and the real warriors lived, scarred and bitter by their experiences.

After a while, Ringiringi continued.

"He would want *utu*, you know. Balance. Revenge. Whoever it was that killed his brother, if he could, he'd find him and kill him. It's his duty to do that. They need to retain their *mana*. Doesn't matter if you do a good deed or a bad one, it must be repaid in kind."

Frank nodded.

"I understand. But would he want *utu* or vengeance?"

Ringiringi shrugged. "No difference really."

If it was utu he was after, thought Frank, he had it.

He said, "Where's this big feller now? Could he be out looking for someone who had killed his brother, do you think?"

Ringiringi shook his head. "No. He were killed during the early part of Titoko's war. Up near Patea at Turuturu Mokai Redoubt. Took a few of your boys with him I heard."

"Do you know anything about him?" asked Frank, noting that when Ringiringi had said "your boys" he was siding with the *Hauhau*. "Where he was from. His *iwi?*"

"The big feller was a war chief, even though he weren't from our *iwi*. Came from up near Waitara, as I said before. Don't know what *iwi* though. He had a ceremony he would perform sometimes before a fight—a sacred weapon he would place on the ground until it pointed to someone. I seen it myself once. He would go into a trance and chant until the bloody thing moved by itself. When it stopped and pointed at some poor bastard he would haul the bugger up and ask him if his heart were strong within him."

"And surely a man would answer yes, if he valued his life," said Frank. He was waiting to hear how this story would enlighten him on his brother's beheading.

Ringiringi took a pull at his pipe.

"Most did, most did. Because they knew if they didn't they would be taken out and tomahawked to pieces. When they left to fight, he would be there, chanting *Patua, kainga! Patua, kainga! E kai mau! Kaua e tukua kia haere! Kia mau ki tou ringa.*"

"Kill them, eat them, kill them, eat them, let them not escape," translated Frank. "That was the chant of Titokowaru as well. I take it my brother refused to say his heart was strong within him?"

175

"Well, he wuz confused, like. Asked what the big feller meant, and said he didn't come over to kill and eat his own kind. Then he went off to the hut he wuz given, and in the night, as I said, the big feller went in and killed him."

"But you agreed?" said Frank, trying not to think about Will's fate. "You would have eaten British flesh if they had asked you to?"

Ringiringi's face showed a quick flash of humor.

"British, I would. But I'm a Yankee, aren't I? Born in Eastport, Maine."

When Frank said nothing, Ringiringi added, "Just fooling with ya. I wouldn't eat human flesh, and they didn't make me. If they beat them—the *Pakeha* that is—in battle, they would bring back a piece of flesh, usually the heart, ripped from the body of the first man they killed in the fight. They would offer it to their *Tohunga*. All he did was light a flame and singe it a bit, then throw it away. One time, after the fight at Papatihakehake I saw a bloke cut open the body of a dead *Pakeha* and tear the heart from it, but he wuz already dead, and no one ate his heart. Just ceremonial I suppose."

They traveled in silence after that. Frank let his passenger off at Tahoarite and watched him squat by the side of the road and start sucking on his clay pipe again. He was several miles from his former companions, and Frank wondered how he intended to return to them. Walk back, probably. The Maori, which Bent had become, were great for traveling long distances overland on foot. Bent, or Ringiringi as he had become, seemed to have settled for a simple life, but Frank wondered how it was possible to survive as part of another world so different from his own.

19

Return Through the Gorge

The Napier mail coach to Palmerston capsized coming through the Manawatu Gorge last night. No one was seriously hurt. No blame is attached to the driver. If the capsize took place at any part of the side cutting which forms the road on the Palmerston side of the Gorge, then it is surprising that the coach, horses, driver, and occupants escaped complete destruction. The road is a very narrow one, cut on the side of the hill, and overlooking the river, with a sheer descent of some hundreds of feet to the rocks and water below. It is about the worst place in the world for a capsize to happen, as, if the coach had gone a single foot over the outer edge of the road, in a few seconds it would have been lying at the bottom of the river, smashed to pieces.

Wanganui Chronicle, 8 September 1877

When Frank pulled his coach in at Murphy's Hotel Mette was sitting on the step with her bag, waiting for him. He'd been driving through a light drizzle, but the skies cleared as he approached Murphy's Hotel. Mette always brings sunny skies with her, he thought. It was as if her sunny nature affected the weather. He'd dreamed about her the night before, but felt the dream slip away as he awoke. Later, he'd fallen back to sleep and dreamed that he was being pursued through a dark forest by a dark, shapeless force. He'd tried to turn and see who was pursuing him but he could not. Once more he forgot the dream, recalling only a vague image of the throat-slashing gesture he had now seen twice, once from the man holding Will's head, and once from Anahera. Was there a connection between the two men? What was it?

As he climbed down from his seat, he noticed she looked unhappy, which dampened his own mood. He had no other passengers and helped her up beside his perch, assuming that's where she'd want to sit. When he passed her an old army blanket from the box behind him over her legs, she set her bag down forcefully and tucked the blanket around her knees.

He'd been looking forward to the opportunity to talk to her. The return trip was somewhat easier as the slope was mostly downhill and was easier on the horses. He sat her on his left, away from the steep drop now to be on his right side. The return journey was on the inside of the road and if they met another carriage or cart that vehicle would have to pull to the edge of the ravine. The return journey was always easier because of that.

She waited until they were on the way out of town, and then said angrily, "That woman did not want to come back to Palmerston with me."

"She'll come later then?"

"She will not come at all," she said. "She is going to live in Wellington with her fancy man and his sister, who I do not believe is his sister, and the children will be sent to where, I do not know. I am afraid they will be in the poorhouse immediately, and so will Agnete when her Mr. Williams," she practically spat his name out, "her Mr. Williams tires of her."

Frank sat in silence for a few minutes, digesting this new turn of events. He was amused at her turn of phrase. What was a fancy man in her eyes?

"Will you tell Pieter?" he asked finally. "He'll want to go and bring her back from Wellington, don't you think?"

Mette sighed.

"He would if he could, I suppose. But I will tell him a good version of the story and leave out the bits that make his sister sound like a, like a *taeve*. Not that I suspect that his sister is going to live in a *bordel*—what would you call it—a whorehouse. No, I will tell him simply that his sister is going to stay with the sister of a friend in Wellington and she does not need any help or money at the moment as the friend is assisting her."

Frank glanced at her.

"She may need money and help eventually," he said. "If things go as you suspect. Don't you think he should be somewhat ready to help, if—when —the occasion arises?"

Mette stared past him towards the river, which was still beside them. They were not yet in the gorge and she was already afraid of the drop she would see as they rose higher.

"I will think about it," she said. "You are right. He should know that everything is not perfect. She is a horrible woman, but she is his sister after all. Pieter can also be difficult, but he is underneath a kind man who would always do his best for his family."

They traveled for a while in silence. Then Mette said, "Sergeant Frank, would you like some bread? I purchased some at the bakery in Woodville. It is fresh bread which I have

179

not eaten since I left Haderslev, and quite delicious."

She took the bread, wrapped in a piece of newspaper, from her bag and tore off a piece for him. He chewed it appreciatively.

"Now," she said, settling back. "I would like you to tell me something."

"What?" he asked, surprised.

"Tell me about yourself when you were a small boy. I know nothing about you except that you were a soldier and that your brother, who was also a soldier, was killed—murdered—by *Hauhau*. Where did you live when you were boys? What about your family—your parents—do they still live there?"

He thought for a minute, working out what he could tell her.

"My father was also a soldier," he began. "He served under the Duke of Wellington and fought at the Battle of Waterloo. Do you know about that?"

"Of course I do," she said. "The Duke of Wellington defeated that nasty little man Napoleon."

"Yes he did, with some help from my father. And before that he—my father—was in Spain, and that was where he met my mother."

"Ah," she exclaimed. "That is why you are a little dark for an Englishman, with brown eyes. Mostly they—Englishmen—have very pale skin and light blue eyes. They look very much like the Germans, so I am pleased that you do not look like that."

He glanced at her, wondering why she should be pleased, and she continued, "And your father married your mother and you and your brother were born while he was still a soldier?"

He shook his head, distracted. "Just a minute while we get

onto the tracks here. We're on the way back up the Gorge and I'll need to concentrate more."

"Then quickly tell me about your life, when you were born, and when your brother was born."

"Quickly? Very well then, I'll try." He gave the horses a light tap and pulled back on the reins to slow them down. "After they were married my father left the army. He was highly skilled with horses, and became a groom at the stable of an important man, a politician, and his old commander from his army days. After he'd been a few years in the stables, the coachman on the estate died and my father took that job. So we grew up on the estate of the politician, and he allowed us to be educated with his sons, at least until they went off to boarding school. Rugby, they went to, one of the oldest British public schools, and they weren't home much after age eleven or so. Even after they left he encouraged us to read, and allowed us to use his library. We ate with the staff in the downstairs kitchen, but were also treated very kindly, almost like family. When the boys did come home they used to make me play rugby with them, but that stopped when I outgrew them and they couldn't bring me to the ground with a tackle. I learned about horses from my father, which has proven useful."

"And your mother," asked Mette. "What about her. How did she like leaving Spain and living in such a cold and unfriendly country as England."

"She died," he said shortly. "In childbirth. Giving birth to my brother. I can barely remember her."

"How very sad," said Mette. "I think I would have liked to know your mother. How brave she was, leaving her country and going to live in another country away from her family."

"Like you," he said. "How did you come to leave Schleswig? You weren't going to be inducted into the army surely, like the boys."

She looked down at her hands, and he saw, with embarrassment, a tear splash onto her hand."

"It was not me, but my brother and my father," she said. "He was a gentle man, very kind to Maren and me and our brother Hamlet. First the Prussians took Hamlet to be a soldier. They were fighting against the French and they needed all the young men they could find. Hamlet left to fight in August and in September he died in the Battle of Sedan, although it was a long time before we heard about it. We hoped all the time he would come home, that he would live." She paused, and then added, "Little Hamlet, Maren's boy, is named after him."

"And your father?" he prompted.

"He was taken to be a soldier just a few months after Hamlet," she said. "And he was killed at the Siege of Metz. It was terrible for my mother. Maren and I were just little girls. She tried very hard to keep the remainder of the family together, and she kept teaching us as our father had been doing…what is that on the road?"

Frank had been looking at her, not paying as much attention to the road as he should. He looked to where she was pointing and cursed, pulling back on the reins to slow the horses before they ran into the barrier that was now across the road, from bank side to cliff side.

"Damn it," he said. "A fallen branch. How are we going to get around that?

In front of them a tree limb had fallen across the road, completely blocking their path. The horses slowed and came to a stop, stamping and whinnying. Frank threw the reins across the seat and climbed down, leaving the horses standing where they were.

"Wait," called Mette. "Won't the horses run away if you aren't holding the reins?"

He shook his head, not looking back at her, and strode towards the branch. He attempted to lift it, but it wouldn't budge. Mette climbed down and joined him.

"What will you do?"

He was walking along the length of the branch, from the edge of the drop to the rise on the other side, staring intently. The rise was not steep at this point, and he hopped up onto an outcrop of rocks and stared down at the branch. He dropped into a squatting position suddenly, looking down at the branch, and said, "Damn."

"What is it," asked Mette, scared suddenly.

"Mette, get over as near as you can to the hill, immediately."

She ran over to the hill and he followed, stopping beside her.

"What is it?" she asked again.

"The branch has been cut with an axe," he said. He was leaning back against the hill, his hand over his eyes, scanning the area. "This isn't an accident, it's an ambush."

"Is it the *Hauhau*?" she asked, her voice quivering.

"Could be," he said. "Although the Armed Constables are keeping a pretty close watch on the entrance and exits to the Gorge. Bushwhackers, maybe. Either way, we're in trouble."

"Does he want to kill me because of the pig?"

"If it is the *Hauhau* he'll be after me," answered Frank. He had not told Mette of his encounter with Anahera. "I may have been involved in something that upset him."

Mette moved closer to Frank.

"Do you have a gun, Sergeant Frank?"

He nodded. "Yes, but it's in the box under the seat. Didn't think to keep it on me, unfortunately."

"Then I will go and get it. If he needs to kill you for revenge, he may not want to kill me."

She started to move towards the coach, but he grabbed her arm and held it firmly.

"I'm not going to let you do that. I won't even consider it."

He looked around again, scanning for movement. Everything was quiet; only sound of the rushing of the waters far below.

"If we move nearer to the coach we'll be under the edge of the hill," he said finally. "We'll have to move quickly, before they—he—realizes what we're doing. Then once we're under the hill I can get around the other side of the coach and up into the seat to get my weapon."

"Will he shoot you when he sees you?"

Frank shook his head. "I doubt that he has a gun, if it is the *Hauhau*. He seems to prefer his kills to be more personal. But if it's bushwhackers, yes they will have a gun. Guns. The *Hauhau* is a better proposition really. He'll want to fight hand-to-hand, for the honor of the killing. Or at least throw his tomahawk at me, if he has another one. Let's move."

He held her hand and they ran the short distance to where the bank rose straight up. He pulled her behind him, and stared around again. Nothing moved, and there was no sound other than the ever-churning waters of the Gorge.

"Stay here and lean back as far as you can," he said, almost whispering now. Then, taking one more look around, he dashed towards the rear of the coach.

The gunshot was so unexpected that Mette gave a small

scream. She saw the edge of the coach splinter. The horses threw back their heads and whinnied, their eyes white with fear. Frank was around the other side now.

"Are you all right, Mette?" he yelled.

It took her a minute to reply. Her throat was dry with fear.

"I, I, yes," she croaked. "Is it the *Hauhau*? Does he have a gun now?"

"Don't know who it is, but he has a gun."

He lifted the lid of the box under the seat of his coach slowly, and reached in to grab the gun. Another shot echoed around the gorge and the box splintered.

"Are you hit Frank?"

"Stay there, Mette. Don't come out," he ordered. "A splinter from the box hit me in the hand. It's nothing, just a scratch." He pulled out his kerchief and wrapped it around the side of his hand.

Everything was quiet for a few minutes, and he started to edge around the front of the coach and under the horses. He squatted there, patting their haunches to keep them calm. He managed to release one, with the idea that he could ride the attacker down, but as it came free from its traces it wandered a few steps towards the branch. That at least gave him some cover. Keeping low, he came up from under the belly of the other horse and sprinted towards Mette. This time there was no gunshot. He arrived back at her side and leaned against the hill, panting. He had a white kerchief wrapped around his hand, and blood was seeping through. Mette helped him tie it around his hand to staunch the blood.

"What are we going to do?" she asked. "If it's bushwhackers I have some money. I could throw it out onto the road and we could call out to them that they can have it if they let us go."

185

"There'll be more money in the mail bag," said Frank. "They could take that if they wanted. I don't think it can be bushwhackers, they would have shown themselves as soon as they realized I don't have my gun on me."

"So what can we do?" asked Mette. "Will someone else be coming through the Gorge today? Can we stay here and wait for someone to arrive, someone perhaps who has a gun?"

"Depends who it is," said Frank. "The *Hauhau* wants to kill me, bushwhackers want the mail for the money they might find. No reason for bushwhackers to kill either of us. As far as I know, no one else wants to kill…" He stopped suddenly and stared at Mette.

"What is it Frank? Does someone else want to kill you?"

She reached out and touched the mark under his eye. "Is it something to do with this? You had a fight with someone, didn't you?

He nodded.

"It can't be him," he said. But she could see in his eyes they he knew something.

"Would he want to kill you? Why? What did you do to him? Who was it?"

As if in answer to her question, someone slid down the hill behind the fallen branch and said, "I have you in my sights, you fucking limey bastard."

Mette gasped. "Gottlieb?"

Karlsen arose from behind the branch, his face an angry mask of hatred. He had a revolver in his hand aimed at Frank. "I won't miss from this distance," he said. "I'll shoot you right where you kicked me, you arsehole. Then we'll see how she likes you."

"Gottlieb?" said Mette again. "Why are you here? Why do

you want to hurt Frank?" She moved in front of Frank and spread her arms out to cover him, but Frank thrust her aside.

Gottlieb sneered at her.

"Thinks he's better than me," he said. "Bloody limey prick."

"That's because he is better than you," said Mette. "That's no reason to shoot him." She was more relaxed now. This was just Gottlieb, not bushwhackers or the *Hauhau*. He would not be able to molest her when Frank was here. He was just full of wind and would calm down and go away if she talked to him.

"I beat him up, a couple of days ago," said Frank quietly. "He really does want to kill me, or at least to hurt me."

"Why did you do that?" she asked, still looking at Karlsen. "Was it because of what he did to me?"

"I did nothing to you," said Karlsen. "The bloody bed stopped me before I could enjoy myself."

Mette heard Frank let out his breath.

"What you did was not nothing," he said. "Even if you, if you." He stopped and started again. "Men, decent men don't attack women while they are sleeping. Decent men don't spy on women when they are washing clothes, and decent men don't take pleasure with themselves while spying on women."

Mette turned and looked at him, her eyes wide.

"You knew he was the man who attacked me and you hit him?" she asked. "Thank you Sergeant Frank. I am happy that you did that."

Karlsen moved his gun from Frank and aimed at Mette.

"Shut up, cunt," he said. "Or I'll kill you too. Get the fuck out of the way."

She gasped and put her hands over her mouth.

"Gottlieb, this is not right. What will our pastor and the Monrads think when they find out you are using such terrible words? And what would they think if they know you have killed us?"

Frank had been wondering the same thing himself, at least the second part.

"You'll be an outcast," he said. "This is not a large country, and you won't be able to hide forever. They'll find you and hang you."

Karlsen gestured with his revolver.

"Move out from the hill. Over to the middle."

Mette held Frank's hand, and they moved slowly forward, both of them expecting a shot, and the pain it would cause, at any minute. They came to a stop in front of the horses. One of the horses, the one that Frank had released, dropped its head onto his shoulder, and then lifted it up and whinnied softly. Perhaps Frank can get the horse to charge into Gottlieb, Mette thought. She hoped he had a plan, at least.

Karlsen gestured his gun at them again, this time towards the edge of the drop.

"Move," he ordered.

They moved nearer to the edge. Mette's hand started shaking as the drop came nearer. Her head felt very light, as if it would fly off her body. She could see the river, tumbling on its path far below her feet. She had a feeling that the river was sucking her downward and she just had to let go and fall, and everything would be over with.

"*Gut*," said Karlsen. "Now you can both jump off the edge. Keep your hands held together and when they find you they will think it is some kind of stupid fucking lovers' suicide."

They both froze, staring at their attacker in shock. Then Mette said quietly, "Gottlieb, let us both live and I will marry you. I swear I will marry you and we will have many children

188

together and a long life. But you must let <u>both</u> of us live or I will not marry you." She felt Frank's hand tighten on hers.

Karlsen made a noise that sounded like *tuh*.

"You think I want his leavings, you whore? If you want to see him live, then you jump first. Then he will be alive when you die."

Mette gave a little sob.

"So," said Karlsen. "Which of you wants to jump first, or do you want to jump together. It makes no difference to me."

"Why don't you just shoot us," said Frank through gritted teeth. Then, to Mette he added quietly, *"Wefen Siesichseitwarts."*

She didn't move. "He speaks German as well," she said sadly.

Karlsen laughed.

"Ich spreche sehr gut Deutsch. Ich bin Deutsch aus Schleswig. Throwing herself sideways will not help at all. I have enough bullets for both of you and I can shoot you one at a time without a problem. Don't think you can save her by dying yourself."*

His face darkened.

"Enough of this bullshit. Jump! Jump! And do it together."

"Gottlieb, I cannot," cried Mette. "I do not want to die. Please don't make me do this. My family, my sister, all those people I know, they will be so sad if I die."

Karlsen raised his gun to eye level and began to walk towards them, a look of hatred contorting his face. Frank prepared to make a last minute lunge at him, knowing that the odds were not good. He did not want to die either, but if he had to he intended to take Karlsen with him to the bottom of the Gorge. Mette made a sound and he turned and saw her slip over the edge of the drop. Ignoring Karlsen he leapt forward. The road sloped down and out for two yards, then dropped

189

directly into the cataclysm below. She had stopped her fall a foot from the edge of the road, and she clutched on to a clump of grass, her body fully on the slope.

"Mette," he said. "Hold tight, I'll pull you up."

"Back away," snarled Karlsen, aiming his gun at Frank. "I will pull her up. I want you to jump together. Get over by the back of the coach. Stay away from the front. I know you keep your guns there. If you make a move towards me, I'll push her back over the edge."

Frank didn't move.

"Go, go, said Karlsen, or I will push her down all the way."

Frank backed towards the back of the coach, remembering as he did that he had put Anahera's tomahawk in the rear boot. One chance, he thought. One chance.

Karlsen leaned down and reached for Mette with one hand. His gun was trained on Frank, but he was looking at Mette who was out of his reach. He knelt and stretched his arm to her.

"Swing up and grab my arm," he said. Mette did not reply.

"Swing up, you stupid bitch," said Karlsen. "Don't you want to live a few more minutes? Don't you want to die with this bastard?"

Frank watched as Karlsen strained towards her, waiting for an opportunity to move. Karlsen had Mette by the hand, his attention fully on her. Frank leaped for the foot box. Karlsen heard him and spun around, letting Mette go. She grabbed the edge of the slope and slipped back down, her feet over the edge of the abyss, but holding on to a gnarled tree root that had been in place for a hundred years. Karlsen started to bring the gun up towards Frank, but the tomahawk was in Frank's hands now. He reached back and threw it as hard and as straight as he could.

The tomahawk hit the side of Karlsen's head and stuck there. He stood, not moving, a puzzled look on his face. Blood leaked down his cheek and he raised his hand part way towards it, but a light seemed to be fading from his eyes. Frank was about to lunge at him when Karlsen swayed and staggered sideways, disoriented. He took one step towards the rim of the gorge, and then suddenly was over it, plunging down towards the water, soundlessly. The river continued to roar beneath them, the horses stamped their hooves, and nothing else moved. Frank caught a brief glimpse of Karlsen in the water as he was tumbled back through the Gorge in the raging water, and saw him disappear beneath it. He bobbed up once, the tomahawk still embedded in the side of his head, then disappeared for ever. When he surfaced eventually, downstream in the Manawatu River, Frank realized, the fact that he had not died naturally would be obvious.

He dropped to the ground and lay face forward, reaching out to Mette. She looked up at him, a hopeless look on her face.

"You can't reach me," she said. "You will have to let me fall."

He edged forward, his hand still inches from hers. "I'm not going to let you fall," he said. "I'd rather die myself than let you go. Not now."

He moved further forward, but knew that a few more inches and he would not be able to keep himself on the bank, but would slip into the gorge, taking both of them down. He looked around for something to hold on to, but there was nothing. He was afraid that if he got up to look for something he would come back to find her gone.

Something pressed against his back, followed by the sound

of heavy breathing.

"Keep holding tight, Mette," he said, rolling over. "One more minute. I'm coming down to get you." The horse he had released was standing beside him, its reins hanging to the ground.

He took off his coat and threw it on the ground, put the reins around under his armpits and edged forward over the drop. "Hold on, I'm coming."

The horse shuffled forward and held fast, taking Frank's full weight as he slid forward. When his hands were both within reach of hers, he held her tightly by the wrists and said quietly, "You can let go now."

"I can't," she said. "I can't do it. I'm scared."

The bush she was holding on to gave way suddenly. But the horse held in place, with a soft whinny.

"Now boy, pull us back," he said, and made a clicking noise with his teeth. The horse backed away from the drop taking the two of them with him. When his body was almost on the road, he gave Mette a tug and pulled her over the edge with him. The front of her dress was torn and dirty and he face was white with shock. She lay on the ground, sobbing.

He patted the horse on the neck and said, "good boy, good boy," then sat down beside her. She sat up and scrabbled further away from the edge.

"I thought I was going to fall," she said, and began to shake uncontrollably.

He picked up his coat and wrapped it around her shoulders, holding her tight. The shaking became violent. "But you didn't fall," he said. "You hung on and now you're safe."

He could feel her chest heaving and her breath coming in shuddering gasps. He put his hand to her face and pulled her against his chest, and put his face against her head.

"I've got you," he said. "You're safe."

"You saved me," she said. "But it was all my fault. I did not pay attention when he asked me to dance, and I gave him false ideas. And now he came for me, to get revenge."

"It was never your fault, Mette. Don't ever think that," he said into the top of her head. As he comforted her he felt a calmness he had not felt for a long time.

She had started to relax, and put her hand up over his where it held her face. They sat like that for several minutes, saying nothing. She turned her head towards him, looking at him, still holding his hand against her face, her eyes searching his.

He bent towards her, unable to stop himself, his lips brushing against hers briefly.

"Do you need help here?" said a loud voice.

They sprang apart, both flushed. Frank's heart was pounding.

Coming from the direction of Palmerston, two large fair men in broad-brimmed hats had arrived in a dray pulled by a bullock. Mette sniffed and rubbed her eyes, and spoke to them in Danish, her voice quavering. The men looked at each other and back at her.

"I think I know what you say," said one in English. "But we are Swedish and I think you are Danish. We are farmers from the Wairarapa and we have been in Palmerston and Foxton buying some equipment for the farm. We have a new plowshare that will be very nice for our land." He gestured to the back of the dray. "Should we move this tree together? We have an axe in our dray. We found it just there on the ground."

"Thank you," said Frank. "We were unable to get by and were worried."

With the two men helping, Frank managed to remove the smaller branches and throw them in the ditch. Then they took the remaining large branch, dragged it to the edge of the gorge and threw it down. It fell to the water and was swept away in the rushing current, much as Gottlieb Karlsen had been just minutes before. The two Swedes showed no curiosity about how the branch had got there, and why they had found an axe in the road.

The men went on their way to Woodville and Frank and Mette climbed onto the coach and started back towards Palmerston. Before they did, Frank tossed the axe far out into the Gorge.

"Best we don't leave this here," he said.

"Was he dead?" asked Mette.

Frank nodded. "I think so. He had a tomahawk stuck in his head, and if that didn't kill him the water would."

She looked at her hands and said nothing.

He flicked his whip over the horses' heads and they were on the road home. But now he had his carbine sitting at his feet, handy if he needed it again. If Anahera was out there somewhere, waiting to attack, he would shoot to kill before Anahera could raise his *mere*. One murder attempt was enough to survive in one day.

20

A Body Under the Ferry Punt

...one man who fell on to the rocks in the river was very badly cut about the head and bruised all over his body. He was taken to the Bridge, where Mr. George Ross, the toll collector, did all in his power to relieve him by giving him painkiller and vinegar, but after a short time his friends decided to take him on. When they left the Bridge the man, was lying at the bottom of the cart, evidently very much hurt.

The Manawatu Times, 29 August 1877

As they reached Palmerston they were both quiet, thinking about what they had to do next. Despite what they had been through, the Mail Coach was a little over an hour late and Frank was able to release the horses from their traces and take them into the paddock behind the Royal Hotel, where Hop Li had left a bucket of oats, as if nothing unusual had happened. Mette watched him as he walked away, but he did not look back. They had decided between them to say nothing about what had occurred. The Manawatu River had taken Gottlieb's body, just as it had probably taken the bodies of Paul and Jens.

Mette felt ill. She could not celebrate Gottlieb's death is spite of what he had done to her.

Pieter was waiting for Mette in front of the hotel, pacing up and down anxiously. He helped her dismount, climbed up and carried her bag down from the roof of the coach and took it silently to the bullock cart. They climbed onto the seat of the cart, he flicked his whip over the heads of the bullocks, and they were off to the clearing.

"Mette, said Pieter finally. "Where is my sister?"

Mette scrabbled in her pocket and took from it the money Pieter had given to her. "Here is your money, less the shillings I gave to Agnete and the small amount I spent on a room and some bread in Woodville. Agnete is not coming."

He took it and looked at her, waiting for more information.

"She did not want to come," she said. "I told her you would make a home here for her and for her two children, but she is going to Wellington to stay with a, with a lady friend."

"How much of money did you give her?" asked Pieter, after a pause.

"A little. Just a few shillings—the ten-shilling note in fact. I did not feel she needed money and I knew that you needed it more for your own family, for Maren and Hamlet and the new baby."

To her surprise, Pieter turned to her, his eyes welling with tears.

"Was there a man there, Mette? Please tell me the truth. I know my sister very well. Has she attached herself to another man?"

Mette bit her lip. "I am afraid to tell you this Pieter, but yes, there was another man. I met her in the church at the funeral of her husband, and she was holding the arm of an

Englishmen. A not very nice Englishman I think. Your sister Agnete said she was going to Wellington to stay with the sister of this man, a Mr. Williams. Perhaps she was."

Pieter wiped away a tear that had fallen onto his cheek.

"My sister Agnete is a bad woman. She has used men since she was a young girl, even our father. I hoped that New Zealand would help her find a husband and allow her to settle down. She met Mads on the boat, just as I met Maren, and she married him very quickly. An older man who loved her and wanted to care for her."

"I asked her to let me bring the children to Palmerston," said Mette. "The Englishman was very keen for me to do that, but she said no. I am afraid of what will happen to them."

Tears were now running freely down Pieter's cheeks, and he made no attempt to wipe them away.

"I must go to Wellington and bring back the children," he said. "Not now, but when Maren has had our son. I will have to leave my work for a few days."

Mette refrained from saying that the baby might be a girl, or from offering to go to Wellington to bring back the children. Clearly this was not a job suitable for her. It was the job of a brother or a male relative, or perhaps....

"You could ask Sergeant Frank to go down to Wellington and bring her back," she said before she could stop herself.

But again he surprised her.

"That is an excellent idea, Mette," he said. "I will talk to him once Maren has had the baby. He will know how to deal with this Englishman you mentioned. He is an Englishman himself."

Frank fed and watered his horses and went to check if Mette had found Pieter. Wiremu Karira was waiting out the front of the Royal Hotel, wanting to talk to him.

"I've just heard that a body has been seen in the river, up near the ferry crossing," he said. "It's stuck under the ferry and no one wants to go in after it. I thought you might ride up there with me and give me a hand."

"Do they know who it is?" asked Frank.

"All they can see is a dark shadow and some hair floating," said Karira. "Could be anybody."

Frank fetched his horse and he and Karira headed out towards the ferry crossing.

"Not one of my missing boys, is it?" he said after a bit.

"Wrong place," said Karira. "Up river. Your missing boys would be downriver, unless they went into the river at a different place than we thought."

"I found a boot," said Frank. "Right where they were supposed to have crossed. I think they're in the river, and they went in where everyone thinks they did. No idea where they can be though."

"They must be somewhere downstream," said Karira. "Somewhere between where they crossed and Foxton. They could easily have been carried down to the estuary. If I were you I would start there and work my way up. I can help you search for them if you like. I know the river well and we can use my *waka tete*. It's down at the wharf in Foxton."

"I'd appreciate the help," said Frank. "Who else could it be? Under the ferry. Anyone missing?"

"One of the men on the road crew seems to have vanished," said Karira. "Sergeant Jackson went looking for him. Could be him. A Scandi I think."

Frank said nothing. Probably it was Karlsen, surfacing quickly from the torrent. If the tomahawk was still in his head the Armed Constabulary would be out in full force looking for the killer. He would have to give some thought to a story, if one was needed.

"Karlsen," said Karira. "Gottfried Karlsen."

"What?"

"The man who disappeared, the one from the road crew."

"Aah," said Frank. "Karlsen. Yes."

"The man you beat up a couple of days ago," said Karira, a slight smile on his face.

Frank gave him a sharp look.

"Heard about it from Jackson," said Karira. "Well done."

When Frank still said nothing, he added, "Jackson went looking for him. I think he wants to beat him up again. Doesn't like the reputation of his road crew being disparaged. Doesn't help him get road contracts."

"You don't think Sergeant Jackson…" said Frank.

"Killed Karlsen and threw him in the river?" asked Karira. "Could be. He was mad as a kakapo when he left."

Frank was thoughtful the rest of the way. The ferry crossing came into view, the ferry stuck half way across the river, the ferrymen sitting there staring at the banks. Two coaches were waiting for the ferry to complete its aborted crossing, passengers walking back and forth, stamping their feet and looking irritable.

Karira commandeered a small rowboat and they rowed out to the stranded ferry.

"Where is he?"

One of the ferrymen pointed under the side of the ferry.

"Down 'ere," he said. "You can just see 'is legs."

Frank could see a dark shape that looked like a pair of legs beside the bottom of the ferry; the rest of the body must be caught underneath. The draft was shallow here, not more than a fathom, and the ferry floated a mere foot above the river bottom. The legs were dark, possibly brown, but he could tell little more. Karlsen had been wearing dark coloured trousers when he had fallen into the gorge. Frank could not remember the exact colour – buff perhaps.

Karira stripped off his shirt and boots and jumped into the water. Some of the women on the dock turned away, although one young woman who was a passenger on the ferry leaned over the railing and stared down at him until an older woman yanked her back.

"I'm going to tug on his legs, see if I can get him lose," he said.

He disappeared under the water for a minute, then came up, wiping water from his eyes.

"Not yet."

One more time seeming much longer, then he appeared again.

"I think I have him."

The body rose slowly and floated just below the surface. Frank pulled it by the shirt, desperate to see the head. It circled and he saw a bloody gash on the side, but no tomahawk. He pulled again and the body turned slowly over, the face now barely above the surface, the lips pulled back in an agonized grin.

Frank fell back onto the seat of the rowboat, horror-stricken. Not Karlsen. But his old friend "Jack" Jackson stared at him with sightless eyes.

Karira pulled himself back on board and they dragged Jackson onto the boat.

"Looks like Karlsen killed him," said Karira. "Jackson was

looking for him, and he must have found him. They got into a fight and Karlsen hit him, probably with an axe."

Frank said nothing. Could that be what had happened? And what would they think when Karlsen's body appeared, if it ever did. How would they explain two men killing each other with a blow to the head? Such a thing was unimaginable.

Frank was nowhere to be found the next day when Mette came looking for him, wondering if there had been any consequences to their adventure the previous day. She walked into town after Pieter left for work, much to Maren's chagrin. The Assistant Constable was the only one at the Police Station, and he knew nothing. Hop Li at the Royal Hotel also had no idea where Frank might have gone.

She drifted over towards the bookstore, drawn by the thought of all the wonderful books inside. Last time she'd been there Frank was waiting outside for her. Perhaps it would happen again.

On the window she noticed a poster, and she stopped to read it. *Academy of Music*, it read. *This evening. Mr. George Sawkins will deliver his second Theologico-Astronomical Lecture on "Satan." In which the myth of evil to the doctrines of the ancient Sun Worshippers, visits Pandemonium, examines the titles and characters of that Old Serpent, the Devil, and treats of...*

She heard someone behind her, and turned to see Mr. Robinson looking at her over his glasses, an amused smile on his face.

"Am I to assume that you are interested in coming to see Mr. Sawkins?" he asked.

Mette glanced back at the poster. "I see it costs one shilling to sit in the back row," she said. "Even if I could afford it, I don't think I would want to attend. It sounds very scary and exaggerated."

Mr. Robinson looked relieved. "I'm happy to hear that you are not interested," he said. "These fire and brimstone raconteurs should be banned from small towns, in my opinion. All they do is excite the populace and put foolish ideas into their heads. Now my dear, would you like to make an old man happy and take a cup of tea with him? Come into my shop. I have a kettle on the hub at this moment."

Mette preferred coffee, as did most people from Schleswig, but she knew that the English loved tea so she was happy to take a cup. She followed him into the shop and watched as he set a kettle full of water on top of a coal fired oven, marveling at the fact that water could be heated so easily.

Eventually they sat down with a cup of sweet tea, with real sugar and milk; Mette was in paradise.

"And why are you in town today?" Mr. Robinson said as she finished her tea.

"I was looking for someone," she said. "Well, actually I was looking for Sergeant Hardy. I came back with him from Woodville on the mail Coach yesterday. He was going to the Police Station to see if there was any news about the man the posse chased up behind the sawmill."

"Ah," said Mr. Robinson. "The man the Armed Constabulary have warned us about. No news, I don't believe. Although there has been another murder."

Mette stared at him in shock. They had found Gottlieb's body so soon?

Mr. Robinson was looking at her curiously.

"Whatever is the matter," he said. "Did you not know that a body was found?"

"A body?" asked Mette, her throat tight.

"Trapped under the ferry punt," he explained. "One of the road crew was found with a gash on his forehead that looked as if he had been hit with a tomahawk. Constable Price believes the man he chased with the posse is the man who killed him. The Armed Constabulary have taken charge, however, and I'm sure they will discover the perpetrator."

Mette's nails were dug into her hand and she could feel the skin breaking. If they discovered it was Frank, surely he would hang. Her whole body felt weak at the thought of that. How could she ever bear that?

"And the Armed Constabulary will search for the person who killed, Gott…this man?" she asked.

"Constable Price thinks—as I do—that in this case the Armed Constabulary needs to be in charge. He has sent them up to Ashhurst to search for the killer. You need not worry, my dear. He is no longer our problem. Good riddance to bad rubbish, I say."

He saw that Mette looked puzzled and added, "I mean to say, it's just as well that the man is up in Ashhurst and being sought by the Armed Constabulary. If anyone can find him, they can. I believe we can all stop worrying. It's someone else's problem now."

Mette finally let her hands relax and sipped her tea without saying anything. Her heart was still pounding. If the Armed Constabulary thought it was the *Hauhau* who had killed Gottlieb, then perhaps they would spend all their time looking for him and not think of anyone else. Of course, if the Hauhau was captured and condemned to die, then Frank would feel obliged…. She could not think of it.

"There is something I wanted to ask you," he said.

She managed to clear her head and look at him questioningly.

She had never felt so comfortable with anyone before, other than Frank.

"You said last time we met that you wanted to write down recipes, and notes about how to use different plants you have found in the bush," he reminded her.

"Yes, I did say that, and I would love to do it—if you would just give me one of those lovely pens," she said, smiling to show she was not serious.

"I have an idea—two ideas really—I want you to think about," he said. "Don't answer right away, but tell me next time you are in town. First, I would like someone to work in this shop. I have another bookshop in Foxton and I can't open both at once unless I find someone I trust to be in one of the shops. The job comes with a room out the back—a tiny room, but sufficient for the needs of one person. I'm sure you would be quite comfortable there, and safe as there are neighbors close by. The second idea is that I would like you to write down your recipes and thoughts so that I can publish them in a little pamphlet. I have a small printing press back in Foxton, and I would sell the pamphlets in both my bookstores. We could share the proceeds—about half what we made each, I should think would be acceptable."

Mette opened her mouth to speak, and he put up his hand. "No, I said you were not to answer directly, but that you should tell me next time you are in town."

In answer, Mette stood up and went to look at the room at the back of the store, and came back with her eyes brimming with tears. "It is exactly perfect," she said. "I will not tell you my answer now, as you request, but I am very excited at the thought of living in Palmerston and working in your bookshop." She would be near Sergeant Frank, she thought, and that would make it even more perfect, if only…

She lingered for half an hour outside the photography studio next door to the bookshop, looking at the photos in the window, hoping she would see Frank, but she did not appear. She wondered if he had heard that Gottlieb had surfaced so quickly in the Manawatu River, trapped under the ferry punt dock. When he did not appear, she started the long walk back to the clearing.

21

In the Estuary with Karira

Whitebait! Whitebait! To-morrow (Tuesday), from 12 to 3 Palace Dining Room, Queen-street, opposite- City Hall. J. Lee, Proprietor.
  Auckland Star, 27 August 1877

The Armed Constabulary took charge of Sergeant Jackson's body. Despite the continued disappearance of Gottlieb Karlsen, Captain Andrews was quite sure it was the act of the man they were searching for, the Avenging Angel, in the face of Karira's insistence it was more likely that Gottfried Karlsen had killed Jackson.

"They think it's because he's wearing the blouse of the Die Hards," Karira said to Frank. "And that it's just another of the vengeance deaths. He wondered what you people did to make him angry with you, as he seems determined to kill as many of you as he can."

It was possible that Anahera had killed Jackson, but Frank wondered why he would want to. Did he want to kill all Die Hards, or just some he had seen at some point? And when would that be? Frank could remember several events where the Die Hards were involved. Any one of them could have aroused a feeling of revenge in the other side. But this lot of killings must have something terrible connected to them. He thought of the name Adams again and wished he could remember where he knew it from.

One consolation was if Karlsen was assumed to have have killed Jackson, then he was dead himself and justice had been served. Frank felt confident that whomever they decided was the killer—either someone who had killed before, or someone who was dead—no one would be looking for him as the killer of Karlsen – if and when his body turned up. They had a neat little triangle of possibilities and he wasn't in it. He rode out to tell Mette that they were in the clear, but she was not at home. Her sister Maren took a message saying that his friend Sergeant Jackson had been found drowned. She promised to pass on the news, but looked at him strangely, as if wondering why Mette would need to know about that.

Frank and Karira rode down to the Foxton wharf the next day and collected Karira's *waka tete* to explore the estuary of the Manawatu River. Frank enjoyed learning how to paddle in the Maori way. He had only used a rowboat or a punt before this adventure. The *waka tete* was amazingly light and fast in the water, and smaller than the large *waka* he had seen Maori use for trading up and down the river. The bow was raised and carved with an approximation of a face with the tongue protruding, reminding Frank of the *Haka* Anahera had performed after the visit to the *Pa*.

"How came you to be a constable," Frank asked him as they began the search. "I spent some time in the Armed Constabulary in '68 and '69, after I was out of the Imperial Forces, but I wasn't happy with some of the things we did, and left. I worked on the docks in Wanganui for a while, and on a horse farm. I became a coachman back in '72."

"One of my *Hapu,* my extended family members, was an early Maori constable," said Karira. "Up in New Plymouth. He was a member of George Cooper's detachment of the New Ulster Armed Police Force, helping negotiate land sales. Then in '53 he joined the Native Police force, the first Maori to do so. He was appointed to the Native Land Court in the early sixties, and later promoted to Sergeant in Charge of the Native Force. My father was always very proud of the connection—we never met him, as we were distant family, but we knew about him—and that encouraged me to join the force when I was old enough."

"Constable Price said you were educated in England," said Frank. "You went to one of the Public schools, did you?"

Wiremu gave a wry grin. "No, I was sent to live in London with a friend of Governor Gore-Browne, whom my father knew, a Mr. Nichols, a Solicitor, and he set me up with a tutor. I was there for just a few months. Not the best place for a young Maori lad to live, London. My tutor and Mr. Nichols treated me well, but I was pointed at in the street, and invited to visit homes of wealthy people as a specimen for the folks there to gawk at. I came home as soon as I could. That was when I joined the force."

"An uncle of mine served briefly with Gore-Browne in Afghanistan," commented Frank. "During the invasion that stopped the Russians coming down into India." He was sensing that he and Karira had a lot in common. "Gore-Browne is the reason I'm in New Zealand, because of his response to the Waitara problem. The Die Hards were brought here to deal with that, mostly. Without him I'd probably still be in India."

They paddled in silence for a minute, both thinking of the

pasts that had brought them to this point in their lives. "How do you enjoy the work?" asked Frank eventually. "The work of a constable?" He had been thinking of looking for another line of work, and the Police had entered his mind, if only briefly.

"I hope you're not thinking of joining the constabulary," said Karira, with a lopsided grin, "believe me, you would not enjoy it. Too much paper work and drudgery; too much time waiting around, dealing with drunks, or separating arguing husbands and wives." He pointed to the far side of the river where a willow tree dragged its branches across a stretch of water and onto a sand bar. "Let's look under that one."

"I've been thinking I might set up on my own," said Frank as they manipulated the *waka* across the current. "As a private investigator. There seems to be a need for someone to work outside the Constabulary, to work for individuals—like the sort of thing we're doing now." He hopped out of the *waka* and lifted the branches, standing in soft sand, while Karira poked a long stick he had brought with him for the search under the water beside the sand, working his way around beneath the branches. Nothing there. He dropped the branch, hopped back into the *waka*, and they backed out into midstream again. They were in the broad sandy mouth of the Manawatu River, which wound around a sandbank into the Tasman Sea just west of Foxton. The wind was blowing them inland, which would be helpful when it came time to return upstream, but made moving hard going.

"What are the chances they got down this far," he said.

Karira shrugged. "Not good," he said. "But best to leave no stone—or branch—unturned."

They struggled on for a while, and then pulled up the Foxton Wharf, about a mile from the mouth, intending to ask in the town if anyone had seen anything—clothing, hats, or even part of a skeleton. By now it was possible that the bodies had been cleaned of their flesh by eels. Men clustered on the wharf holding nets, and were clearly preparing to row out to the middle of the river with them, or had already done so. Several held buckets containing something shimmery.

"What's going on?" asked Frank.

"Ta wheetbeet air roonin'," said a red-haired Scot, standing with a bucket over either arm. Frank looked at Karira for translation. All he had understood was that something was running. Scots were always difficult to understand.

"He says the whitebait are running—the fish fry. They come downstream at this time of year and out into the Tasman Sea. The settlers catch them in nets and cook them up in a batter with eggs and flour. Taste awful I find, but the settlers like them."

Karira pulled his *waka tete* up to his mooring on the far side of the wharf and they collected their horses. Frank was beginning to feel comfortable with the young constable, and to trust him as well. As they headed back towards Palmerston, he said cautiously, "What are you hearing from the Armed Constabulary, about the body, about Sergeant Jackson."

Karlsen, the workman from the crew, has still not appeared," said Karira. "They're coming around to my way of thinking, that he's the one who killed Jackson. He must have got a jump on him. Probably gone north by now, well out of our district."

"I'm sure that's the case," said Frank.

"A bad character all around," said Karira. Spying on the women at the *Pa* when they were at the river, as you know." He looked at Frank curiously. "Is that why you beat him up? The other men said you caught him in the act, but that you were looking for him."

"Yes, I caught him spying on the women," said Frank. "but it was worse than that. He also attacked a young woman in the night, one of the Scandinavian women. Tried to rape her. I'd prefer if you didn't mention it to Constable Price, however. No need to bring Me...her into it."

"I won't," said Karira. "And Hakopa said to tell you he's grateful. No telling what the men at the Pa will do to him if he's found alive."

Frank reined in his horse, and Karira followed suit. They faced each other.

"Look Karira," he said. "I'll come clean, because I trust you. Karlsen set up an ambush for me in the Gorge. Dropped a branch across the road, and when we got down from the coach he forced us to the edge, my passenger and me. My passenger was Miss Jensen, whom he had attempted to rape, which is why I beat him up. He tried to force us to jump into the river. I grabbed a tomahawk from my coach and threw it at him. It hit him on the side of the head and he fell into the river. I have no doubt that he's dead. But it was self-defense. We both would have died if I hadn't managed to kill him first."

Karira was quiet for a long time.

"I'll say nothing," he said eventually. "You've done a good thing for my people. I would not like to see you hang for it, or to go to prison."

"I could prove self-defense, I would think," said Frank. "What with the evidence of the other men in the road crew, and the women at the *Pa*."

Karira nodded. "But do you have any evidence that a branch was dropped across the road? How do we know that you didn't just kill him and take him up to the Gorge and throw him into the river?"

Frank told him about the two Swedish men.

Karira looked thoughtful.

"I would say you achieved *utu*," he said. "I won't say anything to Constable Price unless Anahera is caught and charged with Karlsen's murder. Unlikely, I would say, as he's murdered soldiers, and they'll try him for that. A Scandinavian road worker won't bother them so much."

They were both silent for a time, then Karira said, "The Armed Constabulary will keep searching for Anahera. He's proving a hard man to track."

"Miss Jensen thought she saw him at the *Papaioea Pa*, when we were there recently," said Frank. "Just before he did the Haka for us. She didn't tell me at the time, so…"

"*Papaioea*," said Karira. "My *marae*? What would he be doing there, I wonder?"

Frank shrugged. "He may have a contact there."

"Perhaps it's time to talk to my uncle, to Hakopa," said Karira. "By the time we get back to Palmerston the evening meal will have started at the *Pa*. Let's drop in and talk to him, see if he knows anything. He'll want to thank you for beating Karlsen. He probably wouldn't mind if he knew you'd killed him, truth be told."

They arrived at the gate to the *Pa* an hour later. The *marae* was empty but light spilled from the meetinghouse. Karira led Frank inside, where a row of men sat at a head table and the rest of the *hapu* sat on the floor in front, all eating. A group of women brought the food in baskets, overseen by Princess Moana. She glared at Frank and Karira and gestured towards the head table, where the men made room for them on either side of Hakopa.

"*Ahiahi pai*," said Hakopa, nodding and smiling at Frank. He was scooping food from a basket and spooning it into his mouth with his hand.

"*Ahiahi pai*," said Karira. He reached for a piece of pork, and gestured to Frank to do the same. "Do you mind if I talk to him in Maori?"

"Please do," said Frank. I'll understand some of what you say, and you can fill me in later with the rest."

Karira began to speak rapidly in Maori to his uncle. Frank was lost in minutes, understanding just the pleasantries exchanged in the first few sentences. He listened with half an ear and looked around to see if anyone was looking at him strangely. A movement behind him made him turn, and he saw that Princess Moana was behind them, pretending to be busy with instructions to the women serving the food, but obviously listening intently to the conversation. He tapped the table idly, his eyes on Karira. Karira glanced at him, and Frank flicked his eyes briefly towards Princess Moana.

The meal came to an end, and many of the men pulled out clay pipes and began to smoke. Frank kept his eye on Moana, and saw her seize a basket of food from the end of the table and weave her way from the room. The post meal seemed to last forever, but finally came to an end. Karira stood and shook Hakopa's hand, and Frank followed suit.

"What did you learn?" he asked, as soon as they were clear of the gates of the *Pa*. Karira had offered to escort him home, to protect him from Anahera, in case he was still in the area rather than up in Ashhurst.

"He says he knows nothing about a man involved with our *Hapu* wanting vengeance on anyone," said Karira. "Especially not on soldiers. He says even the *Hauhau* have turned to peace, and a man who was out to revenge himself on soldiers, if that's what he is doing, would be outside the usual scheme of things. An idea from the past. He himself is entertaining some members of Parliament himself next week. Walter Johnston, the local Member of Parliament, and John Balance, the Member from Rangitikei. They're bringing a land agent from Poverty Bay to meet him. To talk about land availability in the area. Hakopa wants to work with the government and the settlers, not to fight them. He wants to be a modern man. Admirable, I suppose."

"Princess Moana seemed very interested in what you were saying to your uncle," said Frank. "Is it possible she's Anahera's contact at the *Pa*?"

"She does come from an *iwi* up in Poverty Bay, where he's killed already" said Karira. "The Ngati Maru. She met Hakopa in Wellington last year, when he was down there visiting some of his government connections, and they married amost immediately."

"So she's a recent bride?" said Frank. "Is she his first wife?"

"He was married for many years to a woman from our own *hapu*," said Karira. "She was never able to have a child, but when she was forty years old she finally fell with child. She died in childbirth less than two years ago. Hakopa was distraught. I was very surprised that he remarried so quickly – I believe Moana set out to catch him. I always wondered why. She seems more suited for life in an active, political *Pa*, not a backwater like this."

They had reached the Royal Hotel, and Frank dismounted. "I saw Moana leave with a basket at the end of the meal," he said. "Perhaps she has been helping him—Anahera—with food."

"I'll keep an eye on her," said Karira. "See if she does that after every meal. If necessary, I could follow her to see what she is doing."

They parted, Karira to return along the dark track to the *Pa*. As he disappeared up the track, a memory jumped into Frank's head, and this time it stayed there. Adams. The pursuit of Titokowaru. He and Captain Porter had been riding around checking on what had been a very successful foray against the Hauhau at Otoia, Tito's encampment up the Patea River. They'd come upon a group of Kepa's—Major Kemp's—men led by a Colonist soldier named Tom Adams with some *Arawa* men who fought under Kepa, Major Kemp of the *Kupapa*. They'd cornered a group who had been left behind to fend for themselves. Women and children, and an older warrior named Matangi. Adams had Matangi pinned against the roots of a tree and was chopping off his head. They'd stopped him, but by then it was too late. The head was off. Frank had wanted to escort the women and children back to Wanganui, but Captain Porter had refused to give him permission. There was too much else to do.

He remembered one of the women, who pleaded with him to save her children, and how he had been heartsick that he had not been allowed to guarantee that she was not killed, or worse. Was she somehow connected to Anahera? And why would Adams own a Die Hard cap, when he was a member of the Colonist army?

22

Anahera and Hop Li

The Tuapeka Times records the following instance of honesty on the part of a Chinaman: A neighboring runholder paid off his Chinese cook, and in doing so gave "John" £6 more than he was entitled to. The Chinaman reappeared at the station in a few days, and much to his late employer's surprise handed back the £6 saying "too muchee." Chinamen are usually good cooks, but not always honest; one who is both must be a valuable man to his employers.

Manawatu Times, September 29, 1877

As he walked his horse behind the hotel to the paddock, Frank could hear Hop Li clanking pots in the hotel kitchen. He knew his friend would hear him feeding and watering his horse, and wondered if he would come out. He often did. A sack of oats sat ready, hanging from the doorknob, for anyone arriving by horseback late at night, and Frank unhooked it.

Copenhagen was tired and sweating after her long day, and he picked up a brush from the back step to rub her down. He lifted the saddle off and laid it beside the step, his gun still resting in the holster on the side of the saddle. When he was done, he walked her around the paddock, talking to her softly, calming her. It was a beautiful night, with the sky a dark velvet blue, with millions of stars looking down at him. Whatever Princess Moana and Anahera were up to, he had forgotten it for the moment. Sometimes it was good to be alive, to feel at one with the world.

The paddock behind the hotel sat at the edge of the bush, thickly treed all the way to the track to the Pa. Above the bush he could see the moon rising, casting shadows over the paddock. A cloud passing in front of the moon made the trees seem to move. For a moment, he though he saw one separate from the rest and come towards him. He stared hard, but it was a mirage. Just nerves, he supposed, but he wished he had kept his gun on him. The trees curved around behind Hop Li's garden, where runner beans and Chinese Gooseberries were strung out in rows on poles.

But then he thought he saw a shape. Still the moon? He couldn't tell. But time to get into the safety of the hotel, where half a dozen men, some with guns at their disposal, would come to his rescue. He stared at the bush and at the garden one more time, then removed the reins from Copenhagen, rubbing her nose.

He heard a footfall behind him, and turned, smiling, expecting to see Hop Li. Instead he saw a giant shape outlined against the light from the hotel.

"Hop Li?" he said, hopefully, knowing that it could not possibly be his friend.

The shape moved forward, and he could see it was Anahera. His face once more was a picture of rage and he could see the blue *moko* spread across his nose and cheeks. Angel's wings, he thought, not a butterfly as Mette had thought.

"*Ka mate Ka mate*," said Anahera softly, staring at him like a

217

huhu grub he was about to squash and eat. He's declaring war on me, thought Frank. I'm a dead man this time. What would Mette think about his death?

He leapt to one side, and the giant lunged past him, almost falling. This time he carried no weapon. I can't fight this man, he thought. He will kill me. But no one else was in earshot except Hop Li, and calling for him would mean his death as well. With no other plan, he backed towards the hotel. The giant stood looking at him, in no hurry to finish him off. He knew he had him.

"*Kamatekoe,*" he said. You die.

"I know you want to kill me," said Frank, backing away. "But I don't know why. What have I done that you must kill me? What have any of us done that you are killing us?" He was trying desperately to think Maori words to explain that if this was revenge for the atrocities during the Titokowera pursuit, he had not been involved.

"*ka mau i kahore matenga,*" he tried. "I took no heads."

With a roar the giant lunged at him again.

"*Toku tuahine,*" he snarled. "*Toku tuahine.*"

Frank felt the man's hand brush his arm as leapt to the side once more. Not waiting to lunge again, the giant spun around and grabbed Frank by his shirtfront. Holding him like that, he lifted one hand and smacked Frank across the face, letting him go at the same time. Frank stumbled back, tripped on a clump of grass, and fell to the ground. Blood was running down one cheek, and his mouth filled with blood where a tooth had penetrated the inside of his cheek. The giant was on him immediately, lifting him from the ground by his shirt, and hitting him across the face one more time, knocking him to the ground. He's going to slap me to death, thought Frank, almost amusing if it didn't involve him dying.

He managed to drag himself upright one more time, and stood looking at *Anahera*. He was dizzy, disoriented, and knew another slap like that and he would lose consciousness, probably never to wake again. They stood there for a minute facing each other, Frank panting, the other in no hurry to finish him off.

"Hey boss," said a voice from the darkness behind the giant.

Hop Li, thought Frank. Now we're both going to die.

"Run," he croaked. "Get away, Hop Li."

Anahera turned to see who it was. Hop Li stood there, a short compact man, looking at Frank's attacker fearlessly, his hands folded in front of him as if in greeting. Grunting, Anahera raised his arms and ran at the little Chinaman standing there so bravely, apparently intending to kill the easy one quickly before he finished with Frank. Hop Li stepped into his rush and made a quick thrusting movement with his arms. Anahera made a noise that sounded like a tackled rugby player, then he was on the ground, clutching his belly and screaming. Blood oozed between his fingers.

Frank stumbled forward.

"What the blazes?" he said. Hop Li was standing there, one clenched fist raised before him, a short, pointed blood-covered blade protruding between his fingers.

He wiped the blade carefully on his apron and grinned at Frank.

"I not spend ten years in goldfields piling up money without I defend myself," he said. "This is punch dagger. You should carry yourself. Best for stopping a big bugger like this one. Never see it coming." He put the blade carefully back into his pocket. "Now, I must call police, doctor too or man might die."

"By God Hop Li," said Frank. "You saved my life. I don't know how to thank you. I was minutes away from death."

Hop Li shrugged. "Nothing boss, done it plenty time before. I like you. Don't want to see you die."

Frank walked over to Anahera. He lurched to his feet, and Frank could see that the cut extended all the way up the front of his body but not deep. He stood swaying and looking at Frank, blood oozing from the cut.

"I will try to help you," said Frank, pleased to note that his skills at the Maori language had returned. "But you need to tell me why you were trying to kill me."

The man shook his head violently. "*Toku tuahine*," he said. "*Toku tuahine*." Frank did not recognize the words. It sounded like a curse.

Hop Li came up beside him. "I can stab him again," he suggested, looking at the swaying Anahera. "Cut a muscle in his leg. Then he talk."

"Leave him for now," said Frank. Let's get Constable Price and Doctor Rockstrow here. Price will keep him in the lockup and I can talk to him there.

By now, two other men had come out of the hotel and were peering around the corner nervously. One had a revolver held shakily in his hand.

"What's going on here," he called. "Does someone need help?"

"Get the doctor, and Constable Price," said Frank. "Someone attacked me and Hop Li here saved my life."

Anahera gave a roar and the two men retreated into the hotel. Holding onto his stomach he loped off towards the bush and into darkness.

Hop Li looked at Frank. "You chase him?" he said.

Frank rubbed his cheek, which was aching both inside and outside.

"Not now," he said. "We'll get one of those men to get Constable Price, and he can alert the Armed Constabulary. Let's go inside. I'll get my revolver in case he comes back. You can clean me up while we're waiting for Constable Price."

"Where he go, you think," said Hop Li. "Just run off into bush? To the river? Have a *waka* there maybe?"

"I have an idea he might be headed for the *Pa*," said Frank grimly. "I wish there was a way to alert Karira."

"I go there," offered Hop Li. "What I tell him?"

Frank shook his head. "I don't know. We think Anahera might have a connection at the Pa, and it may be the chief's wife. But we have no proof, just a suspicion. I'll let the Armed Constabulary know. They can check to see if he's at the *Pa*."

Hop Li took a cloth and began dabbing Frank's cut cheek with a cloth covered with carbolic acid.

"You pretty hurt," he said. "Price comes, you let the shawl boys go find the giant. You stay here."

"I wish I could do something," said Frank. "Are the Armed Constabulary still here? I thought they were in Ashhurst?"

"Those Irish here this morning," said Hop Li. "Want another card game. They back at the hotel."

"They aren't still looking for Sergeant Jackson's killer, then?" asked Frank.

"They come back," said Hop Li. "Have to protect someone. A porter. Why they protect a porter? He just carries bags."

"Porter," said Frank, shocked. "My god, Captain Porter. Anahera will be after him. That might explain what he was doing in the district in the first place. Killing Jackson and trying to kill me was just a dividend for him."

"You better tell him," said Hop Li, putting his cloth in the sink to be washed. "Captain Porter. He be the next one. If he's with the Irish, he staying at the Oxford Hotel."

23

Captain Porter

Our Distinguished Visitors: Mrs. Te Kooti has honoured Wanganui with a complimentary visit, and left for the Front, yesterday, with her Arawa captors, who seem to pride themselves considerably on their recent, achievement upon the East Coast. What they propose doing with Mrs. Te Kooti we know not, but trust they may shortly have Mrs. Titoko Waru to keep her company. During the past month, Titoko Waru has had it all his own way, in these districts, as Colonel Lyons could make no offensive movement, but merely hold on until the arrival of Colonel Whitmore.
Hawkes Bay Herald, 23 January 1869

Captain Porter was staying at the Oxford Hotel, on Terrace End, not far from the Square. Frank found him playing billiards with three men from the Armed Constabulary. His old commander greeted him warmly. He had not changed much other than becoming greyer. He was a solidly built, upright man with a small pointed beard and faded blue eyes. He had always been known as a strong man.

"Sergeant Hardy," he said, shaking Frank's hand. "Good to see you. What are you doing in these parts? I heard you'd left the Armed Constabulary after the Tito pursuit." He gestured to one of the men to take his turn, and stood back from the table.

"I'm driving a mail coach now," said Frank. "Less adventurous, but I'm my own boss and…"

"Interesting days, those, chasing after old Tito, weren't they?" said Porter. He looked reminiscent. "Good days, those were, good days. I loved the action. Spent time chasing Te Kooti as well, into the Urewas, in '70. I'd do that again without hesitation. Great adventures, those were, cutting down the *Hauhau*, helping him see the error of his ways. My life is much duller now."

"The Armed Constabulary have been looking for someone in this area," said Frank. "Someone who calls himself Anahera, the…"

"Avenging angel," said Captain Porter. "I'm aware of the chap. Comes from up in my district. I live in Gisborne these days, at the northern end of Poverty Bay. That's why the Constabulary are with me. Making sure this Avenging Angel, as he calls himself, doesn't come for me while I'm at the *Pa* the day after tomorrow, or before then for that matter. I have a meeting with Hakopa, the chief at the *Pa*, I and two members of Parliament, to discuss land purchases in this area. We're tidying up some of the waste land in the area—*Pas* and such. I'm a land agent these days, you know Sergeant Hardy. Fighting days are over, unfortunately, as I said. Just fighting about who has the rights to land, and who doesn't."

Frank considered how to approach the topic of the beheadings. He did not wish to rouse Captain Porter's ire with any kind of accusation.

"I've been attacked by the Avenging Angel three times," said

Frank.

"Lucky to be alive then," said Porter. "Why would he want to attack you? Or any of those he's killed?"

"Something to do with my forage cap, I believe," said Frank. "And by extension, something to do with the Die Hards, and I think…."

"Did he perform a *haka* for you at any point?" asked Captain Porter.

Frank nodded. "The first time he attacked me, he did the *haka* first. Gave me time to get to my weapon. Then tonight before he attacked me he muttered a few words of the *haka*. Scared me, which is what he intended no doubt."

"It's what he does," said the captain. "He must do his damned dance before he kills you. One of the men who…" he paused and rubbed his chin. "Of course, it was one of the men who was under my command, in the Tito days. I hadn't made the connection. The Angel did the *haka* for him but didn't kill him. He was interrupted by a group of farmers. The poor man has been scared silly ever since. Doesn't even like to leave his house."

"And the other men who were killed?" asked Frank.

"All ex Die Hards, now that I think of it," said Porter. "You're right. There's a connection to Die Hards. What on earth is so terrible for him that he has to hunt us down and kill us?"

"He lost his cap," said Frank. "One of the times he attacked me. It had the name Adams on the inside. Do you remember that name?"

Porter frowned. "I don't think…no, it isn't familiar to me."

"I do," said Frank. "Although he wasn't a Die Hard at the time, I believe he was wearing the cap. Do you remember during the pursuit we came across one of Whitmore's men with a group of *Arawa*? One of our men, a Colonist, had just decapitated an old warrior, a chief. He was just about to go for the women and children and we came along and stopped him."

"Ah," said Captain Porter. "I remember that day very well. He had the head in his hands and he was taking it back to Whitmore, if I remember correctly. I stopped him and the woman, the chief's daughter I thought, grabbed the head and held it in her arms like a baby. Gave me nightmares, that image. What could have possessed her? You think this has something to do with that, do you? Just about a head? They took so many themselves."

Frank nodded, not looking at the captain. "I'm not sure it's got something to do with that day, but I have a strong feeling that it does. It has to be something – or someone – that he cares about strongly enough to kill so many people. Could it be the old warrior was a relative of his? His father, perhaps?"

The words the giant had spoken when he tried to kill him came back to him and he corrected himself. "No, it was his brother, I think. It was a family word he said when he was trying to kill me. *Teina*, is it, for a brother? Perhaps the chief was his older brother."

"The boys would have been his nephews then," said the captain. "Or his great nephews."

"The boys?" said Frank, staring at him.

Captain Porter looked away from Frank's gaze. "I left Adams in charge, when you and I rode on."

"I remember," said Frank, noticing that the corporal's name was now known to Porter. "He was supposed to escort them back to Wanganui, the women and the children—boys, were they? Did he take them with him to Wanganui? What happened to them?"

"He took the <u>women</u> back," said Porter. "The *Aroha* wanted them, I believe. For slavery. I don't approve, but it's their way. And I thought as he was a white man he would protect her. I have no way of knowing that he didn't. But the boys…"

"Surely Adams would not…" Frank stopped "What about the boys?"

"You must understand, Hardy," said Captain Porter. "So much went on during that chase, on both sides. I don't approve of taking the enemies' heads, but they were taking ours. Took the head of your own brother, if I remember correctly."

Frank nodded, his mouth too dry to speak.

"And the boys," Captain Porter continued, "the boys, well it's hard to tell the difference between a child's head and an adult one, after it's been smoked over the fire. I believe the Aroha decapitated them, and Adams took them back to Whitmore for the bounty."

Frank could hardly breathe. He stared at Porter and said nothing.

Porter put his hand on Frank's arm. "I'm sorry, I really am. But by the time I found out it was too late to do anything. And Adams wasn't one of mine, so I could do nothing to him."

"How do you think Anahera found out what had happened?" said Frank, recovering his voice finally.

Captain Porter shrugged. "He was at the encampment when we cleared it, and after we took control he came back and went on a rampage, killing three of our men. We caught him and put him in prison. He's been there ever since, but he escaped a few weeks ago."

"The poor bastard," said Frank. "I could see why he wanted to kill us."

"He'll be coming after me then," said Captain Porter. "But my constables will kill him before he can raise a spear at me, I assure you."

"He just tried to kill me," said Frank. "He would have succeeded if I'd been alone, but the cook from the Royal saved me, managed to stab the man in his belly. Don't underestimate him."

Captain Porter leaned back and looked at Frank critically. "The Chinaman saved you?" he said. "Should be ashamed of yourself, Hardy, letting yourself be saved by a Chinaman."

Frank said nothing. He had heard this kind of sentiment expressed before. He was deeply in debt to Hop Li, and he knew it. "He may have killed another Sergeant, a fellow Die Hard," he said. "Sergeant Jackson, although he wasn't ever part of the battle. But he had some clothing…"

"Most of my men were Die Hards," said Captain Porter. "Asked for them particularly, because they were such reliable chaps. There were probably Die Hard caps all over the place, during the battle. He could have found one."

"But one specifically with Adams' name inside?" said Frank. "Something helped him make the connection. Or someone."

He took off his cap and looked at it, the front with its embroidered insignia, Die Hard the 57th, the name attached to the regiment since the War against Napoleon, after a general had cried the phrase with his dying breath at the Battle of Albuera. "Sergeant Jackson wore a blouse with the same insignia. He knew enough to recognize that."

"That explains some other killings," said Captain Porter. "I'm sure you're correct. Sergeant Jackson was killed by Anahera, and not by this road crew chap, the one who hasn't been found. He's probably dead at the hands of the Angel as well. Maybe caught him in the act of doing away with Jackson."

"How will you prevent an attack on your own person?" Frank asked. "At the *Pa*. Will you have the Armed Constabulary guard with you?"

Captain Porter shook his head.

"Not with me," he said. "Outside the gates. They never let armed soldiers inside *Pas*. There'll just be me and the two members of Parliament. And we won't be armed."

"And me then," said Frank. I'll be with you. They know me at the *Pa*. There's also a Maori Constable living there, Wiremu Karira, and he'll help us keep an eye on you."

Captain Porter nodded.

"Very good," he said. "And I'll have the Armed Constabulary surround the *Pa* from all sides, not let anyone in. I can summon them quickly with a whistle, if necessary. Have the Maori Constable make a thorough check inside. That should cover it."

"I'll talk to Karira and meet you tomorrow outside the *Pa*."

Frank shook hands with the captain and took his leave. The captain returned to his billiard game. Once outside the hotel, he leaned against the wooden slats of the verandah. He felt sick to his stomach, and eventually he vomited over the side and into a bush. The women taken into sexual slavery, two small boys beheaded. It was too much for anyone to bear. Nothing he had suffered could hold a candle to it. Something was bothering him though, something Captain Porter had said. What was it?

Karira was at the Royal Hotel talking excitedly to Hop Li in the kitchen.

"What's happened?" Frank asked.

"Hakopa had one of his men following Princess Moana," said

Karira. "Apparently he's been suspicious of her for a while, and something I said to him made it worse. Thought she was meeting another man. She's confined to her quarters and he's talking about sending her back to her family in Poverty Bay."

"They saw her meeting another man?" asked Frank. "Did they see the man? Was it Anahera?"

"The lookout followed her to a clearing near the *Pa* and saw her meet another man. It sounds like Anahera, but he took off when he saw they were discovered, and the lookout didn't give chase. So he's on the loose again and mobile. She had bandages with her, and some salve, which makes it probable it was Anahera. Hop Li told me what happened here tonight."

"He's here to kill the land agent Hakopa told you about," said Frank. "The one who's coming to meet with the Hakopa and the two members of Parliament."

"Why would he want to kill a land agent?" asked Karira.

"Because the land agent is Captain Porter, my old commander. He's killing people who were at Otoia with us."

"Why?" said Karira.

"There was an atrocity at Otoia, one that the captain and I put a stop to. The man who did it was named Adams. I remembered where I'd heard it finally."

"He assumed you took part, I suppose," said Karira.

Frank nodded.

"And did you have any part in it at all?"

"I felt guilty," said Frank. "Adamson decapitated a chief, for the bounty, and we came up after it was done. But there was a woman – two women – and three small boys. I wanted to escort them back to Wanganui but Captain Porter forbad me. He was probably right to do so. We had so much to do that day. But the captain believes the boys were also decapitated after we left, and that the women were sold in to slavery, to be used by the men..."

"Could one of the women have been Moana?" said Karira.

"If she is I don't remember her as being one. Although one of them I didn't look at very hard. The other one was beautiful, and she put her hands together and looked at me as if..." He was overcome with the emotion of it all, and stopped.

Karira watched him, his eyes half-closed. "How did he know Porter was coming here?" he asked eventually.

"Princess Moana could have contacted him," said Frank. "They come from the same area, up in Poverty Bay. Te Kooti struck up there as well, when he massacred all those settlers up near Gisborne back in '72. It seems to be a hot bed of dissent."

"Is she involved in the murders, do you think?" asked Karira. "Why would she want to marry Hakopa? She wouldn't know months in advance that Hakopa was going to be entertaining Captain Porter, would she?"

"I can't tell you," said Frank. "Maybe she has a different reason for wanting him here."

"What Captain Porter say," said Hop Li. "When he meet with Hakopa?"

"He's going to the *Pa* tomorrow to meet with him," said Frank. "And I want to be there to stop any attempt on his life by Anahera. The Armed Constabulary will also be there, but outside the gates. They won't allow armed soldiers into a *Pa*. I'll enter with Captain Porter and the Members of Parliament."

"No gun?" asked Hop Li.

Frank shook his head.

"No gun. But if an attack happens the Constabulary will be nearby and Captain Porter and I will do what we can until they get inside."

"You too brave," said Hop Li. "Why you risk your like for this Captain Porter?"

"I'm not sure," said Frank. "He didn't do anything himself, and he was always an honorable man. But I'm not sure that Anahera doesn't have the right of it, when all's said and done. I'd prefer that he doesn't get killed." He saw Karira give him a puzzled look, but did not explain

24

The Powhiri

*...all our operations against the Maoris have been in defence of
our settlements, or in the endeavour to punish natives who have
committed gross crimes we have returned to the natives no small
extent of confiscated land in order to restore contentment to the
Maori mind we have refrained from pursuing murderers who took
refuge with Tawhiao, choosing to wait for time, the great avenger, to
bring about the moans of punishment rather than to risk a struggle
which if once again begun, must end only in the extermination of
the opposing natives.*
New Zealand Herald, 21 June 1877

The Armed Constabulary arrived at the *Pa*, surrounding
the coach carrying Captain Porter, Mr. Johnston and Mr.
Balance. The three men climbed down awkwardly and walked
up and down, stretching their legs. The men were dressed
alike in dark suits with tails, and tall hats, with Captain Porter
distinctive by his height and bearing. Frank had positioned
himself at the bend where Anahera had performed the *Haka*,
pretending to be digging out a stone from Copenhagen's front
hoof with his Barlow knife, and keeping an eye open for

anyone else arriving at the *Pa*; after coach and escort passed by, he climbed back on Copenhagen and followed them to the gates of the *Pa*.

Captain Porter greeted him, and they walked through the winding gateway. Behind them, the Armed Constabulary split into two groups and spread out from the entrance, leaving a man every fifty yards. Frank scanned the palisades and the grassy area inside the *Pa* walls.

In the distance, he could see the small greeting party, a group of young warriors waiting to perform the *powhiri*, the ceremonial greeting haka that Maori performed for visitors. It would be not unlike the *haka* that Anahera had done before he attacked, but more formal, with the violence obviously exaggerated. The leader would carry a *taiaha*, a ceremonial spear, which he would use to make threatening moves towards the group of visitors. Then he would lay down a small item in front of the visitors, and Captain Porter would pick it up to show that they came in peace.

"I've seen far too many of these damned greetings," said Captain Porter as they stood waiting for the *powhiri* to commence. "I wish we could just get to our business."

The *powhiri* group approached. As they did, they began the series of yells and stamps that Frank knew accompanied the challenge. They were almost in front of his group when a woman's voice began intoning the *Kananga*, the greeting that called for the *hapu* to accept the visitors. The *Haka* commenced and he knew they would soon be in the meeting house and in the clear. He kept his eyes on the perimeter, scanning for movement. Once they were inside the meeting house they would be safe, for a time, but until they were he would remain alert. Karira was standing guard inside the meeting house, making sure no one entered.

"That chap at the front seems to be taking the whole thing very seriously," said Captain Porter. "You'd think he was really threatening us." He moved forward and bent down to pick up a small carved *tiki* that the warrior had dropped at his feet.

Frank glance over to see what he meant. The leader of the *powhiri* group had raised the *taiaha*, clutched in both hands, above Captain Porter's exposed head, his eyes wild and bulging, a normal part of the ceremony. Frank was about to make a quiet joke, but it froze on his tongue. Anahera, the Avenging Angel, beardless but recognizable with his distinctive angel wings *moko*, was the man standing there, the *taiaha* raised, the expression on his face, Frank now saw, one of almost insane hatred.

As he moved towards Captain Porter with the *taiaha*, he screamed the words he had said to Frank behind the Royal Hotel when he attacked him: *"Mo toku Tuahine. Mo toku tuahine."*

Tuahine, not *teina*, Frank thought, not brother, but sister. That was who he was avenging. His sister and his nephews. Time slowed down and he felt his body moving in slow motion towards *Anahera*. Without a conscious decision, the childhood years of being forced to play rugby with his father's employer's sons came back to him, and he threw himself towards *Anahera's* knees and brought him to the ground in a tackle. Rain had started to fall and he was face down on the ground, Anahera's feet just before his eyes, when the rest of the *powhiri* team jumped him, forming a scrum over his back, feet pressed firmly into his spine. He forced his face up to see what was happening to Anahera, and saw that Captain Porter and the Members of Parliament were on his arms and legs, holding him down as he writhed with rage. He lay there knowing he had stopped the murder of his old captain. But the words Anahera had screamed echoed in his ears. "For my sister," he had said. "For my sister."

Everyone was yelling and cursing; to add to the chaos, Captain Porter blew hard on his whistle, in a perverted version of a referee.

The Armed Constabulary poured through the gates, rules forgotten, carbines trained on the melee. They were on Anahera in a minute, binding his arms and legs, dragging him from the *Pa*, shouting instructions to the *powhiri* men who still held Frank pressed to the ground. He was released and stood up next to the group that had held Anahera.

Captain Porter stood there calmly, dusting himself off. He had remained totally self-possessed the whole time.

"I shall be with you momentarily," he called after the Constables. Take care of him."

He turned to Frank.

"Nice tackle," he said, his eyes gleaming. "If I ever need a first five eights I shall know where to come. Well done, Hardy. I shall see that you get a commendation for this."

Hakopa and Karira had arrived by now, Hakopa full of apologies.

"My wife," he said. "My wife has brought shame on my *hapu*. She has allowed this serpent into our midst. I cannot tell you how sorry I am. I will send her back to her *iwi* in Poverty Bay."

Captain Porter nodded at him and reached out a hand to shake.

"Why should my wife want you killed?" asked Hakopa as he grasped the captain's hand.

"It was Anahera who wanted to see him dead," said Frank.

"Something to do with a foolish incident during the pursuit of Titokowera," said Captain Porter. "He has a grievance from those days. Insanity, I would say. Your wife must have misunderstood what he was about to do. We'll keep an eye on her in Poverty Bay, but I can't imagine she is very much at fault."

Captain Porter and Hakopa walked through the gate together, chatting amicably, as if the friend of the wife of one had not just attempted to assassinate the other. Frank and Karira followed them silently.

Outside, the Armed Constabulary had the coach ready to leave, door open, coachman with his whip high. The two Members of Parliament were hustled inside. Behind the coach two more Constables had arrived with a horse-drawn cart that carried a cage on the back. Anahera had been pushed into the cage and sat there, his knees up, with barely room to move.

About to mount the carriage steps, Captain Porter stopped and turned to Hakopa. "Thank you for your cooperation in the other matter," he said. "The sale will go through before the end of the year. And again, don't worry about your woman. As I said, we'll take good care of her in Poverty Bay."

Frank felt his stomach turn at the inappropriateness of the words. He walked over to the cage where Anahera was held fast, not looking at anyone but staring darkly ahead.

"*Ta matou he koe,*" he said. We did you a great wrong.

Captain Porter looked at him, puzzled, then turned on his heel and mounted the coach. Wilson, the Irishman, who had been waiting at the back of the coach, winked at Frank, then leapt onto the steps of the coach as it thundered away, still guarding the men inside. As they left, Anahera's eyes held

Frank's in a long, calculating look. It was not exactly friendly. But it was not hate either.

"What will happen to him?" asked Karira.

"He'll disappear into a gaol in Wanganui and we won't hear about him again," said Frank. They have a special gaol for people like him, upriver from the town."

"That is good," said Hakopa. "Better we never see him again."

"What was your business with Captain Porter," said Frank. "You said something about a sale."

Hakopa waved his hand vaguely towards the Pa. "I have sold our land here to the Government," he said. "This *Pa* land. We will move into town."

The waste lands, thought Frank. The waste lands of the *Pa* that Captain Porter had alluded to briefly. That was what had been bothering him.

Karira looked at his uncle, his face blank with shock.

"Is this true?" he asked. "You have sold the *Pa*? The land our family has owned for a thousand years?"

Hakopa looked defiant. "You have said to me many times, Wiremu, that our people must move forward. Now comes that opportunity. They will move to the town and find employment, or to the city. They will become modern New Zealanders."

"You have sold our birthright," said Karira, his voice rising. "For what? For nothing, for a mess of pottage. I cannot forgive you. My father would not forgive you."

Hakopa looked back, his face calm.

"I will have a place in town," he said in Maori. "A large house I will build. You may stay with me when you must leave the *Pa*."

25

Finding the Boys

A Bloated Black Aristocrat: Our old friend, Peete te Aweawe added considerably to his importance while giving evidence of his bona fides as a bondsman for the truculent offender, Kereopa, at the Wanganui Court. Along with other property which he mentioned, Mr. Peete described in graphic style upon his town mansion at Palmerston. He did not tell the Court, however, that although it was a two-storied dwelling it had neither stairs, roof nor floors. Those of his auditors who were in the ken, chuckled inwardly at the grand picture conjured up by the fancy of the imaginative witness.
Manawatu Times, November 12, 1879

October came, and the river was warming as it made its slow journey from the ranges down through Palmerston and past Foxton to the Tasman Sea. Frank and Karira, still suffering from the loss of his ancestral lands, and the move of his *hapu* in to town, had been searching up and down the river in the *waka tete*, stopping to look under stands of overhanging willows or in the reeds that grew in some areas. Occasionally they found a log embedded in gravel, and climbed out of the canoe to look underneath, hoping for signs such as clothing or even skeletal remains. By now, the river would certainly have taken off some of the flesh, and the eels would have helped with that process.

At midday on October 3rd they arrived at Awapuni, not far from the sawmill and the clearing where the Scandinavians lived and less than a mile from where the boys had last been seen. Frank noticed a small, well-constructed *whare* on a slope beside the river, in an area that had been cleared of all undergrowth and bush. A Maori man of about his own age was adzing a piece of wood, concentrating hard on what he was doing.

"That is Parateni Te Tupaki," said Karira. "He's creating carvings for the *Wharenui*, the new meeting house we built at the *Pa*. He refuses to believe the Pa is going to be sold."

"Kia ora Mr. Te Tupaki," Frank called.

The man looked up from the work, put his adze down carefully and came towards them.

"Good morning," he said. "Constable Karira, I was about to come and get you."

Frank pulled the dugout close to the shore and jumped out, pulling it into some reeds so it would stay in place. Karira followed him.

"You were coming to see me?" he prompted.

"Yes. I found something you will want to see."

"What did you find?" asked Frank. He thought he might know what it was, and his heart felt heavy.

"Some clothing, down there in the reeds where your *waka* is resting. *Pakeha* clothing. I did not want to touch it before you looked at it."

Te Tupaki came down to the edge of the river and pointed towards a spot close to where the dugout rested. Frank could see it now as well: the back of a plaid shirt, spread flat, just under the surface of the water, floating in the reeds. It sat between two branches that were caught under the bank. They could not have seen it from the *waka tete*.

He stepped back into the water, not minding his wet boots, and waded over close to where the shirt was visible. Then, he grasped one of the branches and pulled it slowly closer. The shirt rose to the surface of the water, bobbing a little. Above it, Frank could see something pale, reflecting the sun that filtered through the trees. Hair maybe, he thought. He waded in further, until the water came up to his waist. Leaning forward, he could just manage to reach the shirt. He took a handful of material and pulled it closer. The shirt started to move in the water, then, ever so slowly, rolled over.

Frank felt his stomach turn.

The two Maori men had been watching from the bank of the river saying nothing. When the object turned over and they could see what it was, Karira said softly, "*Kua kitea e matou ki a ratou*. We have found the one we looked for."

It was impossible to tell which of the boys it was. The plaid shirt without a collar, the moleskin trousers, and the fair hair indicated that it was one of the boys, but the face had all but disappeared under swollen flesh. The body was bloated so that the shirt was tight across what had been the chest, and what was left of the face was purple and swollen, the eyes covered in flesh, with strips of skin falling away from the cheeks. An eel had been eating at one side of the head and bone showed through.

"I will find Constable Price," said Te Tupaki. "But someone must stay with the body. You will not want to lose him now. After I will find the *Tohunga*. If someone dies in the river, then the river is *Tapu* and the *Tohunga* must pray to the *Taniwha* to restore it."

"You stay," said Karira to Frank. "I'll go to the sawmill and find the brother. What should I tell him?"

"Tell him we've found one of the boys," said Frank. "But don't give him any details. Not yet. Just make sure he understands that you're talking about a body."

Karira nodded and strode off up the hill. There was no pathway to the mill from here, but he would find his way easily through the bush.

Frank sat on the edge of the river and watched the body as it lay there in the water. Paul, he thought, although he did not know why. He wished he had a cigarette right now. He was in the calm before the storm, and he dreaded speaking with Nissen and Sorensen, let alone with Mette. If she had loved this boy, even as a friend, she would be upset, and he couldn't stand the idea of her being unhappy.

Eventually, Constable Price arrived, crashing through the bush beside the river. He had left a bullock cart with a wooden coffin some distance back along the riverside, where the track ended.

"I think it's Paul Nissen," Frank said, pointing to the body.

"Holy Mother of God," said Price, crossing himself. "We'll have to put him into your *waka* and take him back down the river to the cart. Can you help me lift him in to it?"

He and Frank entered the water carrying a large flax mat that Te Tupaki had provided, threw it over the body, and between them managed to wrap it into a cocoon. The stench was terrible, but Frank had seen bodies like this before, even bodies of people he knew. Together they carried the boy ashore, water and other fluids draining from it back into the river.

"He isn't in as bad a shape as I would have expected," said Constable Price. "Not for just over two months in the water."

"Could he have been put into the water sometime after he disappeared?" asked Frank.

Constable Price shook his head.

"More likely the cold. If he was down deep, the water would have kept him preserved, to some extent. Then as the spring came and the river warmed, he would have risen to the surface and started to deteriorate. I expect we'll find the other boy soon as well."

As the three men were lowering the body into the *waka* Frank saw Nissen and Sorensen, accompanied by Constable Karira, hurrying from the bush.

"I have to stop him," he said to Price. "He can't see the body."

Price nodded. "No, he can't. Stop him before he gets here. Go ahead, we can handle the rest."

Frank went up the hill to intercept the two Scandinavians. He could see expressions, both fearful and hopeful, on their faces. As he reached them, his hands forward to indicate that they should stop, Nissen tried to push around him. Frank stopped him, grabbing hold of both his arms and putting his body between Nissen and the men busy down at the river's edge.

"I think it's Paul," he said. "But definitely one of the boys."

"I would like to see him," said Hans Christian, attempting to push Frank's hands away. "I need to be sure that it is my brother."

Frank held firm. "I don't think you should. He's been in the water a long time. It's not something that you want to remember. Best to remember him how he was."

"But how can I be sure in my heart that it is him? How can I tell our mother that I was too afraid to look at him?"

"I'll go down there and bring back something that will help you identify him," said Frank. "Is there anything I can look for?"

Hans Christian looked down towards the *waka*, where Constable Price was still in the process of lowering the body into the *waka* for transportation. He was in a state of shock now, of unnatural calm, his arms by his sides, his hands shaking.

"He has a watch," he said. "In his pocket. Jens too. But they are not quite the same, and I would recognize Paul's watch."

After giving Pieter Sorensen instructions not to let Hans Christian come down the hill on any account, Frank went down himself and waded out to the *waka*. In the left hand pocket of the trousers of the corpse he found an old watch. It had stopped at 5:00 o'clock. The shirt had come out of the waist of the trousers as the body had collapsed, and he pulled it free and cut a piece off with his Barlow knife.

"If he can confirm who it is from the watch and the shirt, we can safely assume the identity," commented Constable Price.

Frank walked back to Nissen with the objects in hand. He said nothing, holding them out wordlessly towards the man. Nissen stared at them for several minutes, then reached forward and gently took the watch. He held it in one hand and stroked it softly with the other.

"This is Paul's watch," he said. "My father gave it to him, just before he left Schleswig. It was the first watch he had ever owned, and he was, he was..."

His face crumpled and he sank to the ground very slowly, almost as if he were a puppet on strings. As Sorensen and Frank stood watching, he started to cry, with loud rasping gasps, his arms across his stomach, rolling back and forward in agony.

Mette took the news much more stoically.

"It's good to know at last that he is found," she said sadly. "I always knew he would be dead, but I was not sure if he had been killed by the *Hauhau*, or drowned, and this tells me he drowned. What about Jens? You will find my cousin as well?"

But Jens' body did not surface. Frank and Karira continued searching until eventually they had to concede that they were not going to find him. They could only assume that eels had disposed of his body, or that he was trapped in a place that was not going to give him up. Frank saw that Hans Christian had accepted the loss of his cousin, even though the body had not been recovered and knew that the sorrow would abate to some extent, helped by his family, his neighbors and his faith.

"What about Gottlieb?" she asked. "Will he be found one day as well?"

Frank shook his head. "Perhaps," he said. "But they'll blame Anahera. I don't like it, but he has killed many people." He thought about the look Anahera had given him as he had been taken away by the Armed Constabulary. It had stayed in his mind. He had a feeling that they would meet again someday. What would the circumstances be, he wondered?

Mette offered to help Hans Christian write a letter to his mother, with words that would soften the blow as much as possible. It would take many weeks to get to her, and many more weeks for them to receive a reply. But Mette knew that when the letter arrived in Aabenraa, it would seem to Anna Nissen as if it had happened that very day. Her heart ached for Paul's mother.

26

The Inquest

It is difficult to conceive what occult influence prompts Dr. Rockstrow, on every possible occasion, to endeavour to trample the Foxton Local Board in the dirt. A short time ago he stated to the County Council that there was no Local Board at Foxton, and only a few days afterwards gave the lie to his statement by sitting on the Board as a member.

Manawatu Herald, April 18, 1879

Coroner Dr. Frederick Rockstrow, the recently appointed medical officer to the Maoris of Rangitikei and Horophenua, arrived at the Royal Hotel and stepped up onto the verandah, knocking the mud from his boots and slapping his hat against his knee to remove some lingering rainwater. Rain! It never seemed to stop in this country. He was confident that this would be a short inquest, a formality. A young man who had been missing for two months with not the faintest trace until now, as the paper he had read with his coffee that morning had noted, had been found drowned.

One of two missing Scandinavian men had been found,

surfacing from the depths of the river where he had been trapped for weeks. Something, the warming water according to Constable Price, had caused him to float upwards, and last week he had surfaced from wherever it was he had been caught, to be found bloated in the reeds at the edge of the river. The second lad was still missing, but Rockstrow intended to declare him dead. It was clear to him they had suffered the same fate, unfortunate as that was.

He saw that several people had preceded him to the hotel, and were clustered on the verandah: some Scandinavian men and women, and Frank Hardy, the ex-soldier who had driven the Royal Mail Coach until recently. Apparently Hardy had some hare-brained scheme to set up as a private investigator in Palmerston. Rockstrow could not see the point of that. Very little happened in Palmerston.

Inside, Hop Li, the hotel cook and man-of-all work was waiting to retrieve the doctor's coat. Rockstrow handed him his still-dripping coat, and asked, "Now, Hop Li, could you have one of your delicious roast mutton-bird dinners ready for me? And a good slab of bread with it, if you have some." The doctor was notorious for his love of a good meal, made clear by the way the buttons strained at the front of his buttoned vest. "We should be done in under an hour," he added. "That should just give you time to have it ready."

Hop Li bowed, his hands held together as if in prayer, and for a minute the doctor thought he was being mocked. But not possible. The man was simply a Chinaman who was completely lacking in a sense of irony, like all of his countrymen.

Dr. Rockstrow was a thickset man of Prussian origin, in his early forties. He was prepared to hear the case with a sympathetic ear but a closed mind. He knew many of the Scandinavians in the area came from Schleswig, a long fought-over territory between Denmark and Germany, and had, like he himself, escaped from their homelands to avoid conscription into Otto von Bismarck's military machine. He remembered his own cold fear when he heard that Bismarck intended that every medical student would serve in the German army, and his desperate train trip across the border into Holland, from which he had not returned, instead sailing from Rotterdam for New Zealand. He believed his mother would never forgive him for not staying behind and doing his duty. It was unfortunate, of course, but he had done well for himself in New Zealand.

The empaneled jurors were already waiting for him in the dining room, which stood in for a courtroom for the day. He saw ten men and nodded to those he knew—which was most of them, as Palmerston was a small town of fewer than 800 souls, very few of them English or German.

To one side, looking anxious and unsettled, stood three men, called to give evidence in front of the jury. An older man, broad shouldered but bent forward, a young Maori, and a tall Scandinavian. He had seen the Scandinavian somewhere before and he struggled to remember. The man was young, aged about 22 or 23. His face was ruddy and his shoulders and forearms well-muscled, formed probably by wrestling with logs at the mill. The coroner guessed he was one of Julius Vogel's farming migrants who'd been given the tree-covered land in Awapuni that had turned the migrants to saw millers, of necessity. It came to him then where he had seen the fellow before. At the Hokowhitu mill, the day the poor chap had cut off both his hands and thrown himself on the mechanical saw.

The Coroner passed over the two *pakeha* and called Papiana Whakapaki to the stand. Whakapaki stood facing the coroner, his head down, with a slightly guilty look on his face.

"What do you remember about Tuesday of last week, Mr. Whakapaki," asked the coroner.

"I remember Tuesday, the 3rd of October."

Whakapaki's head remained down, as he stared intently at his bare feet.

Kindly address me, and not your feet, Mr. Whakapaki," said the coroner loudly.

The young Maori glanced up briefly and continued, "I went to fish for eels in the River Manawatu near Awa Puni."

"And?"

"I discovered a body," nodding quickly towards the back of the hotel where he knew the body lay. "It was lying near the edge of the water. It was swollen and I didn't realize it was a man at first…"

"Yes, fine, we understand," interrupted Dr. Rockstrow.

"In the evening, I went back to my place, and, ah, next morning—Wednesday—I came over to tell Constable Price. But by then he had already heard."

The Coroner nodded, wrote something, and gestured at the man to leave. Whakapaki went back to where the other two witnesses were standing and stood scratching himself under one armpit.

"Now we will hear from—he checked his brief, "Mr. Hans Christian Nissen," he said. The clerk gestured and the tall man from the sawmill stepped forward, facing the judge.

"Remove your hat in front of the court please Mr. Nissen."

The young man snatched his hat from his head, blushing, and clutched the brim in both hands, crushing it.

"Now Mr. Nissen," said the Coroner. Do you recognize the body at present before the jury?"

Nissen looked straight ahead and spoke over the left shoulder of the Coroner in heavily accented English:

"Yes, I have seen that—that body. I recognized it by the clothes and watch as my brother Paul."

"And when did you last see your brother, Mr. Nissen?"

I last saw my brother—alive –on the 24th of July, at the Hokowhitu Mill, where I am working. He came to tell me that my wife was asking for me at home. He told me that he and Jens were going to visit someone. He did not tell me who, but I discovered later it was Knud Jensen..."

"We will hear from Mr. Jensen later," said the doctor. "Don't tell us how you learned about what Mr. Jensen said unless your brother told you at the time he was going to visit him. Did he tell you that they intended to cross the river? Also, did he say how they intended to cross the river?"

Nissen shook his head.

"Answer by speaking, Mr. Nissen."

"No, they did not mention the river or how they were going to cross it. I did not know they were going to cross the river."

"And then you discovered he was missing. When was that?"

"I did not see my brother for two weeks after the 24th of July, so I asked people if they had seen him. No one had seen him. I began searching, and went to all his friends and to our pastor. I looked for Jens too, and then I discovered he was also missing. I was looking for both of them after that. I went up to their *raupo whare* and it seemed as if they had not been there for some days. I talked to Constable Price and he could not find them either. He made the search party along the river, and after that I..."

Nissen glanced at Sergeant Hardy, standing at the back of the room, and Dr. Rockstrow saw Hardy shake his head. A question flitted briefly through the doctor's mind, but he pushed it aside. Keep it simple and straightforward, he thought. He was hungry for the meal that was to follow.

"He was a very young man, your brother?" continued Dr. Rockstrow.

"My brother was nineteen years old on January 6 this year. He was a native of Apenrada, Schleswig and came here a year ago." He paused, and added, with a sigh, "I sent for him. I told him he would have a good future here."

"And you're sure it is your brother?"

"I have no doubt that the body," he paused again and his mouth worked for a moment," that the body is that of my brother. As I said already, I knew him from his watch and his clothing."

One of the jurors, Mr. Thomas King, asked:

"Could your brother swim, Mr. Nissen?"

Hans Christian Nissen shook his head. "I do not know if my brother could swim. I believe he could, but perhaps not well. If he could, why…" He paused for a moment, looked down at his hands, still twisting the brim of his hat, and looked up again, adding, "He was a sober man. A very sober man."

The Coroner gestured to the man to be seated and thought that Mr. Nissen had spoken rather too strongly on that last point. He had some doubts about a young man of nineteen keeping himself sober at all times, even though he was a probably a Lutheran, as were so many of the Scandinavians in the district.

Knud Jensen was next to be questioned.

"I am a laborer," he said when prompted by the coroner,

"and now reside at Stoney Creek. I also have a tent on the other side of the river where I spend some time working. I remember the day when I last saw the dead, ah, I mean to say the deceased man. It was on the other side of the Manawatu River. He came on a visit along with Jens Lund and stayed at my tent for half an hour. They came at about half past 3 in the afternoon and left at about 4 o'clock. It would take them five minutes to get back to the river. They told me they had crossed the river on a log and were going back the same way." He glanced at Hans Christian Nissen and added firmly, "They were both sober. They were sober men."

Jensen and Whakapaki left the room but Nissen remained, still torturing his hat in his hands. "He's going to have to buy a new hat," the coroner said quietly to his clerk, who was seated beside him at the table.

Another Maori came into the room and was called forward by the clerk.

In contrast to Whakapaki, Parateni Te Tupaki held himself erect and looked directly at the coroner. Speaking before he was asked, he said, "I remember Wednesday 3rd October. On that day, I was adzing Totara timber close to the river when I noticed the dead body of a *pakeha* lodged between in the rushes at the river's edge. I informed the police that same day. The body was on the south side of the river, near to Kairanga. There were no Maoris about that place previous to my discovering the body."

Dr. Rockstrow noticed a slight emphasis on the word Maoris.

"No Maoris, or nobody at all?" he queried.

"Nobody, Maori or *Pakeha*."

The coroner wrote for a few minutes while everyone in the

room watched. A juror raised his hand and asked, "Is the river fordable?"

Te Tupake nodded. "At times," he said. "But not when it has been raining heavily in the ranges, as I believe it was on July 26th."

When it was clear there was nothing left to say, the Coroner summed up and the jury returned their verdict:

"That on the 3rd. October 1877 Paul Christensen Nissen was found drowned on the banks of the Manawatu River, near Awapuni, but by what means he got into the river there is no evidence to show."

Dr. Rockstrow thanked them, and then added, "I would like to note that another young man also went missing that day. Although the body of Jens Lund has not been found, two months have passed and we can safely assume that he is also deceased. I will declare him dead. But as with Paul Christiansen Nissen, by what means he came to his death we have no evidence to show."

The jurors were dismissed and the Coroner retired to the small parlor at the front of the hotel to seek the Chinaman who was preparing his dinner. After satiating himself with a hearty meal of roast mutton-bird and kumara, and picking the shreds of flesh from his teeth with a fork, he retrieved his coat and hat and left the hotel. The main square of the town was still a quagmire and he stepped carefully into the mud, shaking his head and sighing, thinking of the cobbled German streets he had left behind forever.

Around the corner in the paddock where he had left his horse, he came upon Nissen, assisted by the coach driver Frank Hardy, loading a coffin onto the back of a bullock dray. He stood watching for a moment, thinking of something appropriate to say. He could not imagine what it would be like to lose a brother and a cousin at the same time.

"Mr. Nissen," he said finally. "Would you like the results of the Coroner's Jury sent to your mother and your aunt—in Denmark, is it?"

The man glanced at him and looked back at the wooden coffin, still hovering half way onto the cart.

"Schleswig," he reminded the coroner.

"Well," repeated the coroner, "your mother and your aunt. Would you like me to send them the findings of the inquest? Perhaps they would like to know that the young men died sober and without interference from others."

For a brief moment, a look of pain came over the young man's face, then was quickly hidden.

"I hoped that the inquest would answer some questions like that," he said. "They were missing for many weeks and then suddenly Paul appeared. Jens is still missing. It does not seem right to me. Where is Jens? Paul could swim, but Jens could not. He would surely drown first. Where is he then?"

Then he added, "I'm going to contact my mother and my aunt. Jens' cousin, Mette, will help me write a letter that will let them know as carefully as possible that the boys have died. I will not tell my aunt that Jens body was not found. He is gone and that is certain, as you said in the inquest."

"Yes, well," said Rockstrow, "they certainly drowned. Constable Price believes they both drowned and I believe he is not without experience in the matter. Not much more to say than that."

Dr. Rockstrow watched as the Dane whipped his bullock and pulled away in his cart, the wood wheels sinking into the mud with the weight of his brother's body. He was thinking of his own mother back in Erfurt, Germany, who did not want to know her boy was alive. He turned and saw that Hardy was standing behind him, watching Nissen leave, his cart dragging through the mud of the Square.

"He needed to know what happened to his brother and his cousin," said Hardy, to himself more than to the doctor. "I wish we could have told him more."

"Well, one would," agreed Dr. Rockstrow. "But what else might have happened to them? They crossed the river and disappeared. Drowning should be the first thing that came to mind."

"They feel threatened," said Hardy. "The Scandinavians. They were given land by the government, and have had to work very hard clearing it. They worry because the Maori might want it back."

Dr. Rockstrow looked at him, wondering why he would care about that. They were just peasants, these Scandies. They should consider themselves lucky to own anything.

"They have good land," said the doctor. "And now there is more land available in Palmerston, with the sale of the *Pa* lands."

Frank Hardy did not reply. He was still watching Nissen as his cart moved slowly away across the muddy Square, the casket balanced awkwardly on the back. This was not the answer he wanted for Nissen, no more than the answer he had found to the fate of his own brother. But Nissen would recover. And then Frank would open his heart to Mette.

27

Paul and Jens Once More

Advertisement. Palmerston Dispensary
  *Nursery Requisites. Feeding bottles Mather's, Maw's, and
Alexandrian India rubber and glass tubing, Assorted teats, Breast
drawers, Nipple shields and shells, Teething pads, Puffs and powder
boxes assorted, Puffs, Violet powder, Fuller's earth, West Indian,
and Colonial arrowroot, Hard's food for infants and invalids,
Mincasia, a substitute for breast-milk; Nelson's and Swinburne's
gelatine and isinglass, Liebig's extract of meat.*
  Manawatu Times, July 28, 1877

Mette was on her knees digging up the last of the winter
potatoes, separating the ones that were good enough to eat
from those that would make good seed potatoes. The work
was soothing and she was enjoying the warmth of the sun on
her face and the process of deciding which potato should go
into which pile.

She heard Maren scream and started back on her heels.
Maren was inside lying next to a sleeping Hamlet. In the
last months of her pregnancy she had become very tired and
usually slept with Hamlet beside her for an hour or two every

256

afternoon, both taking comfort from the contact. Mette had left them back-to-back on the bed, snoring contentedly. She listened for a minute. Maren gave another choked scream and Hamlet woke up and started to wail.

Mette stood up and faced the house, her heart thumping and her hands sweating with fear. What was happening? Had someone now attacked Maren? She called her sister's name tentatively. Then louder, said *"Er du gut*, Maren?"

Her sister groaned, then said, *"Hjaelp mig*, Mette."

Mette rubbed her hands against her apron and ran into the house. Maren was lying on her side, her hands on her stomach, eyes closed, teeth bared in pain. Hamlet had stopped crying and was sitting up, looking at his mother with his thumb in his mouth.

"Maren, Maren, what is it? What is the matter? Are you ill?"

She moved quickly to Maren's side and saw that her dress and the bedding were soaked.

Maren groaned again. "It's too early, it's too early."

"What is too early?"

"The baby, the baby is coming. It is too early."

Mette's heart almost stopped. She knew very little about how babies were delivered. She'd been present when Hamlet was born while a woman from town, Mrs. Hansen, had coached Maren into pushing the baby from between her legs while she and Pieter watched helplessly. It had all happened in a few hours and everything seemed so natural, other than Maren's screaming when the pain hit her, that she'd decided that it would be an uncomfortable thing to go through, but worth it when you saw the beautiful little baby at the end of it. This was not the same.

She touched Maren's arm gently.

"Should you push?" she asked. "Will that help it come out?"

Maren looked at her with pain-filled eyes.

"He has not been moving," she said. "I knew something was wrong. When I was like this with Hamlet he was moving all the time. But this time, not for many days. I thought it must be because it was a girl, but I was fooling myself...agh." She stopped and clutched at her stomach again, then whispered, "so much pain."

"What should I do?" asked Mette. "Tell me what I should do and I will do it."

"Find one of the women in the clearing who has had babies and bring her here," said Maren. "Johanna Nissen, or Frida Jepsen. Frida would be better. She has had three children and one was stillborn."

Mette backed out of the house, then turned and ran. She could see several of the women in their gardens, either digging potatoes as she had been doing, or hanging out washing. She rushed down the path to Johanna Nissen, who was standing holding little Claus and talking to a woman Mette did not know.

"Johanna, Johanna," she panted. "You must come. Maren's baby is coming early. I don't know what to do. Maren says it hasn't moved for a long time and she has been worrying."

A faint look of annoyance came over Johanna's face. She sighed and thrust her baby at Mette. "Take care of Claus for now and I'll see what I can do. If she's losing the baby she just has to carry on and let it come. Even a baby who has died must still be born first."

"You should send for Mrs. Hansen," said the other woman. "She can help. My sister lost her baby and Mrs. Hansen was very helpful. She gave her something to drink which made

258

the baby come out very fast."

"But Mrs. Hansen is in town," said Mette. She was clutching baby Claus feeling totally helpless. She did not trust Johanna Nissen to be helpful, or even kind.

"Run over to the sawmill," suggested the woman. "Find someone there to go into town and bring Mrs. Hansen back. Mette turned towards the path to the sawmill. She had not been on that path for some time, and with all that had happened since then the thought of running to the sawmill made her cold with fear. Just when she thought she was over her encounter with the *Hauhau*, and what Frank had been through with him, she would be forced to confront the dark forest again.

"I'll go," said a voice from behind her. Mette turned to see Frida Jepsen standing behind her. "Mette, can you take care of the children while I'm gone? Pieter and Sofie are in my cottage. I will just tell them quickly that they must mind you, and then I will go to the sawmill as fast as I can."

Other women had started to gather, and two of them headed off to Maren and Pieter's house to give what help they could. Frida Jepsen hurried off along the path to the sawmill. Mette watched her go and shivered. She hoped Frida would arrive safely, even though the *Hauhau* had been captured. The bush represented a place of fear to her, as much as she had struggled to regain her love of the treasure it represented to her. She knew she would have to move into town. She sat down on a tree stump and made the children sit on the ground around her. She took deep breaths and was just starting to feel better when a black shape erupted from the forest and came towards her. She stood up with a little cry, almost dropping Claus in the process.

Frank Hardy stopped his horse in front of her and leaped down.

"What's happening? I just ran into a hysterical woman in the bush. She said something about needing help, but she wouldn't stop to tell me why, or what help she needed."

Mette felt her body flood with relief. He was here. Sergeant Frank was here. Now everything would be well.

"Maren, my sister Maren is having her baby," she said. "Only she thinks it's dead already, and it's too soon anyway. It should have waited almost until Christmas. We need to get Mrs. Hansen to come and help us."

"Wouldn't a doctor be better?" said Frank.

He was met with choruses of "No's" from the women.

"Very well, Mrs. Hansen. Where does she live? I'll go fetch her."

One of the women gave him directions to Mrs. Hansen's house, and he galloped off. Mette watched him go, thinking that she should have been on the horse with him. Of course, then there would be no room for Mrs. Hansen, so it was a foolish idea. She sat back down to watch the children, who were building a house with sticks. Hamlet had joined them and sat watching them, his thumb still in his mouth, his eyes large. She hadn't seen Frank for weeks and she was beginning to think that he did not want to see her, now that all the mysteries were solved—accept the one about where the body of Gottlieb Karlsen was. The Armed Constabulary had announced that *Anahera*, the *Hauhau*, had killed Sergeant Jackson because he was a Die Hard, like Frank.

After a while, Pieter emerged from the bush running, Frida Jepsen close behind him. He ran to Mette with his eyes full of fear, and Mette was reminded of the day she and Pieter had run from the mill to see if Hamlet had been taken by the *Hauhau*. It all seemed somewhat foolish now, thinking that the Maori would want to eat a little boy. She felt so much older and wiser than she had been just a few weeks ago.

"Maren, Maren," was all Pieter could say.

Mette stood up and put her arms around him.

"She's fine, Pieter, and Sergeant Fr…Sergeant Hardy has gone to fetch Mrs. Hansen. We don't know how the baby is doing, but Maren is in pain, just as she was when Hamlet was born. That's what happens."

Pieter slumped his head onto Mette's shoulder.

"I would die without her," he said. "Mette, what will I do if she dies?"

Mette had not thought of Maren dying, but she realized now it was possible.

"She's not going to die," she said firmly. "The baby will be born and then she'll be fine. She just has to suffer for a little while. I am sure she thinks it will be worth the pain. Or she'll think so, eventually."

Pieter sat down on the tree stump where Mette had been seated, and she sat beside him and held his hand. They were still sitting like that half an hour later when Frank returned with a flustered Mrs. Hansen sitting in front of him on the horse. Mrs. Hansen was a strong woman. She had walked beside the bullock carts coming from Foxton back in 1873, three young children by her side and another one on the way, all of which she frequently spoke about. But she had not sat on a horse with such a handsome man before, Mette thought, realizing what it was that was so exciting about riding in front of Frank.

Frank helped Mrs. Hansen down and followed her, still

with her hand in his. Mrs. Hansen was flushed a bright pink, but managed to collect herself to say, "Where is she? Where is the mother?"

Pieter stood up and took over. Together they hurried towards the house. Frank looked at Mette and smiled. She heard Maren give a loud trailing scream and turned towards the house, her heart pounding.

"Should you be with your sister?" he asked.

Mette sat down on the tree trunk again.

"I'm just in the way. I have no thought about what I should do and I don't know how to make Maren feel better."

He sat down beside her, taking Pieter's spot on the tree trunk. She glanced sideways at him, noticing for the first time that he was not wearing his old greatcoat, but a smart jacket, and that his hair, instead of being untamed, had been combed down into a neat part. Even his beard looked trimmer, less wild than it usually did.

"You're looking very fine today Sergeant Frank. Were you going somewhere special?"

He smiled again. "I was, but that will have to wait."

Maren screamed again. Mette put her head in her hands and shuddered.

"It's so terrible, having a baby. I had thought it would be a joyful thing, but Maren is in so much pain, and she thinks the baby has died because it hasn't been moving inside her. She will be sad for a very long time, I think."

She looked at Frank, remembering something. "You said your own mother died when your brother was born. I hadn't thought about it before, what a terrible thing it was. How terrible for your father, and for you. You must have been just a little boy."

Frank was no longer smiling. "I was five. It's one of my earliest memories. My mother screaming, just like...my mother screaming. And my father never really got over it, although he took comfort in Will."

She sat up, a look of realization in her eyes.

"I think I will never marry and have children," she said. "I came to New Zealand to look for a husband, to have children, to start a family and have a good life. But now I see that there is too much pain. And children die. Look at Paul and Jens. What will their mother feel when she hears? That they have died in a country so far away, that will be unbearable for her. Children are born in pain, and they die and there is more pain. I would not be able to stand it. My books will be my children."

He was quiet for a very long time. Eventually he said, "But children live as well. Look at little Hamlet, playing there, and all these other children. Think how Maren loves her little Hamlet."

Mette nodded. "That's true," she said. "But still, it does not balance out, for me." As she said it, she believed it.

Frank nodded slowly.

"If there is no baby, if it has really died, you'll still have your room to stay in," he said. "Not that that's a comforting thought for you."

"I suppose I will," she said. "But I'm not going to stay. I know that now."

"What will you do? Will you leave? Please don't go into service. I would hate to see you as someone's servant girl."

Mette regained her composure.

"I didn't tell you, but I have a job, and it has a room for me to live in as well."

"Not as a servant," Frank said again. "Please Mette, not as a

263

servant."

"I'm going to be a seller of books," she said, and he could see that her usual good spirits were bouncing back again. "Mr. Robinson has asked me to work in his bookstore. He has a nice little room at the back of the shop, with a stove for heating, and even a proper water closet just outside the back door. The room is small, but it will work well for me. And I will always be close to books."

"The books that will be your children, as you said," said Frank. He was looking sad for some reason. A butterfly landed on her fingers and she moved her hand around, admiring the blue and yellow on its wings. After a minute she spoke, not looking at Frank.

"Just living is not enough, said the butterfly. One must have sunshine, freedom and a little flower." She blew gently on the butterfly and it fluttered away. "That was said by our very famous storyteller Hans Christian Anderson," she said, then added, "What about you, Sergeant Frank? Is your life going to change?"

"Not as much as I'd hoped," he said enigmatically. "But I won't be driving coach any more. I've had enough of that." He turned towards her. "Did you hear they're building railway tracks through the Square? Soon we'll be able to take the train all the way to Wanganui, and even up to New Plymouth."

"That's wonderful," she said. "Perhaps when the tracks are built you could become a train driver."

He laughed. "I don't think so. No fun in that. I have a better idea, if it works."

"And what is it, this better idea? I'll only be happy if you tell me you are going to stay in Palmerston."

"I will," he said. "I'm going to open a small private investigation firm. I'll work throughout the Manawatu, even the rest of New Zealand if I must. There are many people who need help. I would rather think and explore than simply drive a coach. Wiremu, Will, Karira wants to become my partner. He'll be an excellent person to work with."

"And will you have an office close to Mr. Robinson's bookstore?"

"I've taken a room in the new building next to the Royal Hotel," he said. "I can sleep and eat at the Royal, and have an office right next door."

Mette clapped her hands. "You'll be just across the Square from me, and we can be friends forever," she said.

"Friends? Yes, that will be good. Friends. Forever."

He stood up. "Well, I must be going. I hope to see you soon, in town."

She watched as he mounted his horse. She was sad, but was not sure why. She felt as if something had been left unsaid, something that she had wanted to be said. He had just disappeared when Pieter came out of the house and called her.

"Mette, come quickly. Maren is asking for you."

She trudged reluctantly over to the house. At least Maren was alive, if she was asking for her. She was not looking forward to seeing a dead niece or nephew, however.

In the house, the women were standing around smiling at nothing in particular. Maren was lying on the bed also smiling. Mette's heart began to beat and she felt the beginning of joy. She rushed over to Maren's side. Maren was lying there, her face white and drained. Pieter was beside at her looking proudly down at her, his face a picture of love. Beside Maren lay two small bundles, one on each side. Mette gazed down at two tiny red faces and it seemed her life was now perfect.

"Mette," said Maren. "You must meet your two new nephews."

One of the babies waved a tiny red fist and squealed; the other joined in.

"We have two new little brothers for Hamlet," said Pieter. "Mette, I introduce you to little Paul and little Jens, the future farmers and landowners of the land that is New Zealand."

Maren spoke for the first time, her voice soft.

"Mette, I will do as you want, and make sure these boys grow up to be strong and brave, but also educated men."

Mette held two tiny hands between her own and smiled sadly. Everything is perfect, she thought. Almost.

After a while Maren fell asleep, helped by the Chlorodyne Mrs. Hansen had dropped onto her tongue, and Pieter and Mette left her to rest, babies beside her. Mette's elation had faded but she was not tired. She thought about Frank and wondered, what have I done?

She intended to walk until she was tired, down through the clearing to the path towards town. There was nothing or no one to be afraid of anymore, and she would not be able to sleep, even if Mrs. Hansen dropped some of the chlorodyne onto her tongue. Her body was buzzing with a strange energy, as if something had happened while she was not paying attention. She was happy that Maren now had her three boys and Pieter, but all she could think of was Frank, who had seemed to move away from her. He had left, and she wanted more than anything for him to return.

As she reached the entrance to the pathway she saw a shape coming towards her, a horse and rider. It was if she was reliving the first time she met Frank, as she ran from the bush and in front of Copenhagen. Was she imagining him? No. It was Frank coming towards her on his horse, and her heart leapt with joy.

She sat down on a log at the side of the path and waited. This time she would get it right. She would not run at him screaming, or say sad things to him about butterflies or the perils of having children. She would stay calm and see what it was he had wanted to say to her. He dismounted in front of her, his face hopeful, a smile beginning. Unable to help herself, she stood up and walked towards him quickly, holding his eyes with hers, and reaching her arms out to him. He opened his arms to her and held her tightly to him.

"I'm sorry," he said. "I left you alone when you were in pain. I thought only of myself. I wanted to return to tell you…"

"Maren is not dead," she said in a muffled voice, her face pressed into his chest. "And she has two baby boys. Paul and Jens she will call them."

"Ah, that's good then," he said, his voice muffled against her head.

"Now would you please ask…say what you were going to say to me when I interrupted you with my silly ideas? I was wrong. There must always be children, no matter what the pain."

She felt something warm and damp push against her neck, followed by the sound of a faint snicker. She looked up at Frank, smiling.

"Copenhagen and I have something to ask you," he said.

28

Epilogue: The White Ghost

Fears are entertained that two young men, named, respectively, Jens Lund and Paul Nissen, have been drowned in the Manawatu River. It appears they left their whare a fortnight ago yesterday for the purpose of visiting a relative living on the Fitzherberton side of the river. "We understand that they paid their visit and set out on their return home, at the same time telling their relative that they had crossed the river on a log. They have not since been heard of, and we learn that a party went in search of them yesterday.
Manawatu Times, 8 August 1877

He was cold and hungry. He had stumbled through the dense bush for hours after Paul sank below the frigid water and away from him, cold and terrified. He had seen the terrible Maori on the far side of the river making the face at him, after watching them in the water, not helping them. Even if he could have made it back across the river he did not want to. He was afraid. He would return to Knud's tent, but there was no track on this side of the river and the woods had swallowed him up. He had climbed up from the river and scrambled between the huge dark trees, hoping always to see a track, or to hear people. Night came and he fell beside a log and slept fitfully. The light disappeared completely and he could see nothing, not even his own hand. The sounds in the dark of the night scared him. What animals were there in this forest? What people?

The next morning, he found the river again, but he was across from the place where the Maori lived, the village with the canoes, people coming and going, and he was afraid. Would they help him, or would they throw him in the river and watch him drown? He did not know. He had never talked to a Maori person in the year he had been in this country. He saw a small boy standing on the dock staring at him from across the river. The boy pointed and screamed, "Turehu!" He withdrew quickly into the bush so the boy could no longer see him.

He found a small stream gurgling down into the river and drank deeply. He wished he had kept the bottle that Knud had given them; then he would be able to fill it up and carry it with him, but it was gone, he did not know where. His clothes had dried now but he was freezing and found it difficult to move. His teeth chattered uncontrollably and he could not stop himself from shaking. He started to think about food—how he would find something to eat. Mette, his cousin Mette, was always finding things to eat in the woods, and she had talked about them. He could not remember much of what she said, although he remembered she said people ate young fern roots when they were very hungry. He pulled out some ferns and tried chewing them. The taste was terrible but he was able to create a mush in his mouth that he could swallow, allaying his hunger briefly. He searched more, and near a grove of pine trees found some brightly covered mushrooms, red with white spots. They would keep him from starving. He pulled out several and sat down with his back against a log to eat. There were some white grubs wriggling around on top of the log, and he brushed them away in disgust. Once he was full of mushrooms, at least as full as he could get with mushrooms, he would start walking through the bush again, back towards the Pa. Perhaps he should not be afraid. The people there must help him. He should not be afraid of someone just because they were different from him.

The hallucinations started within twenty minutes. He saw monsters coming at him, *troldt*. He fell and lay there calling for his mother, his stomach cramping. He leaned forward and retched and then fell back against the log, over and over again, getting weaker each time. Eventually he fell into a nightmare-filled sleep. By evening he was near death. He awoke briefly, the visions gone, his stomach aching from the vomiting, freezing cold. He could not move. His body was without strength. He lay there as the sky darkened and the moon came out. Now he could see the stars. He watched them, not knowing what he looked at, not understanding. Eventually he died. He was just another boy who had been lost in the bush. It would be years before he would be found, and by then he was forgotten.

If you enjoyed this book. would you kindly leave me a review?

Thank you

Wendy

29

Sources

The quotations at the beginning of each chapter are available on Papers Past, a searchable database of newspapers published in New Zealand in the last two hundred years. It was in Papers Past that I discovered a coroner's inquest detailing the death of Paul Christensen Nissen, my great grandfather's brother, and Jens Lund his cousin. The news story led to the creation of this fictional story. Sergeant Frank Hardy and Mette Jensen are my own creations, although sometimes it's hard to believe they were not real people.

The beheading in the first chapter also - unfortunately - happened and further details of the Land Wars can be found on Papers Past or on Te Ara, the online Encyclopedia of New Zealand History.

https://paperspast.natlib.govt.nz/
https://teara.govt.nz/en

For more information, go to my website: www.wendymwilson.com

30

Background History

The Scandinavians in New Zealand

The first Scandinavians came from Denmark in the mid-1860s after the war between Denmark and Germany over the Schleswig-Holstein border lands. Bishop Monrad the ex-premier of Denmark and the protagonist of the recent Danish/BBC miniseries, 1864, fled to New Zealand and settled in Palmerston with his family and others from Schleswig. When the town had a brief scare during the war with Titokowera the Bishop returned to Denmark after first burying his plate in the garden. His son Viggo, who makes a brief appearance in Chapter Five, remained behind.

The next wave of Scandinavians (mostly Danes) arrived in the early 1870s. Sir Julius Vogel, Prime Minister of New Zealand, brought Scandinavians to New Zealand because New Zealand was covered in rain forest and the Scandies were famed for their skill as axe-men. Poor farmers were offered assisted passage and land in return for clearing the bush or working on road or railway track construction. The

Scandinavians arrived expecting farmland where a few trees needing removing and were shocked with what they found. Many turned to sawmilling as a way to survive, including my own great grandfather. "Little Claus," born the week his uncle Paul vanished, was my grandfather.

Maoris at the time called the Scandinavians Yaya because of the way they spoke, and it is doubtful any New Zealander would know this now. The British settlers called the Scandinavians Scandies and were quite dismissive of them; articles from the time made negative comments about their accents. Frank moves from Yaya to Scandies to Scandinavians as he gets to know Mette. In general, the Scandinavians, especially the Danes, are not a group of immigrants many modern New Zealanders would know much about. Various Scandinavian Clubs do celebrate their shared past and have online presences.

The 57th Regiment of Foot: The Die Hards

The history of this British Regiment is explained well in the 1866 article below. The Die Hard name came from an incident in the Battle of Albuera when the colonel of the regiment lay dying, and called to his men, "Die hard, the 57th, Die Hard." The term has become separated from its origins over the years and is now mostly associated with the Bruce Willis movies. The regiment spent almost a decade in New Zealand during the Land Wars of the 1860s. Note that the Land Wars were, at the time, called the Maori Wars and have now been renamed the New Zealand Wars. I have chosen to use the term Land Wars as it is more descriptive and was used at the time as well as currently.

HER MAJESTY'S 57th REGIMENT.

The head-quarters of this fine old regiment having left us, we are now at liberty to say a word regarding the only regiment in the service that can lay claim to having been, during their long and active period of service, amphibious, pedestrian, equestrian, and pedestrian again. In the 17th century the regiment was raised and served as marines, and in that amphibious capacity performed good service to their country. They were subsequently transferred to 'the line, forming the 57th Regular Regiment. During the Peninsula war, at the battle of Albuera, whilst commanded by the late Sir William Inglis, they obtained the soubriquet of "Die-hards." They carry on their colours the following distinction: "Albuera," "Vittoria," "Pyrenees," "Nivelle;" "Nive," "Peninsula," "Inkerman,"' and Sebastopol.

After their return from the Crimea, reduced to the mere skeleton of a regiment by hard fighting and hard service, they had hardly been recruited and put once more in fighting order when news reached England of the Indian mutiny. The "Die-hards" were immediately ordered to embark for India by the overland route, and on their arrival in Egypt were mounted to cross the desert, and thus for the nonce became a horse-regiment.

On the suppression of the Indian mutiny the regiment was ordered from India to New Zealand, and they arrived here at the commencement «f the war in 1860. Had Colonel Warre, C.B., of that regiment, wielded the power unfortunately placed in the hands of General Cameron, he would have made short and hard work of it, and saved to this colony and the mother country many precious lives, and a large and worse than useless expenditure of public money. Whether under General Cameron, General Chute,

274

or their own commanders, the old "Die Hards," whenever they had an opportunity, showed what British soldiers could do amongst the Maori race if fairly let loose on them.

During General Chute's short campaign, the "Die-hards," with the 2nd Battalion 14th Regiment and 18th Royal Irish, proved that they could send out a few men from each regiment who, with a few of our colonial forces, could sweep every pa from north to south of this island, caring but little how many Maoris defended it. Well may the British soldier be proud, as he always is, of being led by a brave commander. There are yet about 180 men of the 57th amongst us awaiting a steamer to convey them to join their headquarters in Auckland. We believe the regiment will leave for England in July or August next and whenever they do, the old "Die-hards" will carry with them the best thanks and wishes of the people of New Zealand.

Wanganui Times, April 27, 1866.

The Hauhau

The Hauhau (pronounced how how), also called Pai Marire, was a Christian-based religious movement that arose in provincial Taranaki in the 1860s during the Land Wars (including the two Taranaki wars between 1861-1867) and gave rise to a warrior-prophet named Titokowera. The term Hauhau was used rather loosely by New Zealanders at the time, and that has changed. Now the term Pai Marire is commonly used and is understood as referring to a peaceful group; they did indeed become peaceful in the 1870s and practiced passive resistance. However, at that time the name Hauhau still brought fear to the hearts of the settlers.

In 1868 a Hauhau/Pai Marire follower named Te Kooti massacred fifty-six settlers in Poverty Bay and he is now seen in New Zealand as having had a good reason to do so. The government officially pardoned him in 1883, during his own lifetime, after spending several years pursuing him in a mountainous region called the Urewas.

New Zealand had fortified frontiers well into the 1870s, but by the early eighties the Maori people had embraced pacifism. The final indignity for the Maori people came in 1881 when the Armed Constabulary attacked and leveled a peaceful village in Parihaka, Taranaki. My intention is to write three books with the same characters, concluding with the attack at Parihaka.

British and Other Troops in New Zealand

Several British regiments spent time in New Zealand. A regiment was sometimes called Her Majesty's Imperial Regiment etc. However, it may be better not to use this term; they were just British regiments. Colonial Troops were also formed, as well as the Armed Constabulary who were a national police force similar to the RCMP (Mounties) in Canada. British soldiers who stayed in New Zealand when the army left often joined these bodies. Settlers usually joined a local volunteer group.

Many Maoris fought with the Colonial or British troops and these were called Kupapa, meaning that they were loyal to the Crown. Frequently Maoris would end up fighting beside Colonial troops against other Maoris and the Kupapa troops were given a red cap to distinguish them from the non-loyal

Maoris. I did not make use of this fact as Army Intelligence in the British Army were also distinguished by a red cap. Loyalty was associated with keeping land and often came with a threat attached.

31

Bonus Chapter: When We People the Land

Want to read the next book in the series? The first chapter is here. To receive the next five chapters sign up at www.wendymwilson.com. When We People the Land will be available soon for preorder on Amazon.

The stoppage by Government of the survey of the Waimate plains, when everything was ripe for success, has raised strong feelings of indignation amongst Europeans. It is looked upon in the light of a disaster. It is considered a breach of faith with the natives on the Patea side of the Waingongoro River, who only withdrew opposition to Government acquisition of land, they claimed, on the understanding that the survey of the plains would follow. The Maoris are in high glee all over the district, and say that the confiscated land will all be returned. Serious complications are expected to arise, and a bounceable attitude is already developing.

New Zealand Herald, 6 December 1877

He awoke with a throbbing headache and a mouth so dry he couldn't swallow; his tongue seemed to be glued to the roof of his mouth. It was pitch black and he was lying on something hard and damp and bumpy. He had no idea how he had got here — wherever he was. He reached down and encountered a dirt floor. Not the stamped-down dirt of a cottage floor, but the stone-filled dirt of a river bed. If he stretched out his legs they hit a wall. He reached cautiously above his head and felt another wall.

pulled himself up and leaned cautiously on one elbow, dry retching through waves of nausea; a faint whiff of chloroform came off his beard. He tried to see through the impenetrable darkness Was he in a tunnel? He raised one hand and stretched it forward. Another wall. And with legs extended, a fourth wall. He was in a space about eight feet by eight feet, with dirt walls and a dirt floor. He tried to stand, but the nausea returned and he fell against a wall, gagging. Leaning there, he reached above his head. Perhaps he been buried alive in some kind of tomb. No. He felt nothing.

With his arm stretched to its full extent his fingers brushed against wooden slats, placed across the top of the hole, with spaces between. Air was filtering through and it seemed fresh. The slats were a foot and a half above his head, maybe eight feet high to his six feet two inches. He jumped and held himself off the ground on one of the slats, but it did not move. Staring up through the slats he thought he saw a faint trace of clouds against a night sky, blocked slightly by the shapes of huge trees.

He dropped back down. Where the hell am I, and how did I get here? That was the question he had to answer. But first, who was he? Had he lost his memory? Sergeant Frank Hardy.

Die Hard. An ex-soldier living in Palmerston, Manawatu, soon to be married.

That stopped him.

"Mette," he thought. What will she think? Does she know I've gone? Is she wondering if I've left her? For a minute he lost his calm, pulled himself up and pressed his face between the slats, yelling. "Hey. Anyone there? What the hell is this place?"

In response, a howl, human, but just barely.

He shivered and lowered himself down from the bars to a seated position, his head in his hands, thinking.

He needed to take stock. He edged around the pit with his hands against the dirt walls until his foot kicked against a pail in a corner. It was empty, but clearly there for slops. Nothing else, however. His cell was devoid of ornaments and fixtures. No windows or potential exits either.

He was still wearing his blue greatcoat, but the new large bore Colt Deringer revolver that he'd purchased in Wellington had been removed from the inside pocket, as had his money clip with Pieter's twenty-pound advance and all his own ready cash. His fingers closed over a small velvet box. The brooch he'd bought Mette at Te Aro House on Cuba Street—a butterfly fashioned out of blue enamel that reminded him of her every time he looked at it. It was a beautiful piece, fitting for the woman who was destined to receive it, but, more usefully, it had a sharp heavy pin made of steel. He tested the point with his thumb and drew blood. Something skittered by his foot; a weta the size of his palm was crawling across the toe of his boot and he impaled it with the pin without much pressure. One good weapon then. And with wetas on offer he wouldn't starve if they forgot to feed him. Not as easy to eat as huhu grubs, but still with some sustenance. He flipped it over. A tree weta, which meant it could have come from a tunnel in the dead trunk of a tree buried in the wall of his cell. Something to check later.

He put the brooch into his shirt pocket and dug inside his coat again. A box of Vestas, almost empty, but something. Deep inside his pocket he found a small twist of humbugs—another purchase from Te Aro House. He opened the packet and sucked on one to help the dryness in his mouth. That was it for his coat pocket. His trouser pocket yielded a few coins, a shilling, two pennies, a halfpenny, and a couple of farthings. He wasn't going to be able to bribe his way out of this predicament.

He sat there, thinking. He'd been kidnapped, obviously. But why, and by whom? When had it happened? He could remember being at sea on the steamer from Foxton to Wellington. Had he returned? Yes, because he remembered boarding the steamer, the SS Stormbird, with Pieter's dreadful sister and her two solemn children. She'd boarded with a large steamer trunk of clothing, wearing a crinoline that barely fit through the doorway of the cabin she had insisted on taking on the saloon deck. She already saw herself as one of the Royal Princesses: Princess Vicky or Princess Louise. He'd badly wanted to tell her that nine hundred pounds was not going to elevate her to the *crème de la crème* of society, even if Palmerston had anything that could be described as society, which – thankfully – it did not.

What had happened in Wellington? He'd booked into the South Sea Hotel on Lambton Quay, after reading in the *Evening Post* that it had a splendid billiard table, thinking he might need to entertain himself for a few nights while he searched for Agnete Madsen. But as it happened he'd found her quickly. Wellington was small, despite the fact it had been the capital of the colony for over ten years – under 20,000 people.

He'd started by asking at the hotel for an Englishman named Williams who kept semi-respectable women in his home who were not married to him or related to him; one suggestion led to another, and by the second day he'd tracked her down. She was living in a rundown tin-roofed boarding house built of wooden planks, on Oriental Parade, not far from the Te Aro Swimming Baths. She'd been surprisingly pleased to see him and when she heard she was about to inherit some money was ready to leave right away for Palmerston. Obviously, Mr. Williams had not been as generous as she'd hoped.

He closed his eyes and dozed, waking with a start to the sound of a trapdoor opening. He staggered to his feet.

"Hey there, you, who are you? What am I doing here?"

A rope sling holding a basket of food wrapped in leaves was lowered down to him. He grabbed the basket and the sling was pulled up and out of view. He strained to look up, but could see no one, and no one spoke to him.

"What the hell is going on. Why am I here?"

A bucket dropped down, empty, and hung there. He stared at it for a minute, then understood its purpose. He grabbed the slop bucket from the corner and replaced it with the new bucket. The slop bucket disappeared slowly into the darkness, followed by a click. He looked at the food and sighed. At least whoever had him didn't intend to let him die here. The basket contained steamed vegetables—kumara, boiled potatoes—a couple of cold pork sausages and a bottle of ginger beer with a glass stopper. Famished, he ate everything, and spent the next few hours with his guts roiling, regretting that he'd eaten so much and so quickly. He was to be fed twice a day, apparently, just like when he was in the Armed Constabulary back in '68 and '69. He'd need to pace his food consumption. He'd become used to eating three meals a day.

Daylight came and the sun rose and bore down on him through the branches. It was spring and the strength of the sun was weak, but in his hole in the ground he began to get warm; the woody scent of totara and pines wafting through the bars added to the humidity. He thought he could also detect the faint smell of blood, a smell he associated with a slaughter house. The smell and the heat got to him, and eventually he vomited into the slop bucket. When he was done, he took off his greatcoat and laid it in a corner. Now he could see the true extent of his prison, the dirt floor, the walls reinforced with occasional slabs of wood. He thought of the sawmills back in Palmerston, busy cutting just such planks on their sharp blades.

Which brought him back to Mette again. He could see her once more as she was the first time he saw her, barely five months ago, standing in the forest clearing with her sister, laughing, her blond hair gleaming in the sunlight. It had been love at first sight for him, even if he didn't immediately know it. Then when she'd run from the *Hauhau* in the bush, into his path … all he wanted after that was to protect her, to keep her safe.

The Hauhau. Anahera. Could one of Anahera's accomplices have captured him? Did he even have accomplices? Captain Porter had told him that Anahera was up the Whanganui River in the secret Armed Constabulary gaol, known to be almost impossible to escape. He was probably still there. But who knew if he worked alone? Princess Moana had certainly been deceived into helping him, and for her pains had been sent back to Poverty Bay to live with her family, her *hapu*. Moana and Anahera were connected to each other through the Poverty Bay tribes. After escaping gaol in Poverty Bay, back in the winter, Anahera had been on a murderous rampage, killing any ex Die Hards, soldiers of the 57th Regiment, who'd crossed his path; he'd eventually found his way to Palmerston, looking for Frank's old captain from the Titokowaru war of the late sixties, Captain Porter, at which point he and Frank had run up against each other.

He considered the possibility of Anahera for a while. Surely impossible for the man to organize a kidnapping from his gaol. He'd be separated from other prisoners, and without enough of the English language at his command to recruit a corrupt guard. Besides which, the man was terrifying; not someone who would charm someone into helping him. Terrorize them, perhaps, but that didn't work when you were in solitary confinement, as Anahera surely was.

The day passed slowly, and as night fell the ritual with the basket and the slop bucket reoccurred, confirming his assumption that meals would come morning and night.

As his cell darkened he heard the skittering sounds of wetas, and used one of his precious matches to find the insect's tunnel. He found one about half way up the wall nearest to the trapdoor, the light from his match revealing a small colony of females and juveniles, and one male who hissed at him angrily. He used the last of his light to find a small rock on the floor of his cell, and pushed it into the mouth of the tunnel. That would keep them in there for a while, make sure they didn't crawl over him as he slept.

He fell asleep thinking about his stay in Wellington. He'd had a brief and somewhat curious encounter at the South Sea Hotel, with a Colonel belonging to one of the British regiments in India. He seemed to recognize Frank, although Frank had no memory of ever seeing him before. Why would someone from India have anything to do with this? He hadn't been in India for almost twenty years, when he was a recent recruit. Surely nothing from that long ago could be coming back to cause trouble for him now?

He stretched out on the ground, which was as hard and uncomfortable as a metalled road. It was not the soft bed he was used to these days, but he would do his best with it. He needed to keep up his strength, in case anything came up of which he could take advantage. The years of rough campaigns came back to help him. He lay back on the hard, uneven ground and fell asleep instantly.

The sun rose and the distant, familiar sounds of a military camp drifted down to him. For a moment, he thought he was back fighting in the Taranaki Wars. He sat up and folded his coat, placing it once more in the corner opposite the slop bucket. The click of a key being pushed into a lock signalled that food was arriving again, and he was instantly alert. He knew he had to find who had him before he could understand why he had been taken. This might present an opportunity.

The key turned in the lock and the trapdoor creaked slowly open. He stood underneath as if ready to receive the basket of food from the bucket, his hands outstretched in a feigned plea. The bucket came towards him slowly, and he braced himself. Slowly, slowly. Then his hands were around the bucket. He gave it a sharp pull and let it go, the basket food tumbling across the dirt floor, and leapt upwards.

His hands connected with an arm. Holding it tightly he pulled down hard, putting his weight behind it. A brown arm, small, and soft, a woman's arm came into view. The surprise almost caused him to let go, but he held on and pulled the woman down further. Her whole upper body was through the trapdoor and her hair tumbled down towards him.

"Who are you? Why are you keeping me here?"

She began to wail.

"*Te tauturi, te tauturi.*"

Boots thumped towards them in the dirt, followed by the ominous sound of carbines being engaged.

"Let her go," said a voice. "Or you're a dead man."

He continued holding the arm for a few seconds, then grudgingly let it slip from his grasp and stepped back. The woman was pulled up by unseen hands, still wailing loudly.

"That's better," said the voice. "Now sit down and be a good boy."

He lowered himself back against the wall. They could see him, but to him they were just vague shadows. Above him the carbines were disengaged and there was a soft muttering. He heard them leave, but one man stayed behind. The fresh slop bucket did not appear.

"Got me eye on you, mate," said the voice. "Don't try anything like that again or I'll shoot you in the leg, hobble you for good."

He picked up the food from the ground, brushing the dirt from the kumaras and potatoes. He knew that voice. Who the hell was it?

Lightning Source UK Ltd.
Milton Keynes UK
UKOW01f2335120218
317766UK00002B/477/P

9 781775 220619